I Never Wanted To Be a Rock Star
a Novel
A Novel

I Never Wanted To Be a Rock Star
a Rock Star
A Novel

Lisa Kaiser

CLYTEMNESTRA PUBLISHING

This book is dedicated to Chrissie Hynde, Stevie Nicks, Christine McVie, Joni Mitchell, Linda Thompson, Ann and Nancy Wilson, Carly Simon, Kate Bush, Liz Phair, Linda Ronstadt, Sandy Denny, the Roches, Janis Joplin, Pat Benatar, Bonnie Raitt, Debbie Harry, Siouxsie Sioux, Ani DiFranco, Joan Didion...

Table of Contents

Prologue

I never wanted to be a rock star.

I loved to sing, of course. I had a pitch-perfect voice and had to hear a melody just once to take it to heart and make it come to life. No wonder why I, the otherwise unremarkable Peggy O'Donnell with my squirrel-brown braids, was chosen over the older kids to solo on "Silent Night" at the Blessed Sorrows Parish School Christmas concert in 1959. I rehearsed for weeks, anxious to impress, terror building under my skin as the date drew closer.

When the final notes of "O Little Town of Bethlehem" faded away and my time in the spotlight had arrived, I stepped off the middle riser to stand beside Sister Scholastica at the piano hitting all the familiar notes of my song. My second-grade class hit a few unfamiliar notes in the first verse while I panted under my damp white blouse and plaid jumper, knees clattering under my cable knit tights. But I knew I could do it. I'd sung it perfectly hundreds of times at home.

"Silent night," I sang alone, imagining myself as an angel with God's heavenly view of Jesus's birth, the holy family filling an ordinary stable with otherworldly light and eternal joy.

I let my voice swell with the simple Austrian melody in the overheated Catholic school gymnasium in Evanston, Illinois, just as I had ad nauseam in my bedroom.

But instead of being received with delight, or even indifference, chuckles began rippling through the audience. I scanned the crowd openly laughing as I sang—even my father was stifling a laugh in his handkerchief while my mother poked him in the ribs to shush him. I dug deeper and held on to my perfect pitch like a life preserver in a roiling ocean, but the laughter was impossible to ignore. I lost my nerve. Rather, I was overtaken by my nerves. I shook in my fuzzy tights while I felt my veins throb and my armpits and palms flourished with sweat. Strawberry welts sprouted along my neck and chest, which only made me seem more freakish. My voice wavered beyond control into purgatory as I finished my verse in total humiliation.

I returned to my place in the middle of the choir while Sister Scholastica was still plunking out the final notes and my classmates were erupting in open rebellion. I mimed the rest of the Christmas carols through my tears and fled to my parents' big black Buick with the crowd's laughter searing into my soul. I vowed never to sing again.

Only later did I discover the cause of my trauma. My classmate Michael McNulty had been channeling Elvis Presley behind my back with sinfully swiveling hips and practiced snarl, upstaging me from the second I opened my mouth. That jerk got his moment of notoriety, but he also cursed me with performance anxiety so debilitating that even four platinum albums couldn't cure it decades later.

No, I never wanted to be a rock star. But I did want revenge.

+++

I fell into it, to be honest. Before I became Maggie Morgan, I was Peggy O'Donnell Morgan, a married co-ed whose only desire was to keep my high school sweetheart, Jerry, out of Vietnam and perhaps teach art to elementary school kids until we started a family. Jerry was back in Evanston, working for his dad's insurance business, while I was making the most out of my scholarship to an art college in Philadelphia. That was as much freedom as I could handle then. Even amid near-constant social upheaval in the late 1960s, I wasn't a revolutionary in any sense of the word. Leave the trailblazing to others. I was happy as a bit player, anonymous in the crowd.

But I wasn't anonymous to Aaron Fields, who always seemed to be on the periphery of my days on campus. When I was studying in the library, Aaron was sleeping off the previous night's excesses. When I was watching my friends sing in dank folk clubs, he was glowering at the bar, doubling up his whiskeys. When I was swooning my way through the art museum on a foggy Saturday afternoon, he was slipping bags of dope to the janitors.

During the dreary November of my sophomore year I'd agreed to help out a pal starting a winsome folk group that was taking its lead from The Mamas & The Papas. Aaron, predictably, was at a party after our debut, the supplier of the grass and psychedelics that made the party swing. He approached, obviously stoned and in rogue mode. He stood too close to me and spiked the punch with whatever was in his flask. "I love corrupting young girls," he whispered in my ear.

"I'm not a young girl." I flashed the gold band on my finger. "I'm married."

He moved in closer. "I love corrupting married women even more. Especially the uptight ones. The ones who really need a good screw."

I left the party, cheeks burning, squirrel-brown pin-straight hair encasing me like a veil in my shame as I rushed back to my dorm alone.

I knew I'd see him again. He seemed to shadow me, full of mirth but always keeping a gentlemanly distance. I pretended not to notice but was aware that my frostiness was only making him more intent on corrupting me. And I had to admit that being pursued, even by a dirty hippie, was flattering to a young woman who hadn't been touched since the beginning of the semester.

"I think it's time for you to quit school and have a baby," Jerry said in a crackly long-distance call before Thanksgiving break. "My dad doesn't have any pull with the lottery, the way he did with the draft board. I'm pretty sure a kid would get me a deferment."

I let his comment hang there for a while, then brushed my sleeve over the receiver.

"You're breaking up. We must have a bad connection."

I hung up before he could say more, but his words stuck with me all night, all through my harmonies with the folk group.

Shouldn't this be my *decision?*

My anger pushed my vocals so far forward that I was singing lead. My mates nudged me and gave me dirty looks throughout the night, but I didn't care. It felt good, in fact, not to give a damn.

Of course Aaron turned up later at a party in a basement bar illuminated by strobe lights and a trippy light show, Cream thundering on the hi-fi system. He circled me, grinning.

"If I was flipping through radio stations and heard your voice I'd stop and listen forever," he said.

"You just want to get me in bed," I snapped.

"I do." His dark eyes danced as he held up two fingers in a peace sign. "But that's not all."

Stuck to his fingertips were two funky-looking scraps of paper. He placed one on his tongue and closed his eyes.

"Do you dare?"

The remaining tab of acid was affixed to his middle finger. I took it into my mouth, letting the drug wash into my system and alter my world forever. Gone were my mundane cares about school, Jerry, or living up to some arbitrary expectations as the LSD melted my shyness, my inhibitions, my self-defeating restraint. Unlimited possibilities flooded my consciousness and soaked through my skin and into my blood, my marrow, my soul. And there was Aaron, leading me into this new reality.

+++

I kept singing, although it scared the hell out of me. It was almost a compulsion. But the rock star stuff—that was never my dream. Aaron Fields, on the other hand, *was* a rock star. It was the only way he could live, rebellious and irresponsible and attention-starved and charismatic, even when he was simply sitting in a chair.

He taught me how to do it.

"Come on, Maggie. Let 'er rip," he'd say as he adjusted my mic and worked his way through a few aimless chords on his Fender. "Put the fury in the Four Furies."

It wasn't easy at first. I felt self-conscious and vulnerable when all eyes were on me. I couldn't hide behind a drum kit or a guitar, and the threat of a disaster was ever present. I had to face the audience—*conquer* the audience—alone, under a spotlight, just me and my perfect pitch.

Four Furies fans only saw my rock star self and weren't aware that my performances were preceded by a panic attack that rocketed through my body and threatened to immobilize me with fear. Eventually, I learned to use that adrenaline to fuel the band. I'd follow Aaron's lead and make myself bigger onstage, ferocious at times, then small and quiet, captivating our fans with my apparent reluctance to reveal my true self to them. I kept enough sincerity in my artifice to tell the story of the song, even when those songs prevented old hurts from healing. That's what kept the Four Furies alive and Aaron and I entwined as a very messed-up couple.

But sure, okay, since I'm being honest, I'll admit that the applause soothed an old ache. It stanched the open wound created by Michael McNulty's antics during the long-ago Christmas concert and made me feel less guilty about abandoning Jerry and sending him off to war. As I calculated, if I could command thousands of fans with my voice and some theatrics, I had some value, some worth. It didn't matter what I had to endure to get some respect.

I didn't want to be a rock star, honestly.

+++

So there we were in Tampa. 1982. Final song of the set, the spotlight on. A pause in the song rehearsed and re-enacted throughout this tour. "Finding His Way" detailed the woes of a straying lover and his patient Penelope waiting for his return. Aaron had written that song to justify an affair with a redhead in Seattle, a stain on our relationship that had been transmuted to platinum. The melody turned my stomach every time I heard it. I felt even worse when I had to sing it, the audience cheering on Aaron's abhorrent behavior and my suffering. Both of us knew that our fans ate up the dynamic, Aaron the asshole and Maggie the masochist, and we'd stretch out the final lines until they ached deep down in the listener's bones.

Aaron, on cue, would gallantly step out of the spotlight and into the shadows to allow me a few moments center stage. As rehearsed, I'd wait a beat or two, then sing a few words *sotto voce* and make the audience strain to hear me before building a crescendo that would erupt into an *a capella* primal scream. Then I'd beckon Aaron back and he'd join me in a tentative harmony that we'd let take flight, his guitar and Pete's bass and Hooch's drums kicking in until the tension could be released only by another standing ovation.

So here was the pause in the song as we'd rehearsed. Aaron stepped away. I put my hands on my hips, planted my feet on my mark. The wind machine at the edge of the stage rippled my highlighted blonde hair and fluffed my champagne-colored antique lace blouse. The crowd readied itself for the final lines of the song—"Finding his way, he's finding his way, he's finding his way"—that, in truth, always made me feel pathetic, as if I was giving Aaron permission to cheat on me as a means to achieve enlightenment.

I waited longer than I was supposed to, the white heat from the spotlight blinding me from seeing anything beyond the microphone. But I knew who was out there. Clones of me, wispy young women in form-fitting bell-bottom jeans, flowy blouses, and jangly silver charm bracelets, presentable hippies who would become yuppies soon enough. Clones of Aaron, guys in jeans and Western shirts and a lump of lapis lazuli hanging from a leather strand around their necks. They came as couples or with friends hoping to get laid. Four Furies fans wanted to be Aaron and me, in good times and bad, a flawed couple that was glamorously larger than life but utterly relatable. They felt they knew us. We had them fooled.

The Tampa audience was mine, as it always was at this point in the show.

But did I want them? Did I want *this*?

Our fans saw the band through their own fantasies—red-hot musicians and a dazzling rock and roll couple fronting the group. In reality, we were forced to drop our private plane and were back in a tour bus because we were in debt, barely speaking, sharing our drugs but hiding our best stashes from each other, feeding our egos with sex and publicity, and never—*never*—being honest with each other.

And I was pregnant. Just four months, long enough for me to get my hopes up and believe that this baby would survive if I gave him a chance.

Something fluttered at the lip of the stage and took me out of the moment. She was one of my clones, by now a familiar one. She'd worked her way up from throwing a red rose to Aaron in Birmingham, catching his guitar pick in Atlanta, and then flashing him in Miami, each time whisked out of the crowd and into a waiting cab by one of our roadies. Aaron thought he was so clever and discreet but of course I knew. In Tampa she swayed to the music, not needing to do anything to draw his attention. He'd been playing to her all night, pulling his focus from me to his new girl.

I did nothing. I let the audience wait, feeling the new life inside of me. I stretched out the pause in the song into something intolerable. Finally, I turned to Aaron at the side of the stage. He was in the darkness, but everyone knew he was there. They felt him. I tilted my head, raised my right arm, and let my trademark silver charm bracelet catch the spotlight and send shimmers into the audience. I pointed my finger, weighted down by an Easter Blue turquoise ring, and finished off the song my way.

"Fuck," I howled at Aaron, finding enough energy at the end of the long note to clip off that final K with relish. I took a deep breath to let myself recover and allow my witnesses to etch this moment into their memories. I knew Aaron felt it, even if he was trying to play it cool.

I took another deep breath and committed to the final assault.

"You," I sang, this final word ragged as I hit the limit of my range.

I locked eyes with Aaron and the crowd went mad. They called out my name until the scattered yelling grew into a chant. I let it go on and on and on.

Slowly, I strutted toward Aaron, the spotlight following me. Aaron grinned and held out his arms to welcome me, setting up a gallant bow to paper over my off-script behavior, but he was just playing to the crowd and the girl who was about to meet him after the show.

I didn't sing another note as I took a healthy swing.

My fist landed squarely on his nose.

I went in for a second blow as he crumpled, the rock god finally conquered amid thousands of flashbulbs recording it for posterity. The unlucky girl could have him. I had our baby.

I gave him a final kick with my stiletto boot heel and exited the stage, the crowd chanting "Maggie, Maggie, Maggie" and ushering me away from the Four Furies and into the future.

Chapter 1

It's Time

Oak Park, Illinois, 2002

Hey. I'm with Aaron in Wisconsin. Don't freak out about it. It's all cool.
Maggie read and reread Sage's email until it didn't make sense anymore.
Aaron.
Wisconsin.
Cool.
Maggie dropped her wire-rimmed reading glasses on the lone unoccupied spot on her desk at Felix Ingles Fellows II Designs. The rest of her glass-top desk was strewn with fabric swatches for pillow shams, small squares of burly carpet, a balsa wood model of a kitchen interior, unspooled floor plans, the *New York Times* opened to the financial pages, and Sage's faded third grade school portrait, his busted-picket-fence grin and spit-licked dark-chocolate hair never failing to bring a smile to her face, even on her most stressful days.

Like today. She hadn't slept much since Sage had taken off eleven days ago with just a terse note on the fridge saying he needed some space. Since then, each day stretched out longer and longer until she wondered if her son was somehow able to bend time and space in addition to having a very unique talent for pissing her off.

Not cool, she thought.

Her anxiety over Sage's disappearance joined the low-level dread she'd tried to keep hidden for months. After a decade of building up a nest egg by socking away a deep portion of her paycheck into a safe savings account, she'd taken the plunge and invested most of it in Kencom, a sizzling energy company whose stock was pushing the Dow to new heights. She'd followed Kencom's surge for months, and after a what-the-hell Saturday night alone emboldened by two bottles of Shiraz while watching a particularly bullish cable news talking head, she invested everything she had in it.

Three weeks and six federal indictments of Kencom execs later, her savings account was as bare as it had been when she'd left the Furies.

Then there was the gloom at work. Felix Ingles Fellows II, the legendary 89-year-old interior designer who had introduced the Midwest to restrained neutrals and carefully curated Asian *objets* back in the 1950s, was in the hospital, disabled by a hell of a stroke. The past two days had been filled with huddles and whispers among the staff as Felix's adult children, Trip and Matilda, silently shuffled through the carpeted corridors to their father's office, closed the door behind them and, it was assumed, were making a full assessment of the health and wellbeing of both their father and their father's firm.

It was the moment the staff had been bracing for as they had watched Felix decline in the past year from a vibrant, brilliant thinker to a frail, forgetful, nap-needing elder. Still, he always had time for Oolong tea or a Tanqueray and tonic with Maggie, who seemed to be more of a daughter to him than his own Matilda. He'd discovered her almost two decades ago when, recently divorced from the three other Furies, she'd been decorating windows for a friend's antiques shop and raising Sage alone.

The pairing worked. Maggie felt more solid out of the spotlight, vowing to thoroughly earn her victories over time instead of falling into the quicksand trap of overnight success and financial instability. Felix adored Maggie and patiently guided her as she gained confidence with each success and rose to the top of his firm.

I want you to have all of this, he'd said to her often, late at night, while the two would mix and match swatches and patterns and dream up designs of fantasy homes, just for the fun of it, just to play. *You're the only one who can carry on my legacy.*

And now, with dire rumors and anxiety roiling the office, Maggie was realizing that the time to let go of her mentor and take over the firm had come.

It's time. It's time.

She buzzed Keith, her assistant.

"Any word on Felix?"

9

"Same as yesterday, I guess. He's got such a strong heart it could be—well, a while. Or this afternoon."

"Is he accepting visitors yet?"

"Just family."

"Have Matilda and Trip set up a meeting?"

"Nope."

She nibbled on her left thumb nail, then stretched out her arms to relieve the ache between her shoulders. Her gold charm bracelet rustled in her office's climate-controlled air, the heart locket and "#1 Mom" charm Sage had given her a decade ago bumping up against the plain jade bead Felix had brought back from Hong Kong for good luck, which was resting on an Irish Claddagh, two hands embracing a crowned emerald heart, a keepsake she'd brought back from her last trip to Galway. The gold bracelet and charms had replaced her silver version from the Four Furies era, long ago boxed up and shoved into the attic with the rest of her rock star life.

Her hand brushed up against Sage's old photo, his smile and eyes and coloring pure Aaron.

I can't let this happen.

Her grey flannel pencil skirt and low kitten heels narrowed her strides as she circled her desk as if the open laptop were an uncaged and very hungry lion on the loose in her office. She imagined the lion prowling around the perimeter of the glass-fronted room, brushing up against the midcentury modern arm chairs to scratch the itches throughout its lush mane, then upending the coffee table and scattering sketches, blueprints, and samples. She shook her head and retraced her steps, mentally whisking away the image of a freed male lion threatening her turf.

Don't freak out. Think.

She repeated the pattern again and again while her mind outpaced her steps.

No way in hell will Aaron get Sage.

She fumbled on the keyboard until she tapped out "Aaron Fields Wisconsin" and pulled up a website featuring a mosaic of a weather-beaten cabin, tangled wildflowers, the shadow of a couple holding hands, and Canada geese sunning themselves on an unkempt riverbank.

"*Namaste.* Join us at the Karma Community, a holistic retreat center nestled along the Kickapoo River in southwestern Wisconsin. We offer a respite from the stresses of modern life and serve to enlighten and inspire visitors seeking a new way of engaging the world."

The website made less sense to Maggie than Sage's email.

She clicked through the site until she found Aaron on the staff page, front and center and grinning in a group photo, naturally the star drawing the most attention. Maggie had seen pictures of Aaron during the two decades since they'd broken up, usually accompanying tabloid stories about the aging rock star's king-size drugging and brief sobriety and perpetual money dramas.

She put on her reading glasses and inched closer to Aaron's photo.

Yes.

His head was tilted a bit, but she knew that his nose still showed the indents of her knuckles from the punch that destroyed the Four Furies.

Cool.

She picked up her phone and dialed the number on the website, her charm bracelet jangling against the receiver, then put it back in the cradle before the call went through. Her heels dug into the carpeting as she rushed through the office to the elevator, her overstuffed work tote slung over one shoulder and her Coach purse and suit jacket crumpled under the other arm.

"Reschedule all of my appointments for today," she called over her shoulder to Keith. "I'll be back in the morning."

Chapter 2

Grab a Flashlight

Tyler County, Wisconsin

Maggie blew past the Karma Community three times before pulling into the driveway. She was wired from gas station coffee on the four-hour drive through northern Illinois and southern Wisconsin, forced to take spaghetti strands of poorly labeled country roads through dairy farms and fields of crops she couldn't identify and didn't bother to anyway. She was focused on keeping enough pressure on the gas pedal to speed without getting caught. Then she would grab Sage and yank him home ASAP.

Facing Aaron Fields after twenty years was a thought she couldn't get to just yet, a blind spot that prevented her from seeing the Karma Community's faded sign hidden behind sunshiny wildflowers on the first pass. The second time she missed it because she was so pissed at overshooting it by miles, and when she located it on her third attempt she was thoroughly furious.

She drove up to the whitewashed A-frame splattered with grape vines, did one last check of her makeup in the rearview mirror before pushing her oversize Jackie O-style sunglasses onto the bridge of her nose, and dialed her office on her BlackBerry.

No signal.

Damn.

She ripped the key out of her silver Saab's ignition.

"Sage!"

Maggie banged through the Karma Community's front door, making the chimes on the dream catcher dangling from the doorknob chatter and shudder. She barged through the reception area, ignoring its life-size statue of a young Buddha holding up a slender golden hand in peace, past the lovely atrium and the gift shop overflowing with rainbow-hued pashminas, self-help books, hand-dipped soy candles, and batik tapestries.

"Sage Morgan-Fields!" she yelled up to the unfinished wood beams, to the sun catchers and the waterfall and the mandala painted on the balcony.

"Sage!"

No one answered back.

"Sage!" Maggie bellowed at the yoga class on the sun deck, which did its best to ignore her during a collective downward dog.

A thirtysomething woman in an orange turban, seated on a saffron-colored cushion beside the misty indoor waterfall, opened her eyes as she broke her meditation.

"He's in the grove," she said softly, then closed her eyes gently.

Maggie ran down the hill, slashing through the purple Echinacea and silvery lamb's quarters and feathery yarrow.

In the circle of hawthorns sat Sage.

"There's no need to shout," he said calmly as she approached. "I heard you the first time."

Maggie stood in front of him, feet planted wide apart in the long meadow grass, and rolled up the cuffs of her white blouse, all business.

"You're coming home."

"I can't."

"Why?"

"I am home."

He opened his arms wide, encompassing in his reach the entire property of the Karma Community—the grove, the hills, the meadow, the chicken coops, the homemade gazebo, weathered Adirondack chairs, the gardens, and the large airy main building and small cabins that dotted the land.

"This is where I belong."

Maggie sized him up, looking for any indication that he'd been brainwashed by Aaron and his merry band of followers. On the surface, at least, Sage appeared the same as he had for a while. T-shirt that should have been in a laundry hamper. Chocolate Lab-colored hair that needed a cut and a scrub. Jeans, scuffed sneakers, hard-bitten fingernails. Not enough scruff on his chin to make him look twenty. Mood that seemed stable now, but Maggie knew from years of therapy could change like early spring weather from placid and sweet to glowering and glum, the kind of glumness that made you want to curl up in bed until it would eventually eat itself up in the darkness or be neutralized by a prescription, for a while, at least.

Maggie pushed her sunglasses to the crown of her head to keep her carefully highlighted hair in place. "This is nonsense, Sage. This is Aaron's ego trip, this guru thing. You don't belong in his shadow, not after everything we've been through."

"It's not like that," Sage said, squinting up at her and pulling handfuls of grass out of the ground. "He's not like that. He's a visionary. And I'm a part of his vision."

Sage laid down, spread eagle. Maggie sat down beside him, exasperated, the fire in her eyes cooling to embers.

"We've been through this before," she said plainly. "Aaron is a fascinating man. A genius, in a way. But you shouldn't get caught up in it. Visit him, listen to his empty promises, and love him from a distance. Then let him go. He'll only disappoint you."

Sage picked up a blade of grass and put it up to his lips. "You're biased. He's not like that anymore. And I know he put us through a lot. I remember. I was there. But do I have to live in the past? I want to move on."

He squinted at her, then looked off into the middle distance.

"Besides, aren't you busy with work? You'll never notice that I'm gone."

Maggie grabbed a handful of grass and threw it into the wind. A few dry blades landed on Sage. She brushed them off and scrunched her skirt above her knees, the coolness of the meadow on her bare legs a welcome balm.

"Felix is dying," she said softly.

Sage rolled his eyes and fixed them on the high cumulus clouds.

"He's been dying forever. So this means you're taking over the firm, right?"

"Don't be crass. Felix is a wonderful boss. And I consider him to be a wonderful friend."

"A wonderful friend who's been dangling this in front of you for years. So now he's dying and you get to be the boss. Congrats. You're getting what you always wanted."

Maggie pushed her sunglasses back onto her nose and straightened out her back, knotted from the long drive.

"I'll explain it all in the car. Come on, let's go."

"Who says I'm going?"

"Well, you can't stay."

"Why not? I'm an adult and I can make my own decisions." He kicked her foot softly, affectionately. "I need to do this." He looked straight into her, serious and determined. "Give him a chance."

Her eyes didn't catch his, though.

Maggie sensed Aaron's presence before she actually saw him.

She watched him take his time walking down the hill to the grove, still skinny at sixty-three but comfortable in his own skin.

Damn he looks good.

Maggie exhaled slowly, counting backwards from ten, attempting to release or at least control the thirty years of silent fury she'd endured as Aaron's companion and ex. She clenched her fingers and felt they could fit right back into the dent in his nose if he dared to pull a stunt.

"Welcome, Maggie." Aaron grinned, but then he always did when life got weird.

Maggie smiled up at him, hoping her eyes didn't betray her tension and anger. She inhaled to the count of eight and searched his face, as she always had, for signs of drinking or drugging or a complicated emotional state she'd have to manage.

"I can't stay. Sage and I are leaving."

She exhaled slowly.

Aaron grinned.

She inhaled deeply, breathing in the scents of four organic gardens, innumerable wildflowers, two biodynamic compost piles, and the faint aroma of what would be tonight's dinner for twenty-four guests at the Karma Community. One more deep breath and she'd make her move; she started from the belly up, the way singers do.

"Sage is finding his way," Aaron said softly.

"I am, mom."

"You know how that is," Aaron said, playing on years of pushing Maggie's buttons. "I can hum the melody if you've forgotten."

Maggie held her breath. *I'll never forget.*

Sage stood up, shoulder to shoulder with Aaron.

"I'm staying. I'm working on some projects with Aaron. *Dad*, I mean. I can't go now."

A gong sounded in the distance. Chimes rang in the breeze. Lights snapped on and off in the rooms of the main building. A handful of people walked through the grove, up the hill, and into the light.

"Stay for dinner," Aaron said, extending a hand to Maggie to help her off the grass. "You must have had a long drive. You must have been worried, too, but you shouldn't have been."

Aaron stood close to her, too close for someone who'd drifted in and out of their lives for two decades like curtains blowing in the morning breeze.

Give him a chance, she thought as she inhaled again. *But who deserves one? The son who was finally pulled into the orbit of his father, or the legend who never was a dad?*

"I'll stay, but just for dinner," she said, surprising herself. "I have business to deal with in Chicago."

Aaron whooped and grinned again. Amazing to see that face, whose features she'd only seen on her son for the past two decades. The perma-grin was Aaron's second-most recognizable feature next to his punched-in nose, practically a trademark. Maggie had assumed that it had developed after years of grass, groupies, and the confidence that was the result of the absolute permissiveness and unconditional worship that came with seventies rock stardom. But Sage had inherited it and now, seeing the two of them together, in T-shirts and dirty jeans, Maggie understood why they were refusing to part.

Damn, he looks good.

+++

The dining room was open and dimly lit, with the long, bare pine tables arranged next to windows to take advantage of the ambient light outside. Guests filtered in, some knowing exactly where to sit, others hesitating a bit before taking a seat.

"It's so cool," Sage said while offering his arm and guiding her to a table. "We all eat together and take turns cooking and cleaning. There's never any friction about who's doing what. And I don't mind doing chores, either. It rocks."

Maggie smirked. "So I don't need to pour my own Kool-Aid? How sweet."

The gong sounded again as Sage pushed in his mother's chair. She felt people looking at her, wondering about her. In her bleached-white blouse, tailored skirt, and low heels, she felt utterly overdressed among the second-hand peasant blouses and pit-stained tank tops and stretched-out yoga togs. Her palms erupted in sweat, a lump hardened in her throat, and her gut knotted into a rolling hitch.

She scanned the room and saw Aaron talking to a tomboy, seemingly around Sage's age, in hip-hugger jeans, a smallish T-shirt, and bare feet. They hugged

16

and separated, smiling. Sage seated Maggie next to the woman she'd blown past just an hour earlier, a thirtysomething granola type wearing an orange turban, heavy-rimmed Henry Kissinger glasses, and a citrine stud in her nose.

"Frances, this is my mom, Maggie," Sage said with pride.

"I know," Frances said, her eyes igniting. "It's so nice to meet you."

She leaned in closer to Maggie.

"I have all of your albums."

Maggie held her breath. It had been years since she'd thought of herself as Maggie Morgan of the Four Furies. It was always there in the background, of course, like a lingering perfume or an ache from a long-ago bone break. But for more than a decade her identity was Maggie Morgan, Felix Ingles Fellows' trusted colleague and protégé, a creative force now coming into her own.

But it wasn't just her public persona. Maggie's love of singing was the other thing she lost in the split. The Four Furies had become so toxic by the end, and their songs so sadistic, that Maggie felt traumatized each time she had to sing them. Even the tender love songs Aaron had written for Maggie became distressing reminders of how optimistic they'd been at the beginning of their relationship. And the mega-hits lost their punch when they merely represented a line on their accountant's ledger.

The gong sounded again and the room went silent. Frances stood up and held her palms aloft and swayed, her eyes closed. Maggie could hear her humming something in a minor key, a melody that seemed both ancient and made up on the spot.

Frances swept her hands over the food-laden table. A little whoosh washed over Maggie, making the back of her neck tingle. She bowed her head, like everyone else, and stared at her chipped dinner plate, the crack slicing through it threatening to split it in two.

Just one dinner here and I can take Sage back to reality.

"Mother Earth, you are so plentiful and generous," Frances said in a solemn voice loud enough to carry throughout the spare dining room. "We thank you for your bounty and promise to share your gifts with an open heart."

Frances hoisted a bread basket over her head as the diners murmured "thank you" and "Blessed Be" and the room came alive again. Napkins fluttered, silverware clanged, and pitchers and serving plates were passed around as the warm June evening sun illuminated the room.

Sage introduced Maggie to the others at the table, proud of the friendships he'd made at the center. Frances practiced energetics, herbalism, and goddess spirituality, could forecast the future, and also worked in the business office. Gilman, a quiet, handsome blond with a deep tan, taught nature-inspired art classes and pitched in to help Aaron whenever needed. Sage pointed to a few young men and women scattered at other tables, but they all blurred together in Maggie's mind.

Aaron sat across the room, glancing at Maggie every so often but mostly, hungrily, at the hip-huggered girl at his side. Maggie did her best to ignore them as a helping of garlicky mustard greens was offered up to her. She passed the bowl to Frances and picked at her plate, pushing the tangy sourdough bread to one side of the crack and the greens and braised carrots to the other.

"Dad and I are fired up about our plans," Sage explained while the berry crumble was being set out. "We're getting a drum circle together. Dad says the guitar depresses him, feels like karaoke. I can never get him to play it. But I'm stoked about our plans. And we're going to hook up with other drum circles around the world and synchronize them, and try to work up some good energy. Really get buzzed. I hope it gets political."

Sage scooped up a huge portion of dessert, obviously not satisfied with greens and carrots.

"But we've got a big thing—a huge thing—in the works. It's going to take a year, at least. It's got to be totally planned out in advance. That's why I'm here."

Aaron obviously doesn't know his son well, Maggie thought. *Sage can't even commit to washing and drying his clothes on the same day, much less plan a year-long project and then actually see it through.*

"I shouldn't be talking about it, though," he explained while chasing a blueberry around his dish. "We're not even in the planning stage yet. Sybylla's helping, too." Sage blushed a bit and looked down at his plate.

Maggie smiled, knowing that Sage's attention to the project would wane long before his interest in this new girl.

"Who's Sybylla?" she asked, trying to seem interested and supportive.

Sage looked at her, puzzled.

"Syb? Aaron's wife. My step mom."

He cocked his head toward that tomboy at Aaron's side.

"And she's just two years older than me. Weird, hey?"

The macrobiotic dinner turned to lead in Maggie's stomach. Aaron didn't believe in marriage. He and Maggie had refused to get married when they were young and in love, and then when they were a famous couple they stayed single because it was sexier. And when Maggie walked out on the band she'd been grateful that she could just pack up and leave, no divorce, no mess, no fuss about taking custody of Sage. Aaron hadn't been interested in anything but his yawning need for more drugs and women and adulation, and Maggie wouldn't have allowed Aaron to be Sage's dad even if he had been somewhat sober and faithful. The damage had been done.

But Aaron always had a different explanation, which he offered up anytime anyone asked—especially in interviews. He and Maggie were married on the soul level, Aaron claimed, and that bond transcended time and space and could never be broken in a court of law or anywhere else—not by Maggie's walkout in Tampa or their decades of estrangement, if you extended Aaron's logic.

As he put it, Aaron didn't believe in legal marriage because he believed in the separation of spirit and state, and he thought the nation's founders would agree with him on this point. Aaron believed in independent thinking, ultimate knowledge, and universal connectivity. The state had no place in any of that, nor did banking and commerce or property or possessions. It had no business legitimizing relationships or newborns, or what he'd put in his body to feed it, medicate it, or alter its state. It had no business knowing how much money he earned or what he did with it. He filed his taxes only when he knew he'd get a refund; he felt he supported enough people through his band and at times outrageous consumption and waste.

And now he's married to a girl who was my age when we started the Furies, Maggie thought as she sipped her chilled mint tea. *What a cliché he's become, the elderly rock star and the compliant, hot babe who makes him feel like a stud again.*

Maggie snuck another look at her former partner, surrounded by admirers seeking wisdom and perhaps a few autographs or more. Cynically, Maggie thought, the Karma Community must be some elaborate tax dodge that keeps him afloat and at least slightly legit.

I think I know where the Furies' money went.

Maggie could feel Sage watching her and she refused to react.

"You've got to move on," he said gently. "Sybylla's cool. She's not like other girls my age, and she and Aaron are happy. She wants me to stay and help out. She says that Aaron and I need to get to know each other so we don't repress things in our other relationships. It's all about *integration*." Sage lengthened that last word as if he loved it. "I don't want to be blocked or repressed. The entire world is blocked."

Maggie spied Sybylla and Aaron getting up from their table, totally in sync.

"You know, some dads play catch in the backyard with their sons. Mine is going to fire up a drum circle with me. You've got to admit that rocks." He wiggled his eyebrows until she laughed.

"It's good to see you laugh again, Maggie," Aaron said over her shoulder. She turned and saw him, his eyes sparkling. She couldn't read him though; he'd faked that sparkle before.

"I'd like you to meet my wife," he said while throwing his arm around Sybylla. A flash of metal gleamed on his left hand, while Sybylla's ring finger seemed bare except for a dull tattoo.

"It's wonderful to finally meet you," Sybylla said sweetly, almost, Maggie thought, genuinely. "I hope you don't think I was being rude or trying to avoid you. I just thought you needed some space."

"I didn't think you were being rude at all," Maggie said, lying.

"We want you to stay the night," Aaron said firmly. "These country roads are impossible in the dark."

"I made up a room for you," Sybylla cut in. "Our poet-in-residence is away right now, so you can have her cabin for as long as you like. You can be our singer-in-residence."

"Our mother-in-residence," Sage suggested.

"Thanks. But I should head back in the morning," Maggie said, trying to cut the conversation short. "I need to visit a very ill friend in the hospital."

"Make yourself at home," Sybylla said. "I put some motherwort tincture next to your bed. Take a dropperful in water to relax."

This is what relaxed looks like at fifty-two, Maggie thought.

"There's some ginseng and lemon balm, too," Sybylla added quickly. "In case you need a pick-me-up. And clothes. Just ask and we'll bring you anything you need."

Maggie had to admit that she looked like she needed a pick-me-up. The eleven days of worrying about Sage and the nonstop anxiety over Felix had made her overwrought and cranky.

"Grab a flashlight, Maggie," Aaron said cheerfully. "The path to your room is dark."

Maggie stiffened and met his eyes.

"Thanks," she said while snatching the flashlight from him. "But I can find my way on my own."

Chapter 3

Rewriting History, Again

Lying in bed with the morning sunlight drifting into her cabin, Maggie felt pressure on her legs before it moved up to her belly. Her eyes wouldn't open; her brain was still in an exhausted twilight and she couldn't lift her head off the pillow. But she reached down and felt something furry and alert, a critter. She forced her eyes open. A big orange tabby stared back at her, looking for company.

But Maggie wasn't much of a companion at the moment. She'd barely slept after a long crying jag, first on the edge of the bed and then on the rag rug on the cottage floor. She'd cried deep sobs, the kind a child does when she loses her mom in a grocery store—freaked-out, darkly existential sobs expressing abandonment and fear. They were primal, a deep howl that reached down into the Earth's core and accessed ancient universal terror. Once they started, they couldn't stop. No amount of logic would clip them.

Maggie hadn't cried like that in years, not when her parents died or during the recent weeks when Sage had gone missing without a clue. She hadn't cried at all when she'd left Aaron and the band—she couldn't let herself think too deeply about the implications of her actions, and too afraid that the tears, once released, would never stop. Instead, she imagined that her spine was an icicle, and that she was facing a cold, cruel world on her own.

But last night's pain was immediate and it hurt and she couldn't control it. Even the motherwort couldn't chase the Four Furies away. They'd been, she saw now, a middle-of-the-road band at the tail end of a corrupt rock era that was itself being eaten up by disco, adult contemporary, punk, and rap. Despite his charisma and talent, Aaron was no Eric Clapton or Duane Allman, and Maggie was no Stevie Nicks or Linda Ronstadt or Carly Simon. But the combination of Aaron's effortless fire, Maggie's coolness, Pete's groove, and Hooch's steadiness worked well enough. It pulled Maggie out of her Philadelphia art college to Boulder, temporarily, and then to southern California with Aaron and the guys, which she loved even if she was ever fearful of another Manson Family rampage or urban riot. Aaron, on the other hand, jumped in with both feet and legs and arms, dealing drugs to support the band at first, then making connections in the industry. He swallowed the scene whole like a snake swallows an egg.

The Four Furies' dynamic worked better than they'd expected, and even the band members were surprised by their quick success and loyal following. The Four Furies' image and sound were of its time yet timeless. Maggie and Aaron were seen as the real deal, a back-to-the-land love match that contrasted with glitzy couples who baited the paparazzi at nightclubs. Shy, remote, ultra-feminine, and out-of-time, even at the peak of the Four Furies' celebrity Maggie looked like she could have been a quiet preacher's daughter on the prairie, not a rock star whose ambivalence toward fame made her more famous. "The Mona Lisa of Rock," as she was dubbed, let Aaron do the talking for both of them in public so she could preserve her voice for the stage.

Maggie kept her cool throughout the Four Furies' lifespan, through their struggle and kudos and demise, Aaron's scores and affairs and stupid deals. She kept her cool when the feminists attacked her for being a throwback, a puppet whose ventriloquist boyfriend put words in her mouth, even when it seemed abusive. Maggie took the criticism and the praise and absorbed it into her system the way her flowerpots soak up the rain. She never let it show. It fed her, in fact.

But then in Tampa in the autumn of 1982, fed up with a life she fell into, she severed the Four Furies' connection with a very clean blade and a very solid punch. Her dramatic departure freed her, but it also made the Four Furies more famous and turned Maggie into an instant legend. Sage had seen the photos of Aaron crumpled on stage, Maggie sticking a stiletto heel in his side, but she waved it off as theatrics, nothing more, and very much left in the past.

And the past is where she wanted to leave it all. She put on her skirt and blouse, heels and charm bracelet, looking more rumpled than the night before, and took a dropper of the ginseng on her tongue, without water. Nasty, but it matched her mood.

The tabby trailed her as she made her way up the path to say goodbye to Sage and then make the long drive from western Wisconsin to northern Chicago, alone, to get back to the office. She didn't like the thought of leaving Sage in Aaron's hands, but there didn't seem to be too much harm in letting him stay, for a little while at least. Besides, Aaron inevitably burned people after charming them, she knew all too well. It was just a matter of time before he'd reveal his true self to Sage and Sage would return home with a clear-eyed view of his dad.

She brushed her hand lightly on the tops of the bushes, careful to avoid the brambly purple barberry, anxious to return to Chicago and visit Felix one last time.

Maggie seemed to be the last one up. The main cabin had come alive at dawn, when chimes rang to call residents to yoga and sun salutations. Three staff members chopped fruit and filled clay pitchers with water from the pump. Aaron sat cross-legged, surprisingly peaceful and limber, next to the indoor waterfall, a beam of sunlight from the atrium illuminating his face. Maggie wasn't sure if he was asleep or transcending some sort of existential limit or, as he was in the old days, simply stoned out of his mind.

"Good morning, Maggie," he said, his tone neither here nor there. "Sleep well?"

"Yes, of course." She hoped he wouldn't notice her puffy eyes and drained, pinched expression. "I'm just looking for Sage before I go."

"He's gathering plants. The lindens are blossoming now and we've got to act quickly. The flowers are very fragile, very precious. I'm sure you've smelled them. We'll make tea with them later."

"I've got to go," she said and turned toward the door.

"Take your time, Maggie. Take a walk. Stay for breakfast. Now that you're here you might as well enjoy it."

"Ah, Aaron. I need to go back. I have a life, you know, and a business. Appointments. Clients. A friend in the ICU. A lot of people depend on me."

"They'll understand."

"They won't."

Aaron stretched his legs out in from of him, his faded Levi's baggy at the knees.

"Go on. Have a glass of lemon water. You should start your day with it even if you don't stay here. It opens up your liver and gets you ready for the day."

"And then I can seize it."

"And then you can seize it." He smiled. "I'm glad you came."

23

Maggie couldn't help herself. The question had been tugging at her for twelve days.

"How did you find Sage?"

Aaron laughed. "Google. Actually, he found me."

Ouch.

Maggie had assumed that Aaron had made random contact with Sage, the same random way he'd call in the middle of the night from St. Louis or Sturgis or Akron wishing Sage a happy birthday three months too late. She hadn't considered that Sage had done the seeking. But she had to admit that their son had been adrift lately. College wasn't working, leaving him behind his friends from high school, and he'd gotten irritated every time Maggie suggested alternatives. She'd even offered to take him on at the firm or arrange something with one of her friends, but he curled up his lip. *Too restless for that,* he had said. *Just like your father,* she'd responded under her breath.

"I was shocked when I got his call, but then I'd tried so hard to make contact, I guess he picked up on my vibe," Aaron said casually.

"Wait, let me get this straight," Maggie said, the ginseng finally doing its thing. "You tried so hard to make contact with Sage. When? On what planet? Here on Earth you had vanished. Poof."

"I tried—"

"Don't rewrite history."

"I tried," he said firmly. "I'm not perfect. But you made it impossible for me to form a relationship with Sage."

Maggie reddened at the insult.

"I did? That's fascinating."

"You did. You took him—you snatched him and I was powerless. You wouldn't let me see him when he was born. I was shocked that you named him Morgan-Fields. I'm sure you just did it to guilt trip me."

Maggie heard footsteps behind her and put her hand to her mouth, rolling her eyes toward their unseen visitors.

"Your parents made damn sure that I knew I wasn't welcome." Aaron's voice rose, almost begging the eavesdroppers to stay put. "Your father never thought that I was good enough for you."

"Don't bring them into this." Maggie's jaw clenched. "They rescued Sage and me. You have no idea how much we suffered."

"I suffered too, Maggie. You took my child. It's not natural."

"You weren't fit to be a father. You were a drug dealer when I met you and a drug addict when I left you."

Aaron closed his eyes, searching for the right words.

"True, I've never been an upright citizen. But you didn't give me a chance. I gave him life, damn it—and you sucked him into a black hole. There is only one Sage Morgan-Fields in this universe and you stole him."

Maggie was silent, stunned. Adrenaline washed through her veins, spiking her blood.

"I didn't steal him. I saved him. Whatever happened to you is your own damn fault."

She clenched and opened her hands by her side, palms sweaty and heated, her gold charm bracelet creating a snag on her slim skirt.

"You almost destroyed me," he said with renewed intensity. "You came damn close to breaking my spirit. I always controlled my drug use when you were around. But then you left, pregnant with my son, and I spiraled down and down and down—I tasted dirt and walked through fire and licked the gates of hell. And I liked it. Loved it, in fact. Why not? Nothing mattered without my son. Nothing mattered without you."

Aaron ran his fingers through his slept-on hair, simultaneously losing his cool and keeping it all under control.

"No shit I was stoned. No shit I gambled. No shit I pawned the guitars."

Maggie thought that Aaron finally looked his age—old, beaten, bitter, the dent in his nose making him look haggard, not rakishly handsome.

"And now you're telling me it's all my fault," she said with defiance.

"No, I'm not. I'm telling you my side of the story."

Maggie glared at him. "You have no idea how hard it was."

"Don't pull that martyr crap. I always had to do your dirty work—cut the deals, play the heavy, make the tough decisions for you and me and the band. You just got to stay at home and save your voice and come on stage for the applause. Too fragile and sensitive to get involved in all of the dirty work."

"You're rewriting history again," Maggie said, her anger escalating. "You didn't want me to get involved in the business."

Aaron took a deep breath and brought himself back to composure.

"It's amazing, Maggie. You cling to the past but you can't deal with it. And because you can't deal with it you're doomed to live it out every single day."

Maggie rolled her eyes and looked at the water stream over the pebbles and settle into the pool.

"Your silence is deafening," Aaron said.

Maggie wouldn't let the old wounds reopen.

"Fighting is healthy, you know. Clears the air. Communicates your feelings. We were really on a roll there."

Maggie shook her head at Aaron, shook it at the whole situation.

"Come on, Maggie. You never could resist me after a good fight," he grinned. "We always had our best sex afterwards."

Maggie took a step back and paused, readying her final blow.

"Believe me, Aaron," she said, lowering her voice an octave. "You are totally resistible now."

He let the insult wash over him and reached out his hand with an open palm.

"Stay, Maggie. For Sage. For me. We always worked best as a team."

She thought he was pitiful.

She slung her purse over her shoulder and turned toward the door.

"Tell Sage I had to go. I'll call him later."

Maggie walked through the reception area to the front door and saluted the Buddha statue with her middle finger. She reached for the doorknob and gave it a good pull. The rainbow-colored dream catcher hanging from the knob latched on to her beloved charm bracelet.

Damnit, she spat, caught.

She gave her bracelet a tug, and another tug and twist, and sprang out the door, tumbling down the front steps and skittering into a heap. Her temple bled into her highlighted blonde streaks and her right foot jutted out the wrong way. A kitten heel kicked out into the gravel driveway pointed toward her Saab.

Chapter 4

She Was Hooked, Too

"I need to," Maggie moaned. "I have to. I … *ow*."

Her right foot, propped up on a saffron-colored yoga cushion, would not budge, no matter how hard she tried to make it move. She leaned forward in an attempt to lift her head from the pillow, but the only thing in motion was a shot of pain through her brow and right shoulder, then underneath her right lung whenever she took a deep breath. The pain sliced through her confusion like a soprano nailing High C.

"You're not going anywhere," Aaron said from across the room, where he was reading a thick book on Native American medicine. "Doctor's orders."

The morning was coming into focus. A pull on a dream catcher, a fall, a trip to the emergency room in the backseat of her Saab, Aaron driving, Sage riding shotgun, Sybylla crouching over Maggie trying to get her to do deep yoga breaths to take her mind off her pain, even though the deep breathing hurt like hell. Despite her concussion's cirrus clouds wafting through her thoughts, Maggie had the presence of mind to refuse any of the Karma Community's herbal medicine, compresses, poultices, or Reiki vibes; she demanded an M.D. and she got one in the ER who treated her for a mild concussion, pulled shoulder, road rash, and a badly sprained ankle.

She moaned as she thought of how much it would cost to clean up the vomit she'd spewed in her backseat on the way to the hospital.

"I need to go to Chicago," she whispered. "I need to go to Felix."

+++

Sage brought his mother's breakfast into her cabin on her second day of seclusion.

"You shouldn't shut yourself up like this," he told her. "It's rude. And then I have to make excuses for you."

Maggie sat in the Shaker-style rocking chair and stared out the window into the tangled barberry lining the path to the main building. Sybylla had brought her a flowy paisley tunic and an A-line wrap skirt that looked like it had been home sewn during the Jimmy Carter administration. An elaborately carved walking stick rested against her chair as she sat with her wrapped ankle propped up on a denim patch-covered ottoman, a pale pink hand-knit shawl wrapped loosely around her shoulders. The emerald was conspicuously absent from the Claddagh charm hanging off her bracelet.

"I'm just not ready," she said slowly. "Everyone heard our fight. They saw me wipe out on the front steps. They know everything."

"Get over it, mom. If there's one place you can let everything hang out, it's the Karma Community. No one cares, you know?"

Maggie watched some pale-yellow butterflies fly over the bushes, then get blown to another patch of the garden.

"Take me back to Chicago. This afternoon. I need to say goodbye to Felix."

"Do you really want him to see you like this?"

Maggie touched the gauze pad on her temple and her tightly wrapped right arm to keep her shoulder in place.

How would I ever explain this mess?

She sighed and took a long look at Sage—unscrubbed and thinner than usual but with a bounce in his step she hadn't seen in ages.

"You should have left me a note," Maggie said tartly. "You shouldn't have taken off like that. I hope you brought your meds."

"I can take care of myself, mom," Sage said, clearly exasperated. "I'm an adult."

The butterflies returned to the window and Maggie sighed.

"Do you really like it here?" she asked.

"Totally," Sage said and sat down on the tidily made bed. "It blows my brain every day. I see how much bullshit there is in the world. And how even thinking about things can change it. Energetically. I mean, we're all connected, you

28

know? And if my ass refuses to, like, sell out, then that's one less sellout on the planet."

"But what are you going to do, Sage? Like, with your life?"

Maggie and Sage had been circling around this question for a few years now. Instead of striking out on his own, in Maggie's eyes Sage merely wanted to prolong adolescence and work in a used-record shop, or detail skateboards, or learn how to tattoo. Now, Maggie thought, these options seemed positively Republican compared to trying to save the world through drumming. With Aaron, no less.

"Don't know," he said. "All I know is that I don't want to be a slave to my job. Maybe you can relate."

Maggie sighed again and continued staring out the window, feeling the time ticking away back at the office. "I just don't want you to have any regrets. I don't want you to be twenty-five and have no skills in the real world and have to struggle to catch up. All because you wanted to hang out with Aaron."

Sage snorted. "Were you talking to me, or to yourself?"

He looked at her directly, then wished he hadn't said anything.

"I'm doing something here, you know, even if you do have a low opinion of it. Besides, the real world is totally overrated."

Not knowing what else to do or say, he got up to go.

"Sage."

The hint of panic in Maggie's voice stopped him cold.

"Was I a good mother?"

He opened the door and the orange tabby rushed in between his legs.

"Yeah, sure," he said, slightly embarrassed. "You just need to chill out."

He closed the door softly and Maggie could hear his footsteps crunch the gravel and twigs on the dirt path. The tabby sniffed the air, then rubbed against the legs of the desk, looking up at Maggie in anticipation of some affection.

"Shoo," she said. "Can't you leave me alone?"

Maggie tried to ignore the cat and inspected the contents of her breakfast tray—sliced apple, almond butter and toast, lemon water, and coffee, a surprise. She took a big sip of it with a Vicodin while the cat stretched out on the rug. "Well, at least you're happy," she said to the drowsy creature. "I'm just the crazy old lady who's making a mess of things."

She nibbled her toast and noticed a notebook and a magazine under her plate. She picked up the notebook and an oak leaf fell out. A message was written on it in magic marker: *Maggie—please draw & write & paint. Join us when you're ready. Pax—Sybylla.*

Maggie scoffed at the peace offering. She never kept a journal, never saw the point of it. She had total recall, both a blessing and a curse, and often felt old emotions rush through her as if the past were as vivid as the present. A journal was simply redundant.

"I should have done more drugs with the Furies," she told the cat. "Then I would have forgotten everything, just like Aaron."

That life seemed far away, about as distant as her early sketches of the characters she met when the band was on tour. She put down her coffee and thought about Felix, so frail now, and her assistant, Keith, hoping he was able to cover for her without doing too much damage. She needed to get back to Chicago or at the very least put in a call to Felix, but her cell phone couldn't pick up a signal so far out in the river valley, and she had winced mightily as she'd walked with her cane from the bed to her chair. Driving back to Chicago was out of the question, today at least.

She put the notebook on the floor and picked up the magazine—the Karma Community's catalog, she discovered. The cover was a photo of the main building, the one Maggie had burst through when she first arrived, the one in which she'd had her blowup with Aaron, the one she'd become entangled in and fallen out of. In the picture, the sun was setting behind it, lighting up the green and lavender hills, an idyllic retreat that seemed untouched by modern stresses.

Maggie put on her reading glasses, opened the catalog to a random page, and found the retreat center's rules: No synthetic perfumes or personal products; no cell phones; no personal calls of any sort, unless they were made in the center's business office; no drugs or alcohol, unless they were prescribed by a doctor or herbalist; no intolerance; no judgment; no fears.

She scanned through the course listings: "Interpreting Signs and Omens in Nature," conducted during a walking tour of the community's grounds. "Releasing Tension through Partner Yoga," a weekend course. "Creating a Protective Shield," taught in one night. And "Deciphering the Mayan Calendar," an ongoing course, presumably ending before the world would in 2012.

"Maybe Sage is right," she said while extending her hand to the cat. "Maybe the real world is overrated."

Maggie recognized some of the topics since yoga and various alternative therapies and philosophies had permeated the atmosphere of southern California in the 1970s. She'd meditated then, and had been in consciousness-raising groups when that had been in vogue, especially among self-respecting feminists, which she had considered herself to be. While she never really got comfortable with letting it all hang out in public, apparently others did and benefited from it. She'd been on a macrobiotic diet, too, but then she had been on many diets that everyone was pushing then—Small Planet, grapefruit, whole grains, wheatgrass, fiber pills, uppers, B-12 shots, cocaine. Maggie tried them all, got cranky and thin, then went off them and got depressed, just like a million other women who were pressured into being thin and blonde and liberated.

Looking through the catalog as she waited for the Vicodin to kick in, she noticed that the Karma Community's courses were packaged with workshops and tapes, sometimes with DVDs or CD-Roms—a definite difference from their seventies forerunners. The Karma Community's course leaders were professionals, academics, authors with major publishers and graduate degrees. Maggie spotted no one who looked at home in the seventies, no acid-influenced masters who seemed as if they'd gone through the doors of consciousness on a stained Persian rug in the back of a van, the way most metaphysical teachers were created back then. The Karma Community's teachers all looked earnest and clean; the old gurus were gamey, crunchy, dangerous. They didn't offer workbooks or videos—they crawled into your head and messed with it, sometimes beyond repair.

Aaron didn't seem to teach any courses, but he appeared throughout the catalog, and Maggie zeroed in on him in a posed group shot of the community's staff. She hated to admit it, but even after all of these years—many of them Aaron's lost years, rougher than she knew—Aaron still had that undeniable spark that made him the focal point of any group. Unlike Maggie, who had to deliberately turn it on before each performance or photo shoot, Aaron just was. Even in the candid shots—especially in the candid shots, when he was relaxed—Aaron's certain something leaped off the page. That magnetism was essential for a rock star, and even for a lover, but it spelled hell for any relationship between two equal adults who had independent and sometimes divergent thoughts and opinions.

Maggie gasped when she saw one picture, of Aaron holding a long-limbed weed and grinning with the sun glinting behind him. It captured the quintessential Aaron that Maggie remembered from early in their history, during their happiest times, both as a couple and as musicians.

The Four Furies—Maggie and Aaron, joined by his old friends Pete and Hooch—had formed in Philadelphia, but the young musicians took a road trip to Colorado, where they perfected their songs and sound and lived off the land, simply and economically. They reveled in that life, even loving their hardships and sacrifices. The Four Furies' first album, *Gone West*, and its lead single, "Home Is Where You Are," got raves for its heartfelt portrait of a quiet utopia in the tall grass on the range. Maggie's alto was simple and unadorned, and the songs Aaron wrote for her spoke of their honest love, their nights under a quilt of stars. Aaron portrayed Maggie as a wildflower just budding or a shy young woman who had no idea of her soap-scrubbed allure, while he played the midnight rambler role all too well.

The untouched image was to be short lived. They moved to California and recorded a series of albums in quick succession, some better than others, but all compelled the listener to eavesdrop on the drama of Maggie and Aaron's relationship.

Maggie looked again at the group shot, now drawn to Sybylla, who was looking at Aaron and laughing. There was something about that openhearted laugh that made Maggie think about meeting Aaron in 1971.

I never wanted to be a rock star, Maggie thought. *I just wanted to hang onto that feeling I first felt with Aaron. The feeling of freedom.*

She adjusted her reading glasses and focused in on Sybylla, lit up like a comet as she gazed at Aaron in the staff photo.

Watch out for her. She's hooked, too.

Chapter 5

Just Ask the Furies

Maggie appeared in the tea room of the main building, grimacing as she balanced on her good leg and her walking stick. Sage had told her the only working land line was in the second-floor office and she was determined to hop or crawl or fly up the stairs to get to a phone and call Felix. She'd unbundled her right arm, still aching from the accident, but held it close to her chest for security. She limped up the stone path, up a few steps to the patio and then through the cool tea room for a rest.

Thank god for pain killers, she thought as she pulled herself up the first few steps, treading lightly on her sprained ankle. Step, pull; step, pull. Rest.

She was sweating through her tunic by the time she got upstairs, then hobbled to the first door in the hallway: locked. Second door: locked. All the doors: locked.

She limped to the balcony and waited, rubbing her hand over the well-worn head of her walking stick, her arm still kind of rubbery from its injury. Lightheaded, she leaned against the wall, taking in a pleasant mixture of bread baking in the kitchen downstairs and Nag Champa incense, which seemed to permeate the second floor. A familiar smell from California. Chimes shimmered downstairs, along with the indoor waterfall, part of the white noise of the center that helped to remove it from the real world. The afternoon sunlight created soft shadows in the whitewashed hallway. Maggie closed her heavy eyelids so she could engrave that cloud color in her memory and mix up a paint that could mimic it in a client's bedroom. Mostly a soft white with just a splash of grey to give it some depth. Some lavender, too. But mostly a soft white like clouds.

She heard a hum downstairs, then a shadow at the foot of the steps.

"Hello? Can you help me?"

Sybylla looked up, startled. She tucked a loose chestnut curl into her red bandana, which she wore like a Polish babushka, and smiled, her teeth just crooked enough to be perfect.

"Maggie. What a surprise. What do you need?"

Maggie licked her lips and hoped that her opiate-coated tongue wouldn't be too sluggish and make her sound stoned.

"I'd like to call my friend in the hospital. Sage told me there's a phone in the office. Could you help me?"

Maggie could see Sybylla relax as her thin shoulders retreated into her T-shirt.

"Of course."

She took the steps two at a time and pulled the keys off her lanyard attached to her belt loop. She smiled at Maggie as she approached, but it seemed canned to Maggie, a smile without her eyes. The smile of a Sphinx, of a double agent, of a ticking time bomb.

"Thank you," she whispered as Sybylla opened the second door on the left.

"Take your time. Just remember to lock the door when you leave." Sybylla eyed Maggie's wrapped ankle, white knuckle-gripped walking stick and flushed cheeks and hesitated before closing the door. "Are you going to get down the stairs all right?"

"I'm fine, I'm fine." Maggie waved away Sybylla's concerns as she sat down on a cushioned desk chair.

"I know you have your own prescription medication, but you might want to try some comfrey, too," Sybylla said. "I'd be happy to make you some tea or a foot bath."

Maggie smiled a bland smile of condescension, the way she always had when she refused to acknowledge Aaron's other women. As long as Maggie kept calm and appeared unbothered by the competition, she'd invariably outlast them all, she learned. And she did.

"No need to worry about me," she said firmly.

"Just trying to help." Sybylla closed the door behind her and Maggie felt like she'd just kicked a kitten.

She locked the door behind her, flicked on the desk lamp and looked at her reflection in the octagonal mirror above the desk. She looked like she was having her worst day. A Band-Aid that needed to be changed at her temple. Unwashed hair streaked with silver and with kinks and frizz from the river valley humidity. Not a trace of makeup. Clear blue eyes but crinkly crows' feet at the corners. Purplish prints beneath them.

I could use a long hot shower and some decent moisturizer, she thought as she pulled at the soft skin at her throat, then smoothed out the wrinkles in her borrowed tunic and skirt. *Some clean clothes wouldn't hurt, either.*

She pulled the phone over the piles of papers on the cluttered desk and stroked her left eyebrow, trying to smooth out the tension that suddenly tightened her forehead. She dialed her office, then a cell phone number.

"Keith, it's me."

"Where have you been?"

"I know, I know. I'm sorry."

"I've been worried about you."

"It's been a rough few days," she sighed. "I was in an accident."

"What kind of an accident? Are you hurt?"

Maggie paused, making Keith wait for her answer.

"I'm pretty banged up, but I'm going to be okay. I'm trying to walk. I can't drive, that's for sure."

"Oh my god. No wonder why—"

"What happened?" Maggie's stomach seized up and her mouth turned sour.

"Felix died." Keith took a long breath, then exhaled into the receiver. "He died right after you left the office."

"Oh god."

Maggie coiled the phone cord around her wrist and felt a hot flash jolt through her, making her mind go blank for a few very long seconds and flushing the pain pill out of her system. She snapped back to reality.

"I didn't think he would—"

"He took a turn and that was it."

"How are Trip and Matilda?"

"Hmmm…" Keith took his time responding. "No tears. All business. The funeral is on Saturday morning at the cathedral downtown. You better be there."

"I will, I will."

She put the receiver back in the cradle before Keith could make her feel worse about missing Felix's final day. Her hands shook as she tried to control her breathing.

He's gone.

The finality of Felix's death was making its way into her brain. Felix, who'd found her toiling away as a window dresser and realized she had the eye and raw talent for something bigger. Felix, who knew nothing about her Four Furies past, only caring that she was willing to work hard to methodically build a future for herself and her young son. They'd laugh about it later, the clueless effete and the ex-celebrity right under his nose, but they respected what the other brought to their partnership. Felix, a mentor who finally found in Maggie worthy successor to groom, not his son Trip, not his daughter Matilda. At the same time, Maggie felt most comfortable in Felix's long shadow as long as she could slow down and work her way up step by step and take care of Sage in peace.

I owe him so much, she thought. *But it's too late to tell him.*

Her last moments with Felix were on the phone a week ago, curt and serious as they finalized a design plan for some client who'd be forgotten next year. Of course she didn't say goodbye or tell him how grateful she was for being folded under his wing.

I hope he didn't die hating me for not being there.

Maggie straightened out her back and thought of what she'd have to face when she got back to work. When was the right time to talk to Trip and Matilda about business? She needed a lawyer, she was sure. She'd have to sign some sort of papers. And would Morgan & Fellows Designs need to be phased in or could she just change the name immediately? She'd never discussed a name change with Felix, but it seemed utterly appropriate. After all, how could she be the boss if her name wasn't on the stationery?

It's time. It's time.

She blinked her eyes tightly, then opened them and took in the contents of the Karma Community's cramped office to change the focus of her thoughts. Piles of catalogs, stacks of printer paper. Incense sticks stuck in the potted plants dotting the windowsills. A tangle of cables coming out of a boxy desktop computer. A nearly obsolete fax machine with a red light pulsing in time with her temple. Posters of wildlife with inspirational quotes. Brightly patterned batik tapestries hanging on the walls that would liven up the three-season room she was planning for Carole and Brett Maggiano back in Chicago. Pictures of Aaron, pictures of Sybylla.

Why aren't Trip and Matilda asking for me?

She stood, her legs tense and stiff, and leaned against the desk to stretch out the hamstring and calf of her uninjured leg.

It's what we've all been waiting for.

She rubbed her shoulder, allowing the torn muscles to burn and sear her with pain. Her right hand fell on an oversized binder with a telltale heft. She scanned the sticky notes and unopened envelopes that jutted out of the binder's edges.

I can't. I won't. I mustn't.

She lifted the cover a crack to see if she was disturbing anything, then opened the checkbook fully. The check stubs attached to the binder rings would tell the entire story, she knew, so she flipped through them quickly, noting the sums and not caring who the checks were made out to or what the unopened bank statements said. She reflexively reached up to her hairline for her reading glasses, which she'd left behind in her cabin, thinking she wouldn't need them just to make a phone call. Still, she could make out the tidy handwriting that surely didn't belong to Aaron.

But the money did. And the numbers denoting the running balance were larger—far larger—than she assumed could be generated by a hippie retreat center in Wisconsin's Kickapoo River valley run by a notoriously hedonistic rock star who claimed he'd been swindled for decades by corrupt managers and record executives and never had paid a dime in child support because he was too indigent to provide any cash for them. The balance was certainly larger than what she had in her own accounts—hell, larger than what she'd invested and lost in Kencom.

Damn it, Aaron. This is my *money. This is the Four Furies' money. This is Sage's money.*

Another knock on the door and Maggie snapped the checkbook shut.

"Maggie?" the muffled voice said as the doorknob rattled in place.

"Just a minute," Maggie said as coolly as she could. "I'm just getting off the phone."

The picked up the receiver only to slam it into the cradle to cover her tracks.

All of the sacrifices I made to raise Sage alone, and Aaron's sitting on a pile of money.

She snapped off the light as she opened the door, doing her best to control her breathing.

"I wanted to see if you needed help getting downstairs." Sybylla stepped off the top of the stairs and onto the landing, a bundle of papers in her hands.

"I told you I'm fine."

Sybylla reached past Maggie to open the door, curled her arm in to push the lock on the interior doorknob, then pulled the door firmly shut.

"Everything okay in Chicago?" Sybylla asked with honey in her voice. "Or do you need to go back to your business?"

Maggie took a long look at this young woman who had replaced her in Aaron's heart. She was almost impossible not to like. Just the right amount of innocence to gloss over Aaron's worst flaws and enough steel to keep him from harm. Beautiful, of course, but not intimidatingly so. As welcoming and generous as Maggie Morgan of the Four Furies was insular, unapproachable, goddesslike. With her russet hair, hazel eyes, and constellation of freckles along her cheekbones, Sybylla was the photographic negative of Maggie's fading blonde. Sybylla, not Maggie, was the lucky recipient of Aaron's late-in-life riches and lived in a dreamworld of their own making. Maggie felt a flash rush through her and a wedge of lime rind coat her mouth.

"Don't worry about me, my business is just fine," she said, reaching out for Sybylla's arm. "But you might want to watch yours."

Sybylla's face froze in puzzlement.

"Is something wrong?"

"Something is always wrong when you trust Aaron," Maggie said, stepping forward, closer to the stairs.

"I don't understand." Sybylla's eyes searched Maggie's hard blue gaze.

"Aaron has a talent for betrayal," Maggie hissed. "Just ask the Furies."

Chapter 6

Good Luck with That

Maggie was doing her best to walk unaided. No cane. No sling. No sturdy arm to lean on. No pills. It was time to leave the Karma Community, and she was determined to do it on her own.

That didn't make her trip to the chicken coop to say goodbye to Sage any easier.

She hurt from her toes to her brow but she wasn't going to admit it to anyone. Maggie gritted her teeth and swore under her breath as she walked over the rutted meadow grass to the fenced-in area for the chickens, a cluster of loud and curious creatures who were both interested in and fearful of any strangers. Sage, ripped jeans exposing his distressingly grey underwear, was tossing bits of grass and table scraps to the birds, who were pecking away at the treats. He kept his feed bag slung around his left shoulder, making his thin shoulder blades uneven. From the back, and swapping a feed bag for a Fender guitar, he could easily have passed as Aaron back in the day.

It must be in the genes, Maggie thought, *because he certainly couldn't have picked up those mannerisms from watching Aaron.*

Maggie took a deep breath, then held her right ribs as she winced.

She hadn't stolen Sage, as Aaron had alleged just a few days before. Maggie had the legal papers to prove that Aaron had willingly given her sole custody of their child; in separate documents, she'd agreed to terminate all rights to the

Furies' nonexistent fortune. If Aaron wanted to connect the two, she could easy accuse him of selling his son for future royalties. Although Aaron had tried to make her guilty for taking Sage and raising him alone, she knew it was the right thing to do. She couldn't rewrite history. She saw no need to.

It wasn't easy, but I did it.

Four months pregnant and trying to conceal raging withdrawals from alcohol, coke, and Quaaludes, she moved back into her old bedroom at her parents' house in Evanston. All she wanted to do was to shut out the world, force the sun to stop rising when she was getting ready to sleep and make the evening stretch out into eternity. But unlike the Furies, nature's rhythms wouldn't pause for a rock star who'd gotten used to coming alive in the spotlight, not sunlight.

But it was worth it. Sage was born five weeks early and was scrawny, irritable, and adorable—and all hers. Aaron wasn't there; he'd never be there, if Maggie got her way. She waved away phone calls from her old friends and reporters, and just once let Pete visit to greet the baby. All these decades later, Maggie still smirked at the memory of Pete shaking as he inspected Sage's face, saw a carbon copy of Aaron's, then slumped with relief into the nursery's rocking chair.

No, Sage was all Maggie's. When she'd come home from a long day in the office he'd toddle straight into her arms, grab a handful of her long hair, then inhale, as if she was giving him life with each breath. When he was older he'd get headachy at school with the hopes of going home early and spending the afternoon with his mom, just the two of them, alone in their cocoon, drawing and telling stories, snuggling and laughing. At times she'd even sing to him with a soft voice when he was asleep, the only time she'd let herself be musical.

"Let's run away," she'd sing when Sage was sleeping so deeply he couldn't hear her.

"Into the wild blue
Into a new day.
I'm brave when I'm with you
We don't need money,
Not a red cent.
I've got diamonds and pearls, honey
When we're in our lovin' bed.
Home is where you are
Loving under the stars
Home is where you are
Home is in your arms.
I searched the world for you

To mend my broken heart
To make one soul out of two
And a home we'll never part."

She'd let the words of the Four Furies' first hit, "Home Is Where You Are," drift off into the night. In her darker moods, she'd sing another song at the lower end of her range, "Pandora," known only to her:

"I just had to know.
I had to take a look,
Shine a light on demons,
Fear my feelings,
Let all reason go.
Don't say no."

Then she'd catch herself, and stop, hoping Sage hadn't heard a note.

She wished she could hold on to those old days, even the difficult ones, before his adolescent hormones and angst hit, just the two of them, mother and son.

But that's all over now, she thought and winced again. *It's time to let go.*

"Not bad for a city boy," Maggie said as she came up behind him.

It was true. Sage looked more at home in the Karma Community's fresh air and permissive atmosphere than at home in tidy Oak Park, the safe and affluent and, she had to admit, fairly dull suburb she worked so hard to afford to live in.

"Dude, these birds are nuts." Sage grinned broadly, his hair whisking into his eyes, then clucked back at the chickens, a riot of brown and burgundy and ocher and tangerine and white feathers in constant motion.

Maggie took a deep breath and let the chickens fill the pause.

"I have to say goodbye now," she said softly. "Felix's funeral is tomorrow morning."

Sage squinted at her and threw another handful of grass at the chickens.

"Good luck with that. I really mean it."

"Thanks," Maggie said, knowing that was as much intimacy as Sage could muster.

"Do you have enough meds? Or should I call in another prescription for you?"

"I'm cool. No worries."

"I'm a mom. I'm supposed to worry."

A bottom-heavy brown hen whose flashy feathers extended down to her feet pecked at a grey stone in the dirt, oblivious to the commotion over the grass. Maggie wanted to toss her some treats, or point out the bits already being devoured by her flock mates, anything to redirect the chicken's attention away from the inedible stone.

"I'm probably going to be really busy with work for a while, you know, just doing some paper work and making things official at the firm. So if you don't hear from me it doesn't mean that I'm not thinking about you. It's just—"

"It's just business. I know."

A gentle westerly breeze rippled the tops of the trees in the nearby grove, bringing some relief to the sunny chicken run.

"I can't believe it's really happening."

"What, becoming the boss? It's what you've always wanted."

Maggie watched the hen flick the stone with her beak and walk toward a shady spot near a shallow bowl of water.

"I'm not happy about Felix's death, but I've got to admit that leading the firm is kind of thrilling. I'm pretty sick of playing second fiddle."

"Yep," Sage said, but Maggie wasn't sure he was listening.

"Anyway," she said. "It's time for me to go. Stay out of trouble, okay? You know that Aaron is—" She reached out to touch Sage's T-shirt sleeve and she could feel his bicep harden under the cotton. "Aaron is Aaron, as you'll find out."

"Yep."

Maggie gave Sage a terse hug and a long look at his suntanned face, wanting to imprint this moment in her memory.

"I'm just a phone call away."

Sage turned back to the chickens and mimicked their clucking in a call and response-style rhythm.

"It's time for you to go, mom."

Chapter 7

I'm Felix Now

Maggie cursed Trip and Matilda for choosing the Episcopal Cathedral in downtown Chicago instead of the local Oak Park church Felix had attended for decades. He wouldn't have wanted the fuss and pomp of a cathedral funeral; he didn't seek out attention, instead letting his clients and friends soak up his calm, reassuring presence. But there Felix was, a few handfuls of ash in a mahogany box in front of the high altar of the gold cathedral, the sun shining so brightly that it seemed like the church was lit by amber candles. Like honey, like butterscotch. Maggie wondered if she could duplicate the effect with glazed windows and the right type of woodwork. She'd wait and ask the vicar at the right time.

Knowing that she'd draw attention, Maggie tried to seem cool and composed as well as wounded and in mourning as she hung back in the nave of the church, shyness creeping in. With her black Calvin Klein suit she wore flat slip-ons, her ankle freshly wrapped, and had applied a fresh bandage to her forehead, allowing her professionally blown-out hair to reveal just enough of the gauze bandage. She thought her one-carat diamond studs would seem both respectful and chic. She'd taken a pill to keep the pain at bay after the long drive from the Karma Community to Chicago the previous night had kept her up until the wee hours, sleepless, wincing, wiped out.

"Maggie, you're here."

43

She recognized the woman in the simple navy A-line dress as Matilda, as insular and socially awkward as her brother Trip, but with more spite.

"Yes, I came in last night. It was the soonest I could get here." Maggie showed Matilda her wrapped ankle. "I really shouldn't be driving, but I just had to pay my respects to Felix."

Maggie could feel Matilda inspect her gauze, her foot, her whole demeanor.

"I'm so sorry about your father," Maggie said, dropping her voice and reaching for Matilda's arm. It felt startling to touch the cheap, rough fabric of Matilda's dress after living among hippies who only wore cotton and rumpled linen and denim. Dirty clothes, of course, not like Matilda's tidy garment still smelling of dry cleaning chemicals.

"He was such a wonderful man. A true gentleman." Maggie meant it.

"Yes," Matilda said simply, then brushed past Maggie to greet another guest. "He'll never be replaced."

Maggie took a deep breath and plunged deeper into the church itself, extending her left hand to shake the hands of her clients already settled in their pews, explaining she'd been in an accident and hadn't been in Chicago for Felix's death. Then she squared her shoulders and selected her seat—not so far forward as to seem part of the family, but she wanted to be visible as the next in line to the head of the firm.

She scanned the perimeter of flowers, sprays, and bouquets and spotted her offering: a single pale orchid, its exoticism a tribute to Felix's exquisite eye.

"I saw you on television last night," he'd said to her one morning years ago, triumphant, over his mug of Oolong tea.

Maggie had tried to hide her grimace as she kept her eyes on the latest changes to the blueprint for the McMaster townhouse.

"You were singing like a dream. And you were wearing the most lovely lace shawl over a tube top, of all things. But your bosoms looked heavenly. And your eyes sparkled like aquamarines," he had teased.

Maggie sighed, knowing exactly which TV appearance Felix saw—a late-night concert clip of the Four Furies early in their career. The band had played an entire set, but the TV show ultimately ran just three songs, culminating in "Home Is Where You Are." And the footage of just two lines from that song's chorus made it on to the two-hour paid programming loop that ran late at night, an advertisement for *Hippie Breeze*, a six-disc compilation CD of classic light seventies rock that included the Four Furies' first hit and that snippet of her TV performance, one that had been prefaced by an arm's length of coke to blast through her insecurities, a quickie with Aaron in a bathroom stall to patch things up after grumbling about the set list, and a tumbler of Aaron's Jameson whiskey spilled on her blouse after the quickie, hence the tube top instead of her usual modest prairie girl look. Funny, and horrifying, to think that night would be relived endlessly in the wee hours of the 21st century.

"Insomnia again?" she asked.

"Yes. I was playing solitaire and enjoying a delectable tawny port at two in the morning, and I must have awakened Ronan. He turned on the TV and *voila*—there was my Maggie. I had no idea you'd been so famous. Ronan raved about you. He's going to drag out all of his albums from storage so he can play them for me. He was a fan in high school."

Maggie immersed herself in paint swatches and held each one to the light streaming in through her office window, trying to fixate on the subtleties of each shade of eggshell.

"That's all in the past, thankfully."

"You should be proud of yourself. Not that many women can lay claim to being a rock star in their youth." He had put his hands on her shoulders, paternally.

"It was a fluke, really. Anyone could do it."

"Sing for me," he'd said softly. "You have such a lovely voice."

She had let his compliment hang in the air.

"I don't sing anymore."

"Because of your old lover."

"Yes."

"I saw him last night, too. He was very handsome in a rough sort of way."

"He was. But he was a terrible partner."

"That shouldn't stop you from singing. Don't you sing for Sage?"

She had let the paint samples scatter on her desk and knew that Felix wouldn't let it go.

"That's different."

"Sing for me," he pleaded. "Sing for me the way you sing to Sage."

Maggie had rolled her eyes and smirked, trying to delay the inevitable. Felix always got what he wanted.

"Okay. Here's Sage's current favorite song."

She bit her lip and laughed, joining Felix in his delight.

"Rubber ducky—"

She giggled through the rest of the Muppets' ode to bath time, her voice relaxed as she spoke the words with a light lilt.

"You're a scamp," Felix scolded, flapping the paint samples in her direction, affectionately, playfully, endearingly.

45

How I'll miss you, dear friend, she thought as the cathedral's grand pipe organ swelled with a regal hymn and lofted the urban church onto an otherworldly plane. *I'll do my best to make you proud.*

She motioned for her assistant Keith to sit with her. He silently let his jaw drop as he took in her banged-up forehead and wrapped ankle.

"We need to talk," he stage-whispered over the organ's pomp.

Trip, Matilda, and their families filed into the church and settled into their places in the front pews, expressionless as far as Maggie could tell, formal and weary, as if they were a long-sequestered jury about to return a guilty verdict after a long trial.

Maggie pulled out a handkerchief and let her sweaty palms turn it to mush. She tugged at the jade bead on her charm bracelet and the depression in her Claddagh charm created by the absence of her emerald, and steeled herself for the long funeral service and even longer road ahead of her at Morgan & Fellows Designs.

+++

Maggie hung back in the receiving line, not relishing her first meeting with Matilda and Trip since Felix's death. They were sourpusses with her even on their happiest days, all three of them fully aware of Felix's preference for Maggie's company over spending time with his own children. Now, with Felix her protector gone, she knew she had to smooth over that awkwardness as they transitioned to her control.

She dawdled in the courtyard outside the cathedral's meeting room and let the murmurs of her fellow mourners and the wafts of strong coffee wash over her. She could see the knot of well-wishers in the doorway, Trip's wife Carine acting as a very uncomfortable greeter. As Maggie delayed, a pool of well-wishers formed around her and she let herself receive a pat on the back, squeezed arm, tut-tutting over her bandaged forehead, double kisses on her cheeks. The reverent condolences from Felix's friends and their clients and colleagues made her feel more like his widow, not merely a well-regarded employee. They all must have known that Maggie was the new star, the new center of power, and they needed to get used to it.

As the crowd thinned, Maggie took a deep breath and approached the extended Fellows family, still looking stiff and distant and formal. She kissed Matilda softly on the right cheek, taking in a hint of stale perfume and her sour breath, which couldn't be concealed by the mints she'd popped throughout the ceremony.

"Again, please accept my condolences. You know how much I adored Felix."

Matilda pulled away from Maggie and took in her injuries, her diamond studs, her nipped-in waist in her perfectly tailored suit. Maggie looked over her rival's shoulder and offered her left hand to Trip.

"If there's anything I can do to help you out, Trip—"

He ignored her outstretched hand and raised his chin.

"I'm Felix now. Felix Ingles Fellows the Third, actually." He clasped his hands behind his back and rocked on to his heels. "It's time I claim my Roman numerals."

Maggie clasped her hands, her palms hot and moist, startled by Trip's brusqueness.

"I'm sorry," she said, not able to call this unremarkable man Felix.

"Let's just get this out of the way right now," he said coolly. "My sister and I are entertaining offers for the firm. You're welcome to throw your hat in the ring, as it were. We'll consider it, just like we will consider the other offers."

Maggie flushed, stung by Trip's abrupt change in Felix's long-stated plans to hand over the firm to her.

Damn that Trip. Felix promised!

"We've already received a takeover bid, half a million plus a portion of future earnings," Matilda cut in. "And we'd serve on the board of directors."

Maggie took a step back, unsure if the siblings were being honest or merely playing mind games with her. Both watched her carefully for a reaction. She prayed the pain pill was dulling her reflexes and revealing nothing that would indicate that she couldn't get her hands on a half-million dollars. Not even half a million cents.

"I'm surprised that this is what Felix wanted."

The siblings stared back at her. Trip raised his hand to his mouth to cover a chuckle.

"His will named my brother and me as his heirs in all matters," Matilda said, smirking. "Everything."

"We know our father was fond of you," Trip said, his hand on Matilda's shoulder. "But we're in charge now."

+++

"I'm Felix now."
Damn that Trip.

47

Damn him and his entitlement. Damn him and his name. Damn him and his smirk and comb-over and power to kill my dreams with one whim. Damn him.
And Matilda too.

Maggie opened a bottle of unoaked Chardonnay in the bright kitchen of the Tudor-style cottage that now mocked her for her middle-class dreams. The house wasn't as elegant and restrained as the ones she designed for her clients. She'd wanted a cozy, comfy home, one with lots of pillows and filtered light and small nooks in which she or Sage could hang out and daydream, although they never did anymore, preferring in recent years to retreat into their rooms and carve out separate lives, Sage as a troubled teen and Maggie as the overachieving and underappreciated designer.

All those years of trailing behind Felix and stifling my dreams because I thought it would pay off. Felix told me it would pay off. And damned Trip and Matilda want to play games with my future.

She poured the wine into a heavy coffee mug, not trusting herself with good stemware, and swallowed a full mouthful, not letting it roll around on her tongue first and bloom on her taste buds.

I took a bet on Felix a long time ago. And now that damned Trip doesn't want to acknowledge everything I did for the firm. I brought in clients. I held their hands when things went over budget. I let Felix get the kudos even when I was the one creating the designs.

She rushed to her office off the living room and pulled the drawers out of her desk, feeling the rip under her ribcage deepen. It didn't matter. All she focused on was finding anything in writing that secured her future as Felix's successor. But none of the contracts or scraps of papers or Christmas cards bore any witness to Felix's promises. They'd all been made when the two were alone, sharing private moments, building castles in the air.

You're the only one who can carry on my legacy, he'd told her often.

Apparently he hadn't told his lawyer. And Trip and Matilda certainly weren't going to cough up that information.

Damn that Felix!

She took another big gulp of her wine and strode into her screened-in solarium, her mottled potted plants showing evidence of neglect. She stepped heavily on her injured foot, not caring if she was in pain. She rooted around in a spider plant and found a stub of one of Sage's discarded joints that he didn't think she knew about and lit one, getting the muddy rolling paper stuck to her lips and forcing a big hit of THC into her lungs.

This is just like the Four Furies. Aaron got to be the celebrity and walk away with the money and the fame. I had to go back to work.

She finished her glass of wine and emptied the rest of the bottle into a thermos over her kitchen sink.

Damn Trip. Damn Felix. Damn Aaron. Don't they know who I am?

Four minutes later, with an overnight bag of clothes, a bottle of Sage's medication, and a case of Pinot Noir from the Willamette Valley, she locked the front door behind her.

Maggie Morgan is pissed off and they'll regret it.

Chapter 8

I Know Who You Are

Almost there.

It was the third time in the past week she'd driven this country highway near the Kickapoo River, but nothing looked familiar in the twilight. Tall grass on the road's shoulders, Amish farms here and there, big box stores on the outskirts of small towns. Just a place to drive through, nothing more.

The radio station she'd been listening to since entering Dane County faded into white noise. She punched a button rapidly, skipping over a baseball game, a talk radio shock-jock, a tinny pop song and—of course—the sound of her own voice. As Aaron had predicted three decades earlier, there was something in her voice that would make anyone stop and listen.

"Let's run away into the wild blue," she sang as Aaron's Gibson guitar and Pete's bass and Hooch's drums wound around her impossibly young, clear voice. In "Home Is Where You Are," one of the first songs that Aaron had written for her, she heard their hopes and vitality and daring and pure adoration for each other. Despite the corny lyrics, it was their breakout hit that told the creation story of the Four Furies and fixed Maggie and Aaron in the public's mind as inseparable soul mates living out a rock and roll fantasy.

A sweat broke out along her brow, her armpits, her palms.

"We don't need money, not a red cent
I've got diamonds and pearls, honey

When we're in our lovin' bed—"
She shut off the radio, as she always did when a Four Furies song came on.

She bit on the cap of her pill bottle and shook a tablet into her palm, then took another swig from her thermos to wash it down with wine. She reached over to pluck a Pinot Noir bottle's tapering neck from the passenger seat of her Saab, swerving to stay between the yellow and white lines. Her ribcage groaned. The sun was hazily setting in her eyes and casting deep shadows in the rolling hillsides as she pulled a corkscrew out of her glove compartment.

There's only one way Aaron can make this right.

She put the bottle between her knees and stabbed the tip of the screw through the foil wrap into the cork, steering with her left hand while trying to twist it with her right. The dry cork would have been stubborn even if she hadn't been driving.

She pressed her weakened foot onto the gas pedal as she leaned into a curve in the road, then added more pressure as she pulled. The last thing she remembered was the pop of the cork and the blast of the air bag as her Saab rammed into a pole propping up a billboard sign declaring District Attorney Carl Olsen's re-election bid.

+++

The cell in the basement of the Tyler County courthouse smelled like sweat and industrial disinfectant and hell. The overhead light showed every flaw in this nasty room, which seemed to be smaller than Maggie's office in Oak Park yet held two cots, a sink and toilet, and despair. Maggie reeked of the red wine that was splashed over her during the crash, which made her look like a crime scene stained with someone else's blood. She wished she could change into clean clothes, squirt some cool L'Eau d'Issey on her wrists, scrub the place down with bleach or, at the very least, wash her hands with decent soap that actually produced lather and didn't chap her skin, but of course none of that would happen.

The woman on the cot two feet away from Maggie snored jaggedly, her foul breath further stinking up the humid room.

With fingertips still blackened from being printed hours earlier, she felt along her bare wrist, absent of her charm bracelet, then took an inventory of her injuries: bruised sides, sore shoulder, raging headache, and gauze at her temple from her old cut, where she feared blood was coming through as a result of the crash. She'd never been punched by an air bag and she hoped she never would be again. At least it stopped the corkscrew and bottle from jabbing her in the eye or throat or heart or worse.

I've got to clean myself up and get out of here.

The deputy who'd handled her—a no-nonsense, big-boned gal who took her job seriously—didn't seem like an easy mark. The deputy's tight ponytail, lack of makeup, and the way she wrapped her heavy belt around the middle of her apple-shaped body, daring the rolls of flab to proudly announce themselves through the brown uniform that was designed for a man, all of that said that she didn't give a shit about niceties.

The baby-faced male deputy, though. Maggie thought about him as she patted the dried-out tape affixing the gauze to her temple. He didn't look like a lock 'em up knuckle dragger. He looked like a family man, one who'd gone into law enforcement simply because it was the best-paying job in the county, one that would give his kids some security as Big Ag and Big Box chains bought up everything in sight and offered low-wage, dead-end jobs.

Might as well try.

Maggie knocked on the reinforced plexiglass window embedded in her cell's door.

The female deputy appeared in the window frame, having taken her time to get there.

Maggie took a deep breath.

"I need some new gauze. I'm bleeding again."

The deputy gave her a long look and shook her head.

"I don't see any blood."

"I can feel it."

"It'll dry up if you stop futzing with it."

Maggie's roommate let out a series of snorts and rolled over on the grimy mattress.

"I really do need a fresh bandage. I'm worried about infection."

"Why? You got AIDS?"

"No, but—"

"Hep C?"

Maggie shook her head, recoiling a bit.

"Then you can wait until someone bails you out."

Sage. Oh god. Get here quick.

"Can't I just sign myself out?"

The deputy gave her another long look and narrowed her eyes.

"I know who you are." A fleck of spit splattered on the plexiglass. "Just because you're a celebrity doesn't mean you're getting special treatment."

+++

The key struck metal as it freed the bolt from its holder.

"Hey rock star. You're out."

The female deputy smirked as Maggie rose from her cot, her migraine pounding so deeply she could only squint before triggering even more pain. She held her head high as she followed the deputy to the counter where she could be processed out with a court date, signature, and—finally—the handover of her belongings in plastic bags.

Maggie heard chuckling in the waiting room and her stomach tightened.

How am I going to explain this to Sage?

Maggie rifled through the bag to take an inventory of her purse. Car keys. Wallet. Diamond studs in a tiny plastic baggie. Her charm bracelet in a bigger one. She assumed that the deputies didn't amuse themselves by sorting through her weekend bag and inspecting her bras and panties. She had to assume that, or she'd crumble from the violation.

The deputy heaved the case of wine onto the counter.

"Everything's there except for the pills you didn't have a prescription for. We're keeping them for evidence."

"But they're my son's. He needs them."

"We'll give him a call."

The door swung open behind Maggie as she jabbed the rolled-up documents into her purse.

"Hey now."

Maggie felt a hot flash ricochet from her chest to her limbs and energizing and amplifying her aches and wounds.

"Hey Aaron," the female deputy said, brightening and softening. "How's things?"

"No complaints," he said, his eyes twinkling. "Doubt that Maggie would agree, though."

Maggie squared her shoulders and glared at him.

"I think I'm still recovering from my concussion," she said, then turned to the deputy. "I was concussed a few days ago, you know. And my ankle is sprained."

"Tell it to the judge," she said. "See you around, Aaron. Say hey to Sybylla for me." She let her face fall stern again. "See you in court, Maggie."

Aaron tipped his sweat-stained trucker hat toward the deputy and waved Maggie out the door. "See you, Britt. Come on, Maggie, let's sober you up. You look like hell and smell even worse."

Maggie let Aaron trail behind her as she left the clammy office and walked into the bright noontime sun. She pressed her key fob to unlock her Saab. But the familiar bleep never replied.

"Over here," Aaron said, tilting his head toward a rusted red pickup truck.

"I'm fine. I can drive." She scanned the small parking lot and the cars lined up along the main drag of this unfamiliar small town. "I just don't know where they put my car."

"Your car belongs in the scrap yard. It's totaled. You're lucky to be alive."

Maggie's knees buckled a bit and she dropped her tote bag to the pavement.

"It wasn't. I wasn't—"

"You sure were," Aaron said as he dropped the carton of eleven wine bottles into the truck bed and reached out for Maggie's bag. "You were partying like a rock star," he continued, his eyes twinkling beneath his cap's brim. "In fact, I think you're still drunk."

"I had a concussion," Maggie insisted, being careful with her words. "I'm still recovering."

Aaron unlocked the passenger door and helped her inside.

"And you say I was the bad one. Ha!"

He shut the truck door and gave it a good slap, then pulled into the main drag, a square encircling an imposing brick building. Maggie wasn't quite sure where she was—her legal papers would reveal it to be New Elm, the county seat of Tyler County—but at the moment it was just a small town with a mishmash of buildings dating from the late 1800s to the 1970s, shops with false fronts and mid-century restaurants with big picture windows and a drive-in ice cream shop, probably the last one in existence, she thought.

Aaron drove slowly, well below the twenty-five miles per hour speed limit, his left arm resting on the open driver's side window, his forearm soaking up the noontime sun and deepening his farmer's tan. He nodded or waved to the passing drivers and the few pedestrians on the sidewalk clustered around doorways. They knew him; he knew them. In his stained trucker's hat that couldn't tame his unkempt hair, cheap sunglasses, dirty T-shirt and jeans and well worn-in work boots, he didn't seem remarkable in this small farming town. He was just another guy bailing out a friend who'd partied too hard the night before.

Aaron paused in the middle of the street to allow families exiting the Lutheran church to scatter in safety.

"I forgot it's Sunday," she said. "What a week."

"It's been a wild ride," Aaron said, turning his grin fully on her. "And we ain't done yet."

He turned right at a stop sign and drove a few blocks to the edge of town, where the local streets met the county highway, and pulled into Norm's Norway Inn, a twelve-room, one-story motel with dark brown shingles and red trim, a good-faith attempt to look Scandinavian. Two cars were parked in the corner of the long gravel lot next to the Dumpster and a riding lawnmower.

"You've got to be kidding me," Maggie said, slouching down into the seat and holding her head.

"I'm serious. Serious as cancer. Or serious as a court date with a Republican DA."

Aaron parked in front of Room 102. Its window air conditioner rattled and dripped in the humid heat, forming a puddle near the doorway.

"I don't know what you're thinking," Maggie said, turning on Aaron. "You have no right to—"

"I have no right to sleep with you, Maggie." He held up his hand as if making a pledge. "And I have no intention of sleeping with you so stop jumping to conclusions. But you need to sleep it off and clean yourself up and figure out what you're going to do next. This room is going to buy you some time."

He unlocked the door and handed the key to Maggie. "It's all yours. I'll be waiting here until you're ready to come out."

Chapter 9

Trust Me

Maggie was sure that Room 102's bathroom had been cleaned recently, but she didn't want to touch anything anyway. Not the sides of the shower or its sticky vinyl curtain, or the toilet seat, or the door knob, or even the rough bath towel, for that matter. But all of that was infinitely cleaner than the holding cell she'd been in and, she had to admit, she really needed a hot shower to soak into her bruises and aches and wash them away with her troubles.

She'd forgotten to pack shampoo so she had to use the motel's freebee, which had a pine scent that took her back to the seventies and coarsened her hair. The soap and lotion were just as bad but she finally got the telltale black ink off of her fingertips. She had one last piece of gauze, which she carefully applied over her temple.

What a mess.

In just one week she'd lost and found Sage, lost Felix, found Aaron, and lost her grasp on the design firm. Now she'd wrecked her car, was stranded somewhere in Wisconsin, had cuts and bruises and scrapes from head to toe, and had gotten busted for drinking and driving—and drugging and driving.

And Aaron Fields was waiting outside. Her savior.

All she wanted to do was to curl up in her own bed with a bottle of wine and sleep until her problems melted away and left nothing but a faint stain you could only see in bright sunlight. But she was miles away from home and only she could make her troubles disappear.

Besides, Aaron would still be waiting outside for her no matter how long she lingered.

She didn't bother turning on the lights in the motel room, not wanting to see too clearly the mottled turquoise shag rug, somewhat matching teal-and-black bedspread strategically patterned to hide stains, the dented lampshades hanging off chipped brass lamps, particle board table and chairs, battered TV, and grimy remote control. She'd been in enough of these cheap rooms with the Four Furies to know everything she needed to know about Norm's Norway Inn and she wished she could forget it all. Last-ditch affairs, hookers, suicides, drug deals, gun swaps, on-the-edge families—a rock band passing through seemed somewhat respectable in comparison.

She heard a crack of thunder but saw no lightning when she opened the motel door to reveal the parking lot. Aaron was sitting under the eaves a few feet away in front of Room 105 on a plastic patio chair, his elbows on a battered card table, immersed in a paperback. Even in the dim drizzly light his wedding ring flashed as he turned the book's page and flicked his cigarette stub into a puddle with his long fingers, stretched and slender and knobby from decades of playing the guitar.

Might as well get this over with.

"Hey Aaron."

She tried to look cool and composed as she let herself limp more than she needed to, then pulled up a chair beside him, her hair still wet from the shower, no makeup save for two coats of mascara, clean but wrinkled primrose-colored blouse, and denim capris that stuck to her thighs in the humidity. Her charm bracelet jangled on her right wrist and she'd put her diamond studs in her ears for safety's sake. She'd learned the hard way from years of touring that you never knew who would go through your things when you weren't in your hotel room.

Aaron folded the corner of a page and placed the book on the table. Ken Wilber's bald head and thick-rimmed glasses stared at Maggie from the book's back cover as she tried to figure out how to proceed.

She thought sympathy would work best.

"I want to thank you for bailing me out of jail," she started, her eyes downcast in her best Princess Diana imitation.

Aaron clapped his hands and laughed before she could continue.

"Sweet Peggy O'Donnell," he cackled. "I never thought I'd hear you say those words. I mean, how many times have you posted bail for me. And now— and now! Damn! I didn't think you still had it in you."

Maggie flushed as she felt Aaron search her face to make eye contact.

"I don't have it in me," she protested. "I was concussed. I have a sprained ankle."

"I'll hear none of it, Maggie. Admit it. You were drunk and high and popping open a wine bottle when you crashed your car. You're lucky you didn't wind up with a corkscrew in your eye."

"I was concussed. I shouldn't have been driving in the first place."

"Horseshit," Aaron said, laughing. "You were acting like a rock star. How many times have I heard you say you didn't want to be a rock star and didn't like to be a rock star and you wanted to get the hell away from rock stars and all this time you were a god damn rock star who didn't want to admit it."

"It's not true."

He looked at her long and hard, almost with pride.

"You act like you're so respectable now, but you're still Maggie Morgan. *The* Maggie Morgan."

Aaron laughed again, a chuckle that seemed to carry across the parking lot and over the rumble of the skies and rain.

"Stop lying to yourself, Maggie. The truth shall set you free."

Maggie shook her head and waved away Aaron's offer of a cigarette.

"I am being honest."

Aaron took his time lighting his smoke, forcing Maggie to ruminate on their conversation longer than she would have liked.

"So come clean. What are you doing out here in Tyler County? I thought you had important business in Chicago. A dying friend and business deals and clients and whatever."

Maggie pushed an errant strand of wet hair behind her ear and took a breath as she wondered how candid she should be about her knowledge of his checkbook's secrets.

"I did have business in Chicago. But something came up and—." She fluttered her eyelashes again and looked down. "I need your help."

Aaron laughed again and rested his chin on his palm. Cigarette smoke rose past his eyes, making him squint, then wafted toward Maggie.

"My help? M'kay. Tell me more." He wiggled his eyebrows and grinned, thoroughly enjoying the moment.

Maggie rolled her eyes and focused on the motel sign, which was missing an "E" in "Cable," making the word itself seem garbled and tangled.

"I need money."

"Go to the bank. Get a loan like everyone else."

She knew the only loan she'd get would jeopardize her home, and she wasn't ready to part with that yet. Thanks to the Kencom affair, her Tudor was the only thing standing between her and insolvency.

"I thought you could give me some money."

"Good luck with that. I don't have any," he scoffed and stretched out his legs, letting the rain fall on his work boots.

"I don't need much. I just—"

"I'm sure you have more than me, Maggie. You seem to be doing pretty well for yourself." He took a long look at her and she flushed again. "Are you, you know, in trouble? I mean, other than spending the night in jail for getting drunk and crashing your car."

"I'm not in trouble," she said firmly. "I just need some money. A good opportunity has come my way and I want to take it."

"Wish I could help, but I'm broke."

"I want to buy the firm I work for. The founder just died."

"Fuck the firm. Start your own."

"But it's got a name, a reputation. I've been working my way up for years."

"Fuck it. You've got a name. Why do you want to be in anyone else's shadow?"

"It's always been promised to me."

"Who cares? Promises are worth shit. Be your own woman and fuck 'em."

"You've got the Karma Community," Maggie pushed ahead, the eye-popping numbers from Aaron's checkbook filling her vision and balancing out the six figures she lost in the stock market. "You must be doing really well."

He rubbed the flinty stubble on his chin and waved to a black pickup truck driving slowly past the motel. "It's not a profit-making venture. Besides—"

"You never paid me child support, you know," Maggie cut in. "Never. I did it on my own."

"This again," he sighed. "If I could have helped you and Sage I would have. But you refused to—"

"I would have loved it. Loved it," she said through gritted teeth. "I'm sure Sage would have appreciated it, too."

Maggie let her bitterness hang in the air but she knew that Aaron didn't respond to guilt trips because he never felt guilty about anything. But she didn't want to admit defeat, either, no matter how crazy her plan was.

"It could be a loan," she said finally. "I'd pay you back."

"Listen," Aaron said, pushing the bill of his cap further toward his eyes. "I'm happy to help you with anything as long as it doesn't involve money. I'll drive you back to Chicago. I'll lie for you in court if that's what it takes to get you off the hook. But I just don't have any money to give you. Believe me, I don't have any."

Maggie drew her feet under her and folded her hands on her knees, then crumpled inward. She didn't want to believe Aaron—she knew he was lying about the money—but she knew that she wasn't getting anywhere with him right now.

This is a disaster.

"Maggie, what's going on with you?" Aaron sounded genuinely concerned as he leaned closer to her. "This mess can't be due to a stupid business deal."

She didn't answer him. She didn't want to admit that he might be right.

"I can help you. Really. Hell—I've gotten stuck in tons of shit over the years and I've always pulled myself out. You know that. Whatever trip you're on can't be so bad it's going to be the end of you."

She took a breath, deep enough to make her bruised ribs moan, and tried not to scream.

"Come on, you're Maggie Morgan of the Four Furies. You know how to kick some ass. Hell, I've got the scars to prove it," he said, resting the pad of his index finger in the dent in his nose.

"I don't want to kick some ass," Maggie said evenly, not allowing Aaron to take the conversation off course. "I just want to buy the business as promised and be the boss and live my life the way I always expected to."

Aaron took off his cap and brushed his fingers through his damp hair, which was curling up around his neck and around his ears. Up close, Maggie could see how much of it—most of it—was silver. He reached over the table and held out his hand.

"I know it's not just the money that's making you crazy," he said, his open palm an open invitation. "I've hit bottom enough times to know what it feels like and what it looks like. And how hard it is to explain it to someone else."

Maggie felt tears pooling around the edges of her eyelids and refused to blink and shake them loose.

"Come back, Maggie. Let me help you."

He kneeled in front of her, rain pouring onto his back and soaking his shirt, and took both of her hands in his.

The tears finally fell, making Maggie's vision blur and burn with shame. But she didn't need to see Aaron to know what he looked like, what he smelled like, how their years together had made him who he was, how he laughed, how he fucked, how life was always an adventure when he was around. He was Aaron Fields; he'd been hers, once. And when they'd been together they were superstars. And she hated him.

"Look, I know it's not easy to walk away from the band and have to reinvent yourself," he said softly, his breath smelling like smoke and his skin musky. "There's no roadmap for old rock stars like us. We weren't supposed to go straight and live normal lives and get old. We were supposed to OD years ago and leave a beautiful corpse."

Maggie winced, thinking of how close she came last night to becoming another rock and roll casualty.

"We started the band because we were rebellious and adventurous and creative and couldn't fit in anywhere else. And without the band—"

"But I never wanted that. You did."

He rubbed her palms, searching her love line and life line with his calloused thumb, then flicked through the charms on her bracelet, making them sing.

"You loved it, Maggie. And you were damn good at it, too."

He tried to find her eyes but she wouldn't let him.

"It's too much," Maggie said, her voice cracking. "I just want to slow things down a bit and figure it all out."

He brushed her damp hair away from her eyes and smoothed it into place, revealing her face, both fresh and weary, the image of a queen in exile.

"Trust me," he said. "You need the Karma Community."

Chapter 10

Get Comfortable with Your Discomfort

Trust me.

Maggie didn't mean to crash the cast iron skillet into the sudsy stainless steel sink with such force, but she had to admit it felt good. What was the point of being the substitute dishwasher if she couldn't take out her aggression on the pots and pans?

Trust me. Trust me.

And like a twenty-year-old Peggy O'Donnell Morgan taking her first tab of acid from Aaron's finger, she did.

And now, and now, a rock singer in exile facing who knew what charges in DA Carl Olsen's court, the loss of her dream design firm because of *money* of all things, and Aaron—*Aaron*—reconciling with Sage and calling the shots and giving her shelter. It couldn't get worse.

Trust me.

He got her at her lowest point and she agreed to return to the Karma Community to figure things out in peace.

"Your secret's safe with me. We'll just say you're taking a break," he'd said earlier as he led her up the stairs of the Karma Community's main building to her new bedroom. She wasn't expected to return after departing for Felix's funeral in Chicago, so the cabin she'd stayed in previously was returned to its rightful owner, a paying guest, she assumed. Aaron gave her two choices: take the upper half of a bunk bed in a dorm room with seven other residents or find temporary shelter at night in one of the private bodywork rooms, alone, and sleep on a massage table until someone could stuff a futon into it for her sleeping pleasure.

Maggie lay down on the massage table and folded her hands over her chest, feeling as if she were a stone effigy atop her casket in the tradition of a medieval queen, and took in the scroll of the chakras adorning the south-facing wall, the window open to the east letting in fresh air from the gardens, an electric waterfall installed behind her head and, to her left, shelves adorned with a jagged pink Himalayan salt crystal, geodes, potted succulents, crystals, and framed photos of sunsets over various landscapes. She could have been at her own massage therapist's office back in Chicago.

"Will I get clean sheets?"

"Of course."

"Does the door lock?"

"Only you and Frances will have the keys."

Maggie closed her eyes and tried to imagine herself sleeping in there.

It could be worse.

"I'll take it."

She sat up and Aaron pushed her down again, leaned over, and looked directly into her eyes, then dent in his nose on full display.

"Let's get this straight first. If you're going to stay here, you've got to *be* here."

She propped herself up on one elbow and returned his stare.

"You can come and go as you please to deal with your business, but take as many classes as you need to. Believe me, I think you need a little enlightening."

"Hey," she shot back. "That's not fair."

"I suggest meditation, yoga, and some breath work. Get comfortable with your discomfort. It isn't easy, but it works for me."

"So now you're some amazing guru giving me spiritual advice—"

"I'm not a guru but I've learned from some really great ones," he said airily.

Maggie rolled her eyes and tucked her chin into her shoulder, waiting for the next blow.

"And since you're not a paying guest, I suggest you help out around here. You'll have to contribute in a spirit of community. No pouting, no complaining."

"Of course I wouldn't pout."

"I know you, and you would."

Maggie felt like she was back in her squirrel brown braids and Catholic school plaid listening to a nun's lecture about chewing gum in class, or daydreaming during Mass, or puzzling over the virgin birth.

"No drugging or drinking," Aaron said. "Not a drop, not a puff, not a pill."

"But my wine," Maggie said, pushing him away and looking around the room. "My case of Pinot Noir. Where is it?"

Aaron took a step back and folded his arms across his chest and grinned.

"Narsi and Sahana from the motel thank you for it. They said it'll go great with the grilled lamb kabobs they were planning to whip up for dinner tonight."

"You had no right—"

"Listen." He held up his hand, shutting her down. "If you ask nicely, Frances and Sybylla can get you stoned or high or giggly or mellow just with their herbs. And you'll pass any drug test your parole officer gives you. Trust me on that one."

He paused at the door and tossed the keys, which she let fly over her head and land with a jangle on the bare wood floor. He wedged a business card into the door jamb, which stuck out like a flag.

"I've made an appointment with an attorney for you tomorrow. Erika. She's good people. She'll get you out of your mess and you can go back to Chicago and buy the firm, or get back your reputation or your self-esteem or whatever will finally make you happy."

"Aaron," Maggie fumed. "You don't need to insult me."

He grinned again.

"They're expecting you in the kitchen, Ms. Morgan. I hope you aren't so fancy you can't wash a few dishes."

Maggie threw another pan into the sink as she thought about Aaron's clear delight in ordering her around.

Nothing changes, she thought. *Once an ass, always an ass.*

She picked up the cast iron skillet and took a wire scrub brush to the singed polenta still clinging to the bottom of the pan.

Just a few more days of this, she told herself. *See the attorney. Go back to Chicago. Call bankers for loans. Then buy the firm and pay the legal fines and start my new life as a free woman. Just take it one step at a time.*

She felt a light tap on her shoulder and made her face smooth and tension-free, expecting to find a Furies fan or just a well-wisher who wanted to say hello. She turned to find Sybylla, her face glowing from the heat and steam in the kitchen.

"We don't put cast iron in soap and water," she said, lifting the heavy skillet from the soapy water. "It ruins the seasoning. And never use a scrub brush on it." She grabbed the offending brush from Maggie's hand and Maggie felt the warm suds leave a trail down her forearm and drip onto the spongy work mat below.

Maggie flushed and rested her hand on her hip as she leaned against the sink, unwilling to take orders from Aaron's new wife.

"It's okay," Sybylla said before Maggie could respond. "You'll get the hang of things around here."

Chapter 11

Falling Babies

"Do you think she'll ever leave?" Sybylla asked as she and Frances fluffed and arranged the linden blossoms drying on the table in the tearoom.

"Eventually, I suppose," Frances replied.

"Do you think she'll sue us for her injuries? She must have insurance coverage."

"For what? Dangerous display of a dream catcher? Working herself into such a rage that she fell over her own two feet while she happened to be on our porch?"

Sybylla picked up a pale yellow flower and twirled it between her fingers, the tattoo of a vine circling the ring finger on her left hand becoming covered in its dust. The linden was almost dry, but not quite. When they were sufficiently brittle, she and Frances would pack a batch into paper bags and send them to an herb wholesaler in the area; the rest would go into giant Mason jars and be used for tea at the Karma Community during flu season.

"Does she bother you?" Frances asked.

"Mmm...not really, I guess. I'm just trying to treat her as I would any guest, or any member of Aaron's family."

"Does it bother Aaron?"

"Hard to tell."

Sybylla took a deep breath and filled her entire being with the scent of the lindens. "I wish I could sleep in here," she said softly.

Secretly, she wished she could shake loose the situation between her and Sage and Aaron and Maggie. But she couldn't and she didn't want to talk about it with anyone, even her cousin Frances. Aaron reassured her that he loved her and always would. He'd never given her any reason not to trust him, even when guests got too familiar with him or asked too many questions about the Four Furies or wanted to know how to score some drugs. But he also seemed edgier than usual since Maggie had barged into their lives—restless—and wasn't the up-for-anything but cool-as-hell Aaron she'd been with for the past three years.

"Shh…" Frances said. "No negativity around the plants." She lit her lavender and sage smudge stick and waved its smoke over the linden flowers, humming lightly.

Thank goddess for Frances. Frances had invited Sybylla, her untamed cousin, to the retreat center when had she nowhere else to go. Now, Sybylla was the sweetheart of the Karma Community, and not just because she was married to Aaron. She just loathed cynicism and darkness and was brought up to focus on life's abundance, not to stamp out the life force. Her attitude was transformative and touched everyone, making the center a more welcoming, nurturing place.

Actually, Sybylla's life at the Karma Community wasn't much different from her early years in her parents' home. Sybylla was raised in a small town—if you call eight homes lined up along one main drag a small town—by the eighties version of hippie parents who wanted to live a natural life as far off the grid as possible.

The Pinckney family seemed ordinary enough on the surface—dad Marvin a chiropractor, mom Sara a part-time visiting nurse, and three kids born in five years. But unusually for that part of rural northern Wisconsin, they were multiracial. Sara, from a long line of midwives going back to their roots in Scotland, and Marvin, from Tanzania, never really fit into the mainstream culture of their sports- and deer hunting-obsessed town, but didn't feel the desire to. The entire family lived a simple life according to their own moral code. Ever resourceful, the Pickneys built their house out of used tires and grew most of their food. Sybylla and her siblings were home schooled until the eighth grade and were cut off from pop culture, processed food, and most other forms of consumer society. Sybylla and her brothers spent most of their time in their tree house, reading the classics and creating their own little world in which everything was alive and kicking, active and vocal.

When she hit adolescence, though, Sybylla just didn't fit in anywhere. She was an outcast at high school, despite her natural beauty and sweet disposition. Her social naiveté left her defenseless against the cruelty of her peers' racially tinged jabs. After she dropped out and earned her GED, she couldn't conform to a routine entry-level job, and she wasn't quite ready to become a midwife or massage therapist or vet, ambitions that required years of training.

Instead, her cousin Frances invited her to the Karma Community so she could figure things out without pressure or anxiety. Gradually, as Sybylla spent time there, working with her hands and studying philosophy and spirituality, she channeled all of her curiosity and creativity into the plants, and the planets, and the wonder that is life. As time went by, her wildness turned into simple happiness. That's what Aaron loved about her and hoped would never change.

Aaron—my ferocious, gentle Aaron.

Sybylla was convinced they were soulmates, even if she hadn't been able to admit it when they had met and she tried to discourage him when he wanted to be alone with her. But Aaron persisted, and now she wondered what life would be like without knowing and loving one's twin soul. Lonely and lifeless. Reckless and full of regret. She hoped Aaron didn't regret the marriage now, a year after their quiet wedding in the grove.

"Shh…" Frances said again, looking at Sybylla. "Your thoughts are very loud."

Sybylla smiled. There was no point in even trying to hide something from her unusually perceptive cousin, a woman who could predict the future with stunning accuracy. Classes had been canceled, staff members had been fired, and entire schedules had to be altered because of Frances's bad dreams or stomachaches. Sybylla always listened to Frances' warnings, even if they seemed illogical, and she counseled Aaron to heed them, too.

Frances waved the smudge stick in the air and under the table. She handed it to Sybylla, who walked around the table and then closed her eyes and raised it high, her wedding band tattoo fully visible. She gave the herbs back to Frances, who placed them in a seashell, and the two women watched the embers burn out in sacred silence.

"I can still hear you, you know," Frances said when they were a safe distance from the flowers. "Don't worry so much. Maggie's here for a reason, even if you don't understand it yet."

+++

Sage popped his head into the main meeting space.

"Great timing." Aaron was tangled up in wires with the contents of a toolbox spilling out at his feet. "I need your help."

Sage walked over to the knotted cords, taking in the extent of the problem. "Whoa. Can't we just start cutting?"

"I wish," Aaron said with a laugh. "But we've got some popular teachers coming this weekend and no way to hear them. Where's a roadie when you need one? Here, grab this." He threw a few loops of the cable to Sage, then followed the free cord to its tight knot.

"Grim, hey? I should have listened to Frances about our old tech guy. I met him in Sturgis a long time ago and he came to me for help. But apparently he couldn't handle it here and just shoved this thing into the closet and split. So here we are. All of that bad Qi shut up in the closet. Until now."

Sage picked at a cluster of the cable and tried to see where the loops led.

"How's your mother?" Aaron asked as casually as he could.

"Fine, I guess. Being a bit of a drama queen. You know, the whole situation is about her although she won't admit it."

"Some things never change."

"Whatever." Sage shook the cable a bit. "I think she's worried about what you think about her."

Aaron looked up at Sage, leaving the knot alone for a moment. "I think about her what I've always thought. She's a beautiful, complicated, fragile, and fierce woman. She changed my life. But the baggage, whoa. She has a memory like a steel trap."

"Tell me about it."

"And I'm the kind of guy who needs a lot of forgiveness. Not a great combination."

"So she said."

"You know, it's not like I tried to hurt her. But it seemed that no matter what I did she got hurt."

Sage spooled a bit more cable out of the knot. Incense wafted into the room and wind chimes clinked outside the windows. The two men worked at the knot patiently, trying their best not to struggle with it and inadvertently make it tighter.

"She must have told you terrible things about me."

"Yeah," Sage said quietly, avoiding Aaron's eyes.

"It wasn't an easy situation, having your old lady in your band. I mean, it was great. I loved Maggie and I wanted her there. She was my muse. But the girls, man... they were a big reason why I wanted to be in a band. Every guy's fantasy, you know? I really dug it." Aaron smiled a secret smile. "And then, damn! There was Maggie."

Aaron turned the knot upside down.

"She told me the entire scene was sexist," Sage explained. "That the whole free sex thing was a farce. That the men got off on it, but the women ended up feeling used."

Aaron straightened up and thought for a moment. A kaleidoscope of thighs and breasts and bushes arose in his mind's eye, a swirl of blondes and brunettes and redheads who he'd groped and fucked and made love to, anonymous fans and semi-permanent lovers, Maggie sometimes in the mix, women who'd offered themselves up to him just because he could play the guitar. Just because they could.

"I'm sure she had a hard time with it."

"So, all of that stuff about groupies was true?" Sage asked, half fascinated, half not wanting to know the answer.

"Yeah," Aaron grinned. "And more."

He handed Sage another foot of cable and they started untangling the next section of the clot.

"Did you ever learn the guitar?" Aaron asked, a bit of apprehension in his voice.

"Nah. Not really."

"That's all I did when I still lived at home. That was my ticket out. I mean, think about what it's like to grow up in a small town that your great-great-grandfather founded, where all of your relatives are buried, where half of the men were mayors, where every other prissy Victorian house is somehow connected to you. It's a drag, man. Some inheritance. I booked out to the Haight as soon as I could and never looked back. Then I worked my way back east, and that's when I met Maggie. And the rest is history."

Aaron gave the cord a slight tug.

"Ever listen to the Furies?"

"A little," Sage admitted. "With headphones on."

Aaron smiled, faintly, as he shook out more cord from the loosening knot.

"Did I ever tell you my falling baby theory?"

Sage shook his head.

"I can't remember who told it to me but it was a long time ago. Anyway. The falling baby theory is that we're all babies—totally naked, totally unaware of what it's all about. Innocent. Vulnerable. And we're all, like, falling through space, but at different speeds. So, for a while, you'll fall at the same speed as another naked baby, and you'll hook up or whatever, and then one baby will start falling faster and leave the other one behind. It has to happen. It's gravity. And you can't hang on."

Aaron started spreading the cable around the room, careful not to mess it up again.

"Actually, there's nothing to hang on to. But then you keep falling and you meet up with another naked falling baby and maybe you catch up with someone you fell with before. It can happen, but you can't force it."

"And so on and so on."

"You can't get uptight about it. People come and go. And we're all just pissy little babies. Innocent. Falling. At the mercy of some force that's greater than each one of us."

The knot was almost completely unraveled and Aaron and Sage took a look at what they'd accomplished, the loose web of cords that ran around the room.

"Cool," Sage said.

"Yeah. That idea always stuck with me. It was the only way I could make sense of some things," Aaron said while grabbing the end of the cable. "I don't know. Maybe you don't want to hear that from your father. I'm supposed to be the wise old man, right?"

They started looping the cable again, winding it around Sage's arm and somehow restoring order.

Chapter 12

A Sucker for Vulnerability

"Breathe," Gilman Gorham instructed.

The group of sketchers breathed.

"Focus," he said. "Focus on your breathing."

They tried.

"Now, let your eyes rest on an object, any object. Let it happen naturally."

Maggie's eyes drifted from the clouds in the distance to the birch trees with their shimmering leaves to the patch of grass near her feet and the long leaves and sprightly flower of a dandelion. Her eyes stayed there. She breathed again and for a moment wondered if she was doing this thing correctly. Her foot itched under its elastic wrap and the racket from the drum circle was throwing her off and she felt slightly self-conscious and uncomfortable.

I hope nobody recognizes me, Maggie thought as she wiggled her toes to make her injured foot come alive.

"Focus on what fills your eyes."

Maggie focused so hard the dandelion multiplied and became blurry.

"Fill your body with what you see."

Maggie couldn't believe she wasn't smirking.

"Now close your eyes. Experience your vision on a cellular level. Absorb it into your system."

She had no idea how to do that. Nor, she thought, did any sane person.

"Now, open your eyes and focus again. Pick up your pencils and begin drawing. Do not look at the paper. Do not lose focus on your target. Let your hand go where it will."

Maggie kept staring at the dandelion and stifled a nervous giggle.

She traced an outline of the jagged leaf on the paper, sure that it would resemble a Thanksgiving turkey made from an outline of a child's hand. She hoped that she wouldn't have to show her drawing when it was finished. Or, worse yet, discuss her feelings about her vision or cellular experiences.

"Loosen your wrist, Maggie," Gil said softly. "Don't worry about getting it right. Just let it go."

Maggie tried. It wasn't easy.

+++

Seven people in the hawthorn grove did their best to work up positive juju. Aaron led the drumming, holding a slow, steady beat until he caught a line he wanted to pursue. He played with his whole body, toes tapping, legs rocking, shoulders grooving. Sage watched, trying to pick up on Aaron's riff. Sage tapped lightly, tentatively, trying to not interfere but dying to jump in. He finally did, shockingly, but Aaron only smiled his closed-eyed smile, even when the beat got lost. They recovered. The rhythm kept shapeshifting anyway, one drum leading and others following, just like the Furies changed up their tempo. No worries. There were no rules, because rules just create inhibitions and hang-ups, Aaron said. The drum circle was the antithesis of all that, all the scales and chords that were seared into Aaron's brain. It was freeing. Liberating. It raised the spirits of the Earth. It lifted instincts long buried. It was primal, tactile, and never sounded the same way twice. As the sun rose directly overhead, the drumming filled every outdoor space—the gardens, grove, and sky. The sketchers drew to it. The meditators breathed it into their sacred spaces. The lunch cooks chopped and diced to its pulse, infusing the food with its energy.

Aaron was ecstatic when he entered the main building with his conga under his arm.

"Duncan! Shifrah!" he called out to the couple in the tearoom. "Welcome!"

He wrapped the well-dressed Baby Boomers in a sweaty bear hug.

"Namaste," Duncan said. "Peace be with you."

"I'm so happy you're here," Aaron said with a full heart.

The three had known each other for years, way before Aaron got involved at the Karma Community. They had met in a bookstore in Santa Fe when Aaron was struggling to get clean. The Maguires, big Four Furies fans then working as therapists, had recognized Aaron and invited him to dinner. They were kind enough to ignore his shaking hands and evasive answers, but the next time they met, Duncan cornered Aaron and told him he needed help. They refused to lend him money when he asked, and he wasn't allowed to sleep on their couch or bring his sketchy friends over, but they guided him through the rough spots and led him into a healthier, saner lifestyle.

Now, years later, the Karma Community schedule seemed incomplete without a little of the Maguires' trademark—literally—advice on empowered partnerships. Duncan and Shifrah wanted the entire planet to share in their enlightened happiness so they made a career out of it. Every spring, the Maguires brought in big crowds eager to work out—or perhaps put in—the kinks in their relationships. Fantastic marketers, Duncan, a ruddy peacock of a man, and Shifrah, a cheery Earth Mother type, published their own books, created audiotapes and workbooks, and spoke all over the world. They connected; they merged; they wore down your resistance. They hadn't been on Oprah yet, but they were in touch with one of her producers and were sure that they'd get booked soon—just after the next tape, the next workshop, the next spat that turned into the next book on reconciling and merging and enlightenment.

"We're so happy to be here," Shifrah said, adjusting her lavender raw silk scarf around her shoulders and pushing her springy salt and pepper curls away from her face. "We just got back from a speaking tour of Scandinavia. But there's nothing like being here in the early summer."

They hugged again.

"Where's your lovely wife?"

"I'm not sure," Aaron said, wiping his brow. "But I'd like you to meet someone special. My son, Sage."

Sage stepped forward from behind Aaron.

"Fantastic," Duncan raved. "Are you a musician, too?"

Sage laughed. "I drum a little."

"He drums a lot," Aaron said proudly.

The gong sounded for lunch and Aaron escorted his visitors into the dining room, glad that his son and his family of choice were together at last.

+++

The sketchers heard the gong in the garden, signaling the end of the lesson. Gil dismissed his class and helped Maggie to her feet, then offered her his arm, which she accepted.

He tugged at her drawing, a sketch of a thicket of wildflowers tangling in the wind—sprightly, welcoming, lush.

"I didn't know you could draw," he said.

"I don't, much. At least not these days, other than sketches of interiors for my clients."

"It's a shame you don't." He looked at her carefully. "You're funny."

"How?"

"Your son runs away from home and you follow him. I mean, it's a rite of passage thing. Every kid needs to break away, to rebel against his parents. But you won't let him go."

Maggie swallowed, embarrassed by this sudden intimacy.

"Well," she said, drawing out the word while she recovered from his directness. "We're trying to integrate," she continued, stealing Sage's line.

"Ah, integration. Good idea. When you cut something out you just create more of a desire for it. The shadow."

"Yes, something like that," Maggie said, not believing it.

"I know a lot about it," Gil said, squinting in the sun as they walked the path to the center. "I grew up Amish. Very strict. Very black and white. But even we get some time off to live among the English—the non-Amish. It's called Rumspringa. It's sort of a spring break for us farm kids. Then, when it's over, each one of us has to decide if we'll go back to the Amish or try to live in this foreign world."

He held the back door open for Maggie.

"How did you end up here?" she asked.

"One thing led to another," he said as they walked through the hallway to the dining room. "I left home to understand the outside world and fell in love with it. The colors, the noise—the Amish don't allow artwork, so I filled up my eyes with painting and movies and everything. I started doing art therapy with troubled kids as part of my service to the community. I spent a weekend here on a silent retreat, then kept coming and going for a while until I decided to stay. Actually, I've been here longer than Aaron."

"Oh? And you're not in management?"

Gil laughed. "It's not like that. I don't want to *be* management. I just want to do my own thing, and I believe in communal living and what this community is all about. Besides, Aaron is the public face here. He gets us attention, he generates the crowds. He still has a lot of fans. I'm sure you get the same reaction."

"Not really," Maggie admitted. "I don't give a damn about the Four Furies anymore. And I'm not like Aaron. I don't need all of that."

"I don't know if he needs it," Gil said. "He just gets it."

He held out her chair at the long pine table and she sat down, a flush breaking out along her throat and décolletage.

At the next table, Duncan and Shifrah gasped.

"It can't be," Duncan said.

"That isn't."

They leaned over to Maggie.

"I hope we're not interrupting," Duncan said. "But we're such huge fans. Huge."

"When we made love the first time it was to *The One Great Mystery* album," Shifrah added proudly.

Maggie laughed and waved their adulation away.

"We didn't know you were here. Aaron hadn't told us," Duncan said nervously. "Are you getting back together?"

Maggie blushed. "No, no," she shook her head and smiled. "He's married."

Duncan blushed even deeper than Maggie. "I meant the Four Furies."

The singer and her fan looked away, noticing some movement on the other side of the room to silently change the subject. Sybylla appeared in the doorway with water pitchers; Frances held some roasted radishes in a huge homemade platter.

"Sybylla!" Duncan called out. "Sweet Sybylla!"

They rushed over to her and buried each other in hugs and laughs.

"It must be a lot to carry around," Gil said with sympathy. "Do you still sing?"

"No."

"No? Never?"

"Never."

"Another shame. Singing and drawing talent just tossed away." He put some sprigs of watercress on her plate. "I've got to disagree with those two, though," he said, motioning toward Shifrah and Duncan. "*Stars that Shoot and Fall* was my favorite Four Furies album. It got me through a really rough patch. I lost my girlfriend, I lost my job, my apartment, everything. So I just started driving. I drove for a couple of months, driving and driving, thinking and going crazy. And one of the tapes I had in my car was *Stars that Shoot and Fall*. That song— 'Balancing the Scales'—I could listen to it a million times and it would never get old. There was a dent in the tape from rewinding it over and over and over. It's a great song."

"Thank you."

"I'm a sucker for vulnerability. And I hoped my ex was that sad in my absence."

Gil was just like every other Four Furies fan who assumed that the emotionally raw song was about Maggie's pain caused by Aaron's flings. In truth, "Balancing the Scales" was inspired by a tale darker than any fan could imagine.

Stars that Shoot and Fall was their first album under a new contract, and the label's executives expected a monster hit to take the Four Furies to the next level of stardom. The original version of what would become "Balancing the Scales" was an up tempo raver about Aaron's teenage rebellion. "Rock 'n Roll Destiny" was dumb and fun and definitely not what was expected from the Four Furies, but they all knew that it would be blasting out of every muscle car window during the summertime, a radio hit that would make the Four Furies and the execs fabulously wealthy.

But it never made the album.

Because Maggie got caught.

She had been having an affair with Pete, the bassist, when Aaron was spending all of his time in the studio working on the album, coked up and tense and nervy. It wasn't a love affair, Maggie knew at the time, but it was a welcome relief from the weight of her relationship with Aaron. Besides, it made Pete happy. It wasn't like he had been lusting for Maggie all those years and finally won her, but the sex was great and their illicit affair added a new spark to the band. *Harmless enough,* Maggie thought. *We both know the score.*

It was harmless until Aaron had walked in on the pair naked on the teak deck of their beach house, spent and sweaty and relaxed in each other's arms. Aaron's reaction was swift and brutal. Punches, kicks to the groin. A chokehold. A smashed whiskey bottle, shards wielded as a weapon. Pete pinned to the railing, Aaron's gun at his temple. Aaron had let Pete take off without his clothes, then held the pistol to his own head.

"I can't live without you," he'd said, his finger trembling on the trigger, Maggie kneeling at his feet. "You know I can't."

After a long night of pleading and tears his anger subsided and she slid the gun out of his hand and emptied the bullets into the beach grass below the balcony.

"And I can't live without you, you damn fool," Maggie said, easing him into bed at dawn, when they made love carefully, tenderly. She curled up around him, entwined from tip to toe, hyper-alert and tense, a lioness ever watchful for danger as Aaron slept deeply, totally spent.

Aaron spent the afternoon in the studio, then called his bandmates to come in as the sun was setting.

They sat in a circle as they always did, Peter, demoralized, with a black eye and split lip, Aaron with a belly full of whiskey, Maggie exhausted and shaken, Hooch sensing something was going on but smart enough not to acknowledge it.

"We're playing 'Destiny' again." Aaron handed Maggie a notebook page with new lyrics. "But we're going to slow it down. Way down."

They did as he commanded, transforming the high-spirited hit into a funereal lament.

Maggie stepped to the microphone and looked at her new lyrics for the first time.

"Where were you last night?" she sang.
Same place I was
In someone else's bed
Balancing the scales.
Where are you tonight?
Telling sweet lies
And cutting lines
Balancing the scales."

She took a deeper breath and held out her hands to signal that the band should take it even slower.

"You say I lie and I cheat," she sang, defiantly, without regret, Aaron joining her in a low growl.

"And maybe I do
But baby
I'm balancing the scales."

Maggie stepped back and let the band take over, thoroughbreds raring to go and straining at the confines of the slow tempo. Aaron struck up a mournful solo up the neck of his battered Gibson guitar, Peter urging him on with his pummeling bass, pushing the pace of the song with his intensity, refusing to accept defeat.

"You know no one can touch you," Maggie sang, her voice cracking as her full heartache shone through.

"And I'm all yours," she and Aaron sang together.

"But baby I'm balancing the scales."

By the time Aaron closed out the song Maggie knew that she would never—*could never*—leave him. No one but Aaron could ever capture her feelings so purely and push her to express herself so honestly, shyness be damned. No one but Aaron could transform her private heartache into the stuff of legends. She was balancing the scales with Pete, trying to even the score with Aaron. It wouldn't work, of course. They could continue to cheat and lie and sleep around, but ultimately she had to admit that they belonged together. And Aaron knew it, too.

Maggie rubbed her temple, trying to rub the memory away as she listened to faint minor-key melody filling the air in the Karma Community's dining room, Frances' benediction before their vegan meal and iced lemon balm tea.

"*Namaste*," the room said in uniform as Maggie's memory of Aaron faded away.

"It's a shame you don't sing anymore," Gil said, leaning in close.

Maggie smiled faintly, tears blurring her vision as she glanced over at Aaron snuggling up against Sybylla, their friends circled around them, a picture-perfect scene of hippie paradise.

"You know no one can touch you and I'm all yours," she thought as the song's melody filled her soul.

How wrong he was, she told herself.

She stiffened her spine and ran her finger along her lower lash line to erase any signs of sadness.

"You must have had offers to record again," Gil said. "There's a huge underground of Four Furies fans just waiting for you to make a comeback."

She checked out Gil—handsome, with shoulders like a Viking and blond as a summer afternoon. He didn't seem as loopy as the others here. He seemed sweet and sincere. But real. Pure. A short-term distraction from her troubles.

"So tell me, Gil," she asked, trying to remember how to flirt. She stared into his eyes so intensely she could see her reflection in them. "What do you need to integrate?"

Across the room, Frances shivered.

Chapter 13

The Hungry Ghost

"I hate to do the emcee thing," Aaron said to the overcrowded tearoom after dinner. "But I will. We're lucky to have tonight two speakers who are extraordinary experts on relationships, personal growth, and enlightenment. Tonight's talk is just a preview of their weekend course, and believe me, it's amazing. Just like them. Please welcome Duncan and Shifrah Maguire."

Aaron hugged Duncan and kissed Shifrah on her cheek, then gave them the stage and the attention of the room. A bouquet of wildflowers was placed on their table to their right, along with water, candles, and each of their books and tapes on enlightened partnering. A whiff of burning sage and lavender hung in the air. Aaron joined Sybylla in the back of the room and stood behind her, his arms encircling her waist and his face buried in her spilled-out chestnut hair. Maggie caught a glimpse of them, then looked away and patted Sage's hand.

"Before we begin, we'd like to take a moment to gather our intentions. Take a nice long breath and exhale," Duncan instructed.

"Ah…" Shifrah acted out for the room, making eye contact with the people in the first row.

"Ah…" the crowd responded.

"Get rid of the stresses of the day."

"Ah…" Shifrah continued. Maggie exhaled silently.

"Now relax your body. Wiggle your toes. Then your calves and your knees. Up to your rear."

Shifrah giggled. Sage shifted in his seat.

"Then open your stomach and your chest. Feel the tension loosen. Roll your shoulders. Roll your head around. Get in touch with your body. It's your temple."

Maggie complied only as much as she felt she had to. Sage practically boogied in place and Maggie wondered how much tension an unemployed drummer had to release.

Aaron and Sybylla were relieving their stress in tandem, Aaron's chest pressed against Sybylla's back, never losing contact with each other. It wasn't explicitly sexual, but Maggie knew what they were doing and she thought it was tasteless.

"Encircle yourself with white light," Shifrah said. "Get that healthy glow. Now, extend it out in all directions."

Maggie didn't. But it seemed like what she'd done before going on stage— summoning her powers, making herself bigger like a peacock or, at times, a predatory bird, the creature that matched her mindset during the Furies' shows. Aaron had had his own routine, too, she was sure, but he never shared it with her. He just came out of the bowels of the backstage area either fighting fit or foggy, wasted, freshly blown.

"Include your lover or partner in your energy field."

Maggie winced. What the hell, she thought, and imagined Gil in a circle of light, as corny as that felt. The back of her neck burned. She wondered if he could feel it. *Of course not. This place is rubbing off on me. I'm becoming as nutty and gullible as the rest of them.*

"Thank you," Duncan said solemnly as he arranged a few wisps of cloud-colored hair across his sunburned scalp. "Shifrah and I share our light every morning and night. It's our way to check in with each other, to remind ourselves that our relationship is spiritual. It transcends both of us. And it requires attention."

"But it isn't always easy," Shifrah said.

"Just this morning," she said as she turned to Duncan and they smiled and touched fingertips, "when we were packing for this weekend, we hit a few snags."

"We travel so much that we have a routine. But this morning I tossed out the routine. Instead of being responsible for packing our course materials, I left them on our desk. I started packing our clothes instead."

"Which drives me crazy," Shifrah said with an exaggerated wink. "Duncan is practically color blind…"

"…and I can barely dress myself." He pointed to his garish Hawaiian shirt and pleated khakis with a rehearsed laugh. "But I wanted to do something different today. I didn't want to be responsible for the books and papers. The problem, though, is that I didn't communicate this to Shifrah. I just went ahead and did it."

"And of course I went crazy."

The audience laughed along with the Maguires, Duncan looking slightly guilty. He walked closer to the crowd.

"As silly as it sounds," he said with a new seriousness, "this gave us insight into our relationship. I was tired of being responsible for certain things, for being the 'materials guy.' Now, that role worked, that made sense. But Shifrah had no way of knowing I was tired. I started to resent it. Why am I doing all of the heavy lifting? Why is my job so mundane? Why does she get to do the fun stuff, the creative stuff?"

"Why does Duncan get to do the easy stuff, the job that doesn't require a lot of thought?"

Their eyes caught and the audience was drawn in further.

"The thing is, I was placing my needs above the relationship," Duncan said in a stage whisper. "I wanted to do something that the current relationship wouldn't allow."

He paused for a moment and zoomed in. "Because I didn't think it was allowed, I craved it. I became what the Buddhists call a hungry ghost."

Shifrah joined him and held his hand, forgiving him for his transgressions. "The hungry ghost—the hungry partner—is a miserable creature. It craves and craves, but never feels satisfied," she told the crowd.

"It's hollow and selfish."

"It's envious and greedy."

"It's resentful and manipulative."

A few audience members stirred in their seats.

"It makes demands. Why aren't you satisfying all of my unspoken, uncommunicated needs?" Duncan asked Shifrah.

"Why do you only do what's easy?" Shifrah responded.

"What can you do for me? And why aren't you doing it?"

"And why do you still feel empty inside?"

"The relationship works, but…"

"…but it's rigid, stale…"

"…because I'll only meet you halfway…"

"…if you get there first."

"So I might as well look outside the relationship for my satisfaction…"

"…and take your energy with you…"

"…and still feel hungry, empty…"

"…forever searching for a fantasy…"

"…and only remembering the broken, rigid relationship we once had…"

"…instead of supercharging it with your desire to change it…"

"…I put myself above the partnership…"

"…creating boundaries where there should be abundance…"

Maggie knew it was shtick, but she was paying attention. The hungry ghost thing—eh—she could take it or leave it. But what compelled her was the Maguires' lives as a professional couple, not unlike her and Aaron back in the day. Duncan's and Shifrah's identities were bound up in their relationship; their careers were tied into it, too, as they profited off of analyzing and mythologizing their marriage.

There was a certain amount of security in that arrangement, but it demanded a price: the public confession. Their fans wanted to know about the boredom, tedium, and three a.m. terrors of relationships; they wanted to find the diamonds of meaning in the rough days of kids, jealousy, bounced checks, and scheduled sex. They wanted to know that Duncan could be thoughtless and selfish; they sensed that Shifrah spent too much money but hid the receipts well. These sins made the Maguires real—and gave them more material to work with.

Similarly, Aaron, as a professional boyfriend, had no problem lacing the Furies' songs with clues about his relationship with Maggie, his muse. He could make contact with the fans' private aches because he shared them. The Furies' albums held up after all of these years because a broken-hearted guy like Gil could drive across the country and hear Maggie and Aaron break up and fuck and beg and accuse the way Gil would have, if given a chance. We were all suckers for vulnerability, Maggie realized.

And there Aaron was on the other side of the room, his arms around his new wife while Duncan and Shifrah received hugs and compliments from audience members filtering out of the room and back to their cabins, their journals, their anxieties and dreams. Aaron hadn't been on stage but he was flushed, electric, Sybylla giggling and coy. Maggie knew what was going on.

The endorphin rush after a great performance was always the best part of the night—Aaron and Maggie usually sought each other out in the dark, backstage corners of the venue for sex, or clumsily unzipped in the back of a limo, or simply didn't care who saw or heard them in their tour bus. They'd been playing games on stage for their fans, teasing and torturing each other with their theatrics. Alone, naked, they could be honest with each other. The rock star stuff be damned—Maggie had just wanted Aaron all to herself. The Aaron that only she knew, the Aaron that belonged only to her.

Chapter 14

So Long, Suckers

Sage was still tingling after the lecture. Half of what Duncan and Shifrah talked about went right over his head, but he got it, he thought.

It is about integration, just like Sybylla said. Just like he and Aaron were trying to do. Like when you see something in someone that you just can't stand—that means that it's in you, too, and you can't stand it there, either. Otherwise, you would never notice it. But once you know what's happening, you can integrate that thing that you see in someone else and know that you have it, too, so you can't hate it. Because then you'd be hating yourself, too.

Sage stood off to the side of the dispersing crowd, on the edge in the corridor. He watched Duncan and Shifrah sign workbooks and CDs and hug a few people. He saw Gil, all business, arrange the equipment and chairs for tomorrow's lecture, Duncan and Shifrah's daylong seminar on harmonizing with your partner's energy field. Sage watched his mother slip up the stairs to the business office. And Aaron and Sybylla—they were in their own bubble, untouchable.

Sage ducked outside and lit a cigarette, inhaling deeply and letting the drag fill his lungs. He left the lit-up center behind them as he walked down the garden path to the shed, helped along by glowing paper lanterns poked into the grass. Sage ground out the cigarette stub on the dirt path, then shoved the shed door open. He entered, pulled out a rickety abandoned bike, and pedaled through the hills under the crisp moonlight.

Sage tumbled through the hills on the old bike, which clearly wasn't designed for off-road roaming. The thin tires were slightly flat and almost totally bald, but Sage careened through the grounds without a care.

The brakes were another story. He tried the left one and the right one and neither one slowed him down. He dragged his toe along the grass as he descended toward the creek.

He laughed belly laughs all the way to the water. Then, at the river's edge, he reached into the front pocket of his baggy jeans, extracted the bottle of pills he'd been prescribed since he was seventeen, and chucked them.

"So long, suckers," he called out.

He watched the white-capped brown bottle bob in the river and move its way downstream.

He laughed again and rode up the hill, wobbling all the way up. He circled and looped under the stars and lost his balance looking at them. Not thinking of his earthly surroundings, he didn't see the rock slab that jutted out from the grass, and wiped out at the foot of an old maple tree, getting tangled up in roots and grass and handlebars.

Sitting against the base of the tree, caressing the nubby bark as if she was deeply in love with it, was Frances in her orange turban.

Sage laughed, then winced.

"Ouch." He curled up in pain, which shot from his toes to his ankle to his knee and his hip.

Silently, Frances let go of the tree and put her hands on Sage's knee, concentrating heat there. Sage felt something—something like a spiral, like a burst of light, like an awakening.

Frances put her right hand on his ankle. Then, when she felt Sage's energy shift, she moved her hands up his leg, letting the Reiki energy flow from the universe through her and into his sore spots.

Sage surrendered. He didn't know what was happening, but he knew that something definitely was happening. He felt as if he was on a waterbed, but he wasn't. He was on a threadbare red chaise, a brocade pillow propped against the wooden arm to cushion his head. He and Frances had hobbled back to this place, and now he was floating on something that didn't feel like anything of this world.

Frances pressed a warm damp rag on his knee, something that she'd soaked in an herbal brine for a few minutes.

"What is this place?" he asked, taking in the strange little outbuilding tucked among the walnut and pine trees. Bundles of dried plants and flowers hung from the low ceiling. Jars on homemade shelves lined the walls. An easel was propped up in one corner, a half-done watercolor clipped to the top. And sieves, cheesecloth, racks, bowls, funnels, bottles, pliers, knives, books—the tools of Frances' trade—were piled everywhere.

"It's my herbal refuge," she said, keeping her hand firmly on his knee.

"It's like," Sage said, overwhelmed. "Like..."

"Another world?"

"Yes."

"Good."

She reached over to a jug of water, poured some in a chipped tea cup, added a dropper full of a dark brown tincture to it, and handed it to Sage.

"This should help."

Sage held it close, smelling it.

"It smells like the forest," he said, slightly awed.

"Appropriate, don't you think?"

Sage looked away.

"Did you build this place?"

"Sort of," Frances said as she dipped the cloth into the cooling water. "It was a chicken coop originally, then I took it over and made it my own. Well, Aaron helped a lot. He built the roof and installed the windows. I did the rest."

He put the freshened cloth back on his knee.

"Feeling better?"

"I think so."

Sage leaned back into the pillow, taking in everything. Not just the herbs and jars, but everything—the poppet pinned to the wall, and the quartz crystals in the copper bowl, and the rolling papers and matches on the windowsill.

"Are you a witch?" he finally asked.

Frances smiled.

"Drink."

Chapter 15

The Goddess

Maggie closed the back door of the main building behind her and waited to hear the lock click. She didn't know the code to turn on the security system, so she slid the chain lock in place, hoping that would be good enough to keep her safe for the night. She was alone in the building, the seminar attendees lingering around the campfire and late-night strollers having returned to their sleeping quarters as the strings of fairy lights around the winding paths sputtered in the breeze.

She took off her sandals and allowed the cool tiles to soothe her feet as she walked toward her second-floor massage-room-turned-bedroom at the top of the stairs.

A long day today. Another long day tomorrow. I'd love a glass of wine, but they don't believe in that here.

A tapestry hung in the corridor leading to the main dining room—an exotic goddess wearing a heavy gold, elaborately detailed headdress and breastplate. Her skin was blue, and her ruby-red tongue extended to her chin.

Take that, Jagger. This gal did it first—and better.

The goddess had four arms and a garland of skulls dangling from her neck. One hand was held aloft in a sign of peace, another extended in friendship, the third held a scythe, and the last one gripped a severed male's head by his jet-black hair, blood dripping, his face peaceful. She stood on a man's chest, the conquered man utterly submissive to her.

The goddess didn't look a bit remorseful.

I'll have what you're having. I'm going to need to slay a few men to get what I want.

One by one the lights in the retreat center blinked off in sheets of darkness. The only spot of light was the green light of the security system monitor glowing behind Maggie.

Crap.

"Hello?"

Maggie ran her fingers along the wall, feeling stupid and clumsy as she tried to mentally recreate the floor plan of the building. Corridor, dining room, corridor on the far side, kitchen to the right, stairs to the left. Atrium, gift shop, and meditation room somewhere beyond. Not a problem.

She reached the end of the hallway, took a breath, and searched forward channeling Helen Keller, shuffling her feet, hands extended outward to feel for a chair or table. She made contact with one chair, then felt for another, then kicked a table leg. Pain shot through her already sore bare foot.

"Damn it."

She heard steps on the other side of the dining room and the hair along her arms stood to attention.

"Hello?"

"Hello," she heard.

Not Aaron, not Sage, she thought.

"Could you turn on the light?" She hoped her voice didn't betray her fear and stood silently, holding her ground, wishing she had the blue goddess's knife and bravado.

She heard more steps come toward her, a chair pushed aside, then felt the warmth of another body close to her.

"It's all right," the man told her. "I've got you."

"Who is this?"

She felt warm hands on hers, the callouses not matching Aaron's tough pads from guitar playing. This man's fingers were firm and strong, the pulse in his wrists jumping. He was just as keyed up as she was.

"It's Gil," he said. "I didn't mean to scare you."

Gil. She imagined his broad shoulders, clear eyes, strawberry blond locks that he sometimes pulled back into a ponytail. Handsome. Young. A sucker for vulnerability.

Then she thought of her own body—softer thanks to early menopause, late dinners, and extra glasses of wine—and shrank back from where her thoughts were leading her. It had been almost two years since she'd been with a man and she wasn't sure she was prepared for what her instincts wanted her to do.

"I was scared," she admitted. "A bit."

He pulled her in closer so their thighs touched. She didn't pull away as she felt him swell between her legs. She smoothed down his soft work shirt, then whisked back his lapel to feel his jugular vein throb.

Maybe it's time. Maybe he won't care that I'm not what I used to be.

She brushed her cheek against his whiskers, then pulled her face down into his neck, damp from the long day. He ran his hands along her back, her waist, her breasts.

"I'm staying upstairs. It's not—"

He cut off her whisper with a deep kiss that took her by surprise and sent a jolt through her. She let him kiss her again and again and again until she felt her knees give way. He took her hand and led her through the dining room, out the long corridor and past the reception area to the meditation room studded with pillows and cushions. He leaned her against a cushion on a pile of soft blankets as he lit a votive candle and flicked on the burbling waterfall.

"I've always wanted you," he whispered in her ear as he fondled her nipple under her camisole. "Ever since I bought my first Furies album. I stared at you on the cover for hours and hours and hours."

Unlike Aaron, Maggie never slept with Four Furies fans, always feeling queasy about the power imbalance or the fear that some one-night stand was going to blab to the press and shatter the Maggie-and-Aaron myth. Instead, she sought out other musicians, peers who could understand the aches that she felt as an artist, a mate, a much-desired but lonely celebrity with a love-hate relationship with fame and his fans.

It didn't always go as planned.

She gasped as Gil slid his hand under her shirt and she was taken back to a night in the mid-seventies when Aaron was holed up in the studio trying to meet an impossible deadline for the *Phoenix* album. She'd reluctantly attended their manager's party in the hills without him. She always felt uncomfortable in these social situations, not really feeling a part of LA's musical elite, but at the same time resented being judged as just the pretty face and voice expressing Aaron's genius.

Maggie was grateful when Clark Kavanaugh, the British Guitar God of the moment, handed her a glass of California Chardonnay and ushered her through the party with a gentlemanly ease. Clark had been kind but distant to her on the

90

few occasions they'd met—backstage at one of his shows, at an intimate showcase of his new material on the Strip, in the halls of their management company, Clark tucking his latest platinum album under his arm, shaggy bangs flopping in his eyes, deeply embarrassed.

Aaron revered him as the One Musician Who Truly Got It.

The glass of Chardonnay led to another, then some grass, a bottle of cognac shared on the slope of the canyon at sunrise, and slow, silent lovemaking in one of the host's spare bedrooms as the party dissipated around them. Clark's fingertips were more calloused than Aaron's, but more tender, still.

"Leave him," he whispered. "He doesn't deserve you."

He kissed her again, so long that she thought she'd float away.

"Give me one more night. One more night."

She said nothing as she put her clothes on and closed the door quietly behind her.

Dozens of white roses and an Elsa Peretti open heart necklace in a telltale blue Tiffany box were delivered to her with no note, but the sender didn't need to be identified. She knew, apologized when he phoned, tried to wriggle her way out of it, refused to meet him again.

"I'm in too deep with Aaron. I can't break up the band. I couldn't tour with him if we were split. It just wouldn't work."

"Give me one more night," Clark said, his voice cracking. He could have had any woman in the world and he wanted the one who refused him. "We can be brilliant together."

Clark was willing to rip up his own tour to be with her, shadowing her and protecting her as the Four Furies promoted their new album. He offered to open for the Furies, or at least do a double-headline tour to make things fair. He tried to get her to record with him to give them an excuse to be together. He proposed marriage, just like that, just to have her.

But she just wasn't ready to make the leap.

Aaron noticed the roses and Maggie's worried distance but immersed himself in mixing the album, shrugging off her latest indiscretion.

"Tell the sad little puppy you picked up to get over it and stop sending this crap."

The roses stopped arriving but that wasn't the last message Clark sent to Maggie.

They'd always deny that the song was about her, but the lyrics left no doubt.
"I saw you across the room
Beautiful lady, sad eyes
Sing for me, charms and lace

Your man's a fool."
Then he laid it all on the line in the chorus:
"Give me one more night, I said.
One more night, I begged.
Give me a night to clear your head.
Come back to my bed."
And if the listener were really dense, Clark cleared it up in the next verse:
"We walked in the moonlight.
Didn't talk, just touched.
Your heart furious under your lace,
Don't deny it feels so right."
The single shot off like a rocket fueled by the great Guitar God losing his cool over a woman, unnamed, the one who finally broke him. Maggie knew absolutely it was about her; Aaron didn't flinch when he heard it. They denied it to reporters, but both knew, all three of them knew, the truth. Their shared management team kept the rumors alive to pump up sales.

Maggie and Aaron didn't discuss it as they put the final touches on *Phoenix*. Then, alone in the studio, Aaron did what he did best: He seduced her. Got her to loosen up and relax, praised her vocals as they listened to the new tracks, lowered the lights, and flattered her, kissed and touched her tenderly as he undressed her and made love to her as only a man who knew every inch and nerve ending of her could.

When she heard the final cut of their first single, "Nothing to Hide," she knew why. You had to listen closely, but it was unmistakable. The audio of their lovemaking provided the steady pulse to the song, a full-on duet which Aaron had written years ago and recorded weeks earlier but now, caught in the scandal of the Clark Kavanaugh affair, a song that took on new meaning.

"Baby, I'm a fool for you.
If that's a crime
Then let me do my time.
Baby, I'm true to you.
No other man
Pleases me like you can.
I've got nothing to hide.
Ask me everything,
Won't find anything.
I've got nothing to hide."
"Nothing to Hide" zipped up the charts and pushed Clark's "One More Night" from the top spot. DJs chattered endlessly about the rumors and played

up Maggie and Aaron's sex sounds, which denied them radio play in the South. The Four Furies were denounced from pulpits for celebrating unmarried sex so graphically, giving teenagers ideas—as if they didn't already have them. Maggie, used to hiding behind a good girl image among her hedonistic peers, hated the song, hated the scandal, hated hearing others' opinions on the truth of the affair and dueling songs. She hated performing it, since the audience expected her and Aaron to moan and sigh and pant when they weren't singing about pleasing each other. She hated Aaron for manipulating her and turning their private dramas into public confessions. She alone knew the truth of that song, and Clark's, and she felt like a traitor.

She called Clark to apologize and declare her innocence, but he refused to speak to her and hibernated in his English country house, lost in a heroin stupor. His pain only fueled her desire for him, for the opportunity he presented her if she'd only had the courage then to split from Aaron. But the success and scandal of "Nothing to Hide" kept her bound to the Four Furies, at least until the notoriety simmered down. And deep down she had to wonder why Clark was so besotted. She didn't feel she deserved that kind of adoration from a man as revered as he was. No, flawed Aaron fit her better. At least she didn't have to work hard to be good enough for him.

Decades later in the cool meditation room, as Gil carefully peeled off her clothes and kissed her pale skin from top to bottom, delighting in her softness, adoring and worshipping Maggie Morgan of the Four Furies, she wondered if sleeping with fellow rock stars, and abstaining from sex with fans, had been the right choice. She was a goddess to Gil, a goddess to a lot of men. She might as well enjoy it.

She laid back and let him live out his fantasy.

Chapter 16

Open to Interpretation

Frances sat on the floor at the foot of her bed and inhaled the morning air deeply. She lit the dried mugwort leaves in the small brass bowl, then fanned the embers with a turkey feather. The smoke filled the room quickly, smelling a bit like pot, but not exactly. She inhaled again, holding the air in her lungs and belly, then sighed, and rolled her head forward, to the side, then back and around to the front again, completing a circle.

Frances turned to her right, the east, and welcomed the energy from this sacred direction, the lightness and newness and clarity of the good breeze above her head. Holding the bowl of smoldering mugwort above her head, she visualized all in the Karma Community that belonged to the element of Air—learning, talking, laughing—and filled it with light. Gil flashed in her mind, his paintbrush held high, looking like the romantic and daring Knight of Swords from her well-worn tarot deck.

Frances swiveled to the south and welcomed the Fire element's vibe, its passion and desire and inspiration. She visualized the burning sun rising in the east and traveling across the sky. In her mind's eye, Frances enveloped Sybylla and Aaron in the glow, then let them dance. "Welcome, South, enter," Frances said aloud.

Frances now faced the west, the direction of the Water of life, of emotions and fluidity, of the unconscious and of cleansing. Maggie appeared in Frances' sacred vision, looking at her reflection in a fresh, still pond before cupping her hand and drinking from it. Frances smiled, glad that Maggie showed up.

Frances now faced the north, the direction of the element of Earth, which she imagined as the primeval forest, thick and lush and overgrown, the realm of dirt and trees and flora, the realm of fertility. Sage ran through this wilderness, a free wild child fully alive and aware, a nature spirit about to embark on his hero's journey out of Eden.

Frances bent down and touched the floor with both palms, grounding herself. She welcomed all that was below—roots, mud, lava, underground springs, landfills, decaying life, regenerating power, slumbering animals. She thought of her own grandmother, the wise, nurturing crone who knew healing secrets and passed them on to her daughters and granddaughters.

Frances next raised her face to the sky, the stars, sun, and clouds, the spirit guides and butterflies and airplanes and satellites and kites and birds. All that was above was welcome, too.

Then Frances opened her arms wide as she did every morning, putting the energies in motion, imagining a silvery band encompassing them all like a gyroscope or an atom with herself at the center, like the heartbeat within the great Cosmic Egg. In her mind's eye, the silver bands slid and vibrated and spun while she placed her hands over her second chakra. She moved her hands over her heart, holding the wind, fire, water, earth, roots, and sky inside of her deepest core until she would release them that night. She asked that everyone would be welcome at the center. She asked that everyone feel connected to each other, and to the earth and sky and fire and water and air. She asked for peace and love. *We'll need an extra dose of it*, she thought warily, always two steps ahead of everyone else.

+++

As he rolled over in bed, Sage cursed the morning. His internal clock hadn't adjusted to yoga at dawn and breakfast wrapped up before eight. He did it, of course, and tried to seem enthusiastic about it. Sometimes he did it just to show Aaron that he was into his scene and game for anything.

Sage had never been a morning person, unless he was pulling an all-nighter of video games, beer, weed, and music. Maggie tried to get him up at a decent hour, but it was easier to let Sage sleep in and have the morning to herself, stress-free and determined to face her clients with a brave face. Sometimes, Sage only pulled himself out of bed just before Maggie returned from work in the evening and he went out with his friends. Maggie suspected as much, but didn't dig for proof.

They were on different schedules at home and only occasionally bumped into each other, Maggie's patience tested by her laid-back son. Their schedules did overlap late at night when Maggie had insomnia, though. On those nights, he could hear her TV through the walls and down the long hallway that separated their bedrooms. Sometimes he'd click through all of the channels until he found the one that synchronized with the white noise from her room. Then he'd leave it there, light a bowl, and vicariously watch television with his mom. He always felt strangely close to her in these moments, close enough but far enough away, too. There, but not. That was enough for both of them some days.

Sage loved long mornings in bed, watching cable and eating cookies until he had to go to the bathroom or make phone calls or whatever. That was his favorite time to space out. It was like meditation at the Karma Community, Sage thought, only you watched TV while you did it. He knew that he needed that time off and got cranky when he didn't have it. That's why college had been so hard for him. He didn't have that zone-out time that mellowed him out.

That time freed up his mind. It wandered all over, from girls to sports to fantasies of becoming famous and not giving a fuck. Like in the real world he'd outgrown skateboarding, but sometimes he'd daydream about his own empire, superimposing his face on Tony Hawks' and swiping all of his accomplishments. Sometimes he was a poker champ and played hands that brought him from the brink of elimination to tournament glory.

Sometimes Aaron popped up in Sage's daydreams. But Aaron was always an observer, someone who was in the crowd and amazed by Sage's talent, whether he was playing poker, or directing a film, or day-trading and making millions in a few seconds, or just being surrounded by hot chicks at a party. It didn't matter what Sage conquered; he just conjured up Aaron's applause and praise when he finally did something of note.

That's how he wanted to meet Aaron, as a champ, a player. He still wasn't sure why he contacted Aaron when he did. Well, the stuff about integrating and the rest of that crap, sure. And he had always been curious about Aaron and wondered about the drugs and groupies, where the money went, why Maggie said he'd been a shit to her, and why he didn't give a shit about his son. Sage guessed that it didn't really matter as long as Aaron was cool to him, and he was. Sage just tried to focus on the present, the now. The past was open to interpretation.

+++

Aaron lay between Sybylla's legs, his head resting on her bare stomach. They were in their morning cocoon, their world calm and quiet and bordered by cotton tapestries inside and elm and maple leaves just outside their window. Aaron smiled. Sybylla turned her head to face the filtered morning light.

"We're going to have to tell people, you know," she said softly. "There's no way we can keep this a secret."

"I wish we could," Aaron said while reaching for her hand. "I'd rather keep it a secret until the very end and then amaze people with what we've done. I hate being pressured by people, answering questions and sticking to a deadline. Or a budget." He rolled over and propped himself up on his side so that he could look at his wife.

"Frederick will definitely want us to submit a budget," Sybylla said. "Remember how hard it was to convince him that we needed a fire pit? But we just have to keep reminding him of how it will benefit the Karma Community— attract more people, get them excited, get them to think." Her eyes were really glowing. "Get them to feel, to act."

"I don't think dear Freddie cares about any of that stuff," Aaron said. "He's so unenlightened. I'd love to turn him on to what we're doing, but he's like a rock, a brick. He's dead inside. Inert. He eats shit food, drives a Hummer, and inherited all of his money. When I see him, I just see his energy go down. I can actually see it happening. And then I feel him try to suck my energy and I just have to back away. Poor little vampire."

"But at least he signs the checks every month."

"True. He could invest in anything—a diamond mine in South Africa or sweatshops in Bangladesh. But I guess he's already done that."

"Aaron. Be nice."

Aaron frowned. "Now he's trying to be socially conscious by owning the Karma Community. Whatever that means." He raked his hand through his hair and sighed at the thought of the man who owned a community that was priceless to its residents. "He reminds me of some of the rich dudes I met when the band was together. They wanted to be in the music industry to be cool and rebellious so they threw parties and went to shows and tried to put together deals for new bands. They thought that if they knew artists, they *were* artists. But their money was old money, and they were jive. You knew they were going to go back to Beverly Hills and clean themselves up and drop back into high society. They were only playing at it. They didn't make any sacrifices. Just like when Freddie drops in with his rich friends and demands massages and tea, and then they leave their trash everywhere and disrupt everyone when they're on their cell phones. They're totally unaware, but they feel enlightened and spiritual because they can come here and get in touch with themselves."

"They're trying, I think. Don't be so judgmental. Meet them where they are. Even if that isn't where you want them to be," Sybylla soothed.

"He just wants his friends to know that he's got Aaron Fields on his payroll. It gives him credibility in that scene."

"He could just walk away. He could get sick of losing money on this place," Sybylla contested. "That must mean something."

"It means he has an ego," Aaron said, sorrow and anger mixing in his voice.

"Like everyone else. Like you. Like me. Don't be so quick to judge, just because he's your boss and you have to answer to him," she said gently. "It's a game—Freddie wants to think he's socially conscious, and you want to live here. Play the game. Appease him. Then he'll leave you alone."

"You're right," Aaron said quietly, again proud of his young wife's old wisdom, but still resenting feeling like he was a Dutch financier's puppet, no matter how hands-off Freddie was in the day-to-day operations of the retreat center. "But money and ego—it's always a corrupt combination."

"It's a necessary combination. And without it I'd still be living in my parents' tree house."

"And god knows where I'd be."

"I bet the goddess knows," Sybylla teased.

Aaron kissed his wife's bare stomach, then coolly blew on it to make her giggle. With his second finger he traced a spiral on her abdomen, a large, funny, crooked spiral that circled around Sybylla's navel and then got progressively wider.

"I love our dream," Sybylla said.

"I love our labyrinth."

"It's not just a dream anymore, is it?"

"No, goddess willing."

Aaron continued looping his finger around and around Sybylla's belly and tracing spirals and circles that were invisible to anyone but them.

"The pattern you wanted…" Aaron began.

"Yes, the full moon and the waxing moon and the waning moon…"

"I can't quite make sense of it," Aaron said gingerly.

"But it's so simple," Sybylla said, tucking another pillow under her head. "Start at the bottom, then make a big circle, counterclockwise." She moved Aaron's hand as she spoke, tracing the full moon on her skin.

"Then go inside that circle, and go almost all the way to the top. That's the beginning of the waxing moon. Then come back down and up again, making a smaller crescent, and do it again and again, making smaller and smaller crescents."

"Yes, but…"

"But…"

"But how will we ever lead people out of the moons? We'll trap them in our labyrinth, stuck in the waning moon with nowhere to go."

"Can't they retrace their steps to get out of it?"

"They could, but…"

Sybylla thought for a moment, then grimaced.

"I see what you mean. We'd have walking meditators crashing into each other as they make their way through our labyrinth."

Aaron squeezed Sybylla's hand.

"I know it came to you in your dream, but…"

"It isn't manifesting properly."

Aaron brushed her cheek, attempting to whisk away her confusion.

"I'll just have to ask the universe for another labyrinth design. I know the answer will come. You just have to hang in there with me, Aaron."

"Of course."

"You're not angry with me, are you?"

"Why? You'll get the answer," he reassured her. "We'll build this labyrinth, no matter what. We'll show old Freddie what we can do—together."

Chapter 17

They've Always Gotten Me Wrong

"I'll be back in an hour," Maggie said, kissing Gil softly on the cheek as she exited the Karma Community's pickup truck in a driveway on the sunny side of the highway leading out of New Elm. "I just need to clear up some stuff I'm working on in Chicago."

There was no other way around it: Maggie needed a lawyer to get out of her legal mess in Wisconsin, but she wasn't ready to tell Gil what kind of mess she was in. He didn't need to know, really. She's be gone soon.

She had an initial appearance in court the next day and wanted an attorney to help her through what she thought were some bullshit charges from a small-town district attorney. Although they were bullshit, if left to marinate they could complicate whatever was going to happen with Felix's firm—Maggie's firm, hopefully. If she could convince Trip and Matilda to accept her offer. If she could come up with the money.

Get rid of the legal stuff, then figure out how to get a loan. Maybe a second mortgage. Just take it step by step by step.

The law office of attorney Erika Erikson, the "good people" Aaron had recommended, was in an addition to a nondescript postwar salmon-brick ranch house on about two acres of lawn and gardens along the highway. Maggie pressed the doorbell and waited to be buzzed in as she watched Gil back out of the driveway and head off in to town to do the Karma Community's errands: get fifty pounds of chicken feed, mail the electric bill, return some library books before their due date, pin up flyers announcing some upcoming workshops on the community bulletin boards at the diner, library, and city hall. And then he'd pick her up and deliver her back to the Karma Community.

He's too good to be true, Maggie thought to herself as he drove away. *Too good for me.*

"I've always wanted to meet you," Erika said, swinging the door wide open. "I have all of your albums."

Maggie laughed politely and scanned the woman who'd help her clean up her mess. Erika was tall and well built, a woman who put on muscle, not fat, when she gained weight, with soft brown hair brushed so that her curls turned into waves that frizzed out by the end of the day. Her clear blue eyes were deep set above high cheekbones. She was slightly around Maggie's age, probably one of the few women in her law class back in the mid-seventies. She wore a full skirt, white blouse, with long patterned vest over it with a string of garnets around her neck. Not a trace of pretension, ego, or vanity.

Good people, yes.

"We're on tomorrow's docket for nine o'clock sharp. You have two choices. If you want to get it over with quickly, don't contest the charges and you can go on with your life. But you will have a criminal record, which will affect parts of your life you can't even imagine right now. If you want to fight it and clear your name, we'll have to come up with a strategy," Erika said, showing Maggie into her office, a sunny spot off of the living room, and taking a seat behind her desk. File folders were stacked on every available surface, but there seemed to be a method to Erika's mess, as if a filing system really did exist but only she knew its secrets.

Maggie pushed an armchair closer to the opposite side of the desk, folded her denim skirt under her legs, and dropped her Coach purse to the rough Berber carpet. The oscillating floor fan blew humid air at her, and she was grateful she was only wearing a thin sleeveless blouse with her skirt and espadrilles. Erika poured two glasses of iced tea, which immediately started sweating in the humidity.

"How bad is it?" Maggie asked, shaking out her right arm and allowing her charm bracelet to jingle.

Erika opened a thick file folder marked M. Morgan.

"Since this is your first offense, you're looking at up to $1,000 in fines and losing your license for at least a few months, and possibly doing three months in jail for driving drunk, possessing your son's medication, having an open container in your car, driving recklessly, and damaging Carl's billboard."

Maggie sat back and furrowed her brow. She recalled the image of Carl Olsen, the paunchy balding blond whose campaign billboard she drove into head-first while enjoying a soothing combo of wine and weed and pain pills.

"Jail?"

"It doesn't happen often, but—"

"But what?"

Maggie felt a line of sweat trickle down her back and into the elastic strap of her bra.

"Who knows what Carl will do, given the opportunity to lock you up. He'd love to ruin the Karma Community and teach every godless liberal a lesson."

Maggie brushed her arms softly and wrapped herself up tight, trying to make herself small. The one night she'd spent in a holding cell had been horrible— beyond horrible, something she was trying to block from her memory when it bubbled up. Being sent to jail—even for a night—just could not happen. Not to her. Not to Maggie Morgan of the Four Furies or Maggie Morgan of the soon-to-launch Morgan & Fellows Designs. It was totally impossible.

"That's ridiculous," Maggie said. "I have nothing to do with the Karma Community. I was just driving there to see my son. Besides, I was concussed."

"Could you release your medical records to me? That would really help me cut a better deal."

Maggie knew she wouldn't. Couldn't. She'd cajoled the doctor into prescribing a narcotic for generalized pain from falling on the front steps of the Karma Community. The concussion was Maggie's own diagnosis.

"I'll see what I can do," she said softly.

"Think about it. If you want to get back to Chicago tomorrow, plead guilty and pay the fine and you'll be free. Well, free with a criminal record. Otherwise, I'll try to work out a deal with Carl, but the evidence against you is pretty strong."

Maggie sat back in the chair and looked out the window. Erika's side yard boasted a well-tended flower garden and, further to the back, vegetables that were already spilling out of their raised beds. Sunflower stalks formed a border between her property and the neighbor's back yard, where a girl, about five, romped around an elaborate cedar play set. Maggie watched the tow-headed child make her way along the monkey bars to an elevated fort, then hang out over the balcony railing before sliding down a green wave to the lawn. A teenager sat on the patio, legs splayed in the sun, eyes closed, as the child crept back up to the monkey bars to repeat the circuit.

"So?"

Maggie imagined herself as the little girl going round and round, repeating her steps, as the second in command at Felix Ingles Fellows II Designs. Up the steps to the monkey bars of client meetings, project plans, and handholding, then handing over the money to the boss as she slid down the slide, back to where she started, ignored by those who were supposed to be watching her. It was challenging and exciting at times, but she'd never break the cycle if she didn't hop off and take control of her career.

"I need to go back to Chicago. I'll plead guilty to anything to make it go away."

"You'll have a record, you know."

Maggie waved her hand, dismissing her concerns.

"I'll have a record in Wisconsin. Nobody in Chicago will care."

"Okay, then. I'll call Carl and work something out."

Erika took a long sip of her iced tea as she shuffled through the papers in Maggie's file and landed on a drawing of a circle divided into twelve pieces, with small icons dotted throughout and bright yellow and pink highlighter marker slashed over the graphics. Even seen upside down Maggie recognized it instantly: her horoscope.

No wonder why Aaron likes her so much.

"I just want to confirm, you were born at 5:16 in the morning, right?"

"Yes."

"Great. There are a lot of birth times for you out there on the Internet. I wasn't sure which one to trust, so I called Frances, and she got it from Aaron."

"Do you always use astrology in your law practice?"

"Not often. But I was so curious about you—I've known Aaron for years and, well, I was a huge Four Furies fan. I even wore a charm bracelet, just like you. And I always wondered—"

Maggie stiffened, feeling invaded.

"There's not much to know," she snapped. "I joined a band with Aaron, left to start over on my own, and now I'm here in your office."

Erika scrutinized the horoscope, tilting it and rotating it and looking at it from every angle.

"I'm sure there's far more to the story than that."

Maggie pulled her purse off the floor and dropped it into her lap, opening the flap to retrieve her key chain, weighted down by the key to her demolished Saab. The little girl swung from the monkey bars again, then let go, dropped to the lawn, and started walking up the slide.

"I've been to astrologers in the past, and they've always gotten me wrong."

"Maybe they were using the wrong birth time."

Maggie watched the little girl put one unsteady foot in front of the other on her ascent. She wanted to clap when she made it to the top of the play set, where the little girl jumped around with sheer joy.

"The last one said I was put on earth to suffer."

Erika scoffed as Gil pulled up in the driveway.

"I'd never say that about you. Ever. But if you want me to analyze your chart, we'll have to set up another appointment. Or ask Frances—she taught me everything I know."

Erika stuck out her hand, waiting for a shake.

"I'll pick you up at eight and we can go over to the courthouse in New Elm together. Until then, have the folks at the Karma Community light some candles and pray for you."

Chapter 18

Grasping the Nettle

Maggie closed her eyes as she led Gil's hand under her skirt and tried to relax.

He'd skidded onto the gravel shoulder of the county highway when he'd tried to kiss her and fondle her left breast while taking a curve around a dairy farm. She'd swatted him away as he got back on the road, but still he persisted, a puppy with a bone and too single-minded to care about being punished.

"Please," he'd said. "It's been a long morning."

Maggie rolled her eyes but couldn't hide her smile.

"We're almost there. Can't you wait until we get back to your cabin?"

Gil downshifted the old truck and pulled off onto a work road winding between two soybean fields, then parked roughly.

"No."

"I need to make some business calls."

"I've got some business, too."

Gil slung his arm around her shoulder and kissed her deeply, clumsily. Maggie leaned in, but neither one of them could clear the stick shift between them. Laughing, Gil exited the truck, then held the passenger open for Maggie.

"Here? Someone will see us."

"Who? Some squirrels?"

She laughed, despite herself, and emerged from the truck. She stood against the hood of the truck then motioned to the foot-high soybean plants waving in the noontime breeze, high enough to conceal a couple making love in the soil, but too low to keep their secrets if they wanted to do anything more adventurous. The road was just a stone's throw from the truck and a slim strand of trees divided this patch of beans from another field of crops. The sun beamed in full force from high above, creating no shadows on the ground.

"Yes," Gil said, holding her tight and looking straight into her eyes. They lit up, despite Maggie's playful attempt to push him away. "Here." He kissed her neck. "Now." He pushed her hips closer to him. She gave in for a few kisses and ran her hands along the taut muscles of his back before looping her fingers around his belt, getting a firm hold on his waist, and pulling him even closer. Maggie took a step back to be pressed against the truck and led Gil's hand under her skirt.

Beats calling a banker for a loan and worrying about the DA, Maggie thought. *Besides, I'll be gone tomorrow.* She closed her eyes and responded to Gil. He was hot and fit and so eager to please, and when they were finished she felt a sense of relief, of catharsis, of power. A little like a goddess. She bit his shoulder and laughed.

"I'm glad you couldn't wait."

"I've been waiting for you for years," he sighed into her neck.

She let him kiss her again and felt his hands grasp her hips more firmly under her skirt. The heat and sweat from their bodies mixed with the warm breeze and the noon sun, a bit of Malibu in Wisconsin, Maggie thought. She looked for clouds in the sky, but there were none. Just a blue so pure that it seemed white along the horizon. A car passed on the road and the leaves of the trees in the thin woods bristled in the wind. She closed her eyes, nibbled Gil's earlobe, and tried to stretch this moment out so she could remember it later when things got rough.

"Hey now."

Maggie and Gil turned their heads toward the woods and watched a group emerge from the shade. Frances and Sybylla led the way, baskets in the crook of their arms, with two women and a man in hiking gear carrying paper grocery bags and a spade. Aaron, in his John Deere trucker's cap and scrubby work clothes, stepped out of the shadow and stood still.

Panic, shyness, and excitement mingled in Maggie's veins as she kissed Gil deeply and his hands instinctively grabbed her tighter, daring the group to keep watching. When she was sure she had their attention, she pulled Gil closer, then broke away from their kiss and turned to her audience. Sybylla and Frances had politely turned away, but the rest—including Aaron—were riveted.

Perfect, Maggie thought.

Gil shrugged and let go, then zipped up his jeans quickly and fumbled with his belt. Maggie's tangled silk panties lay nearby in the tamped-down dirt of the work road like a discarded trophy after a one-sided, too-easy-to-matter blowout battle. Gil took a step to fetch them, but Maggie grabbed his arm and held him back.

"Hey now," Frances called out. "We got a little lost but we're heading back."

Maggie pushed Gil away and approached the group with him tagging behind her. The hikers seemed wilted in the sun and still fixated on what they'd just stumbled across, fixated on her deeply unbuttoned blouse, bare legs, and flushed skin. All were aware that she'd just been fucking Gil in broad daylight and that she didn't give a damn who'd seen them, didn't give a damn that she had nothing on under her skirt and that Gil still smelled of her. She tried to check Aaron's eyes, but they were concealed by his cap. He chewed on a long blade of grass.

Just balancing the scales, Maggie thought. *Just like old times.*

"We're on a weed walk," Sybylla explained. "It's part of the curriculum."

The man with the spade, a sixty-something with a runner's physique in hiking shorts, Tevas, and an REI T-shirt, took a step toward her.

"You're Maggie Morgan."

Maggie smiled broadly and put her hand up to her chest, feigning modesty.

"Yes," she said simply. There was nothing else to say.

"I have all of your albums," the man said with awe. He turned to Aaron. "Are you two getting back together?"

"No." Aaron's answer came too quickly.

"Never," Maggie said. "That's all in the past."

She flashed Aaron a big smile, mocking his trademark grin. He winced, then let out a low whistle like a slow-chugging train.

"We're all cool now." Aaron clapped his comrade on the back and walked toward the woods. "Come on, folks, let's pick some food."

Gil slung his arm around Maggie and kissed her ear. "Ever been on a weed walk?"

Maggie shook her head and kept her eyes on Aaron.

"It's basically just foraging for food and medicine. You know—dandelions, mugwort, mint, plantain. But you never know what you'll find."

They followed the group into the shade, where Sybylla was kneeling before a tree with thin bark and light-green leaves. She pulled something out of her basket and placed it at the trunk, then patted the tree and stood up in one fluid motion, just as she did in her daily yoga practice.

"Tobacco," Frances said, edging up toward Maggie. "She's making a sacred offering before taking something away. A way to give thanks."

Maggie wanted to roll her eyes but willed herself to remain still.

Frances knows my real horoscope, Maggie thought. *Who knows what else she knows about me.*

"Interesting," she said, trying to look interested.

"It is," Frances said firmly. "It really is."

Sybylla and the women kneeled in the soft dirt and used Swiss Army knives to slice off curled fern shoots, which they put in their paper bags. The man dug into the soil around a broad-leaf plant, but Frances shooed him away.

"Not now, Brian. Wait for September to gather the root."

Gil took Maggie further into the woods, where a dribbling creek barely wetted the dirt but seemed to help to cool the air and remove them from the heat of the soybean field. A frog jumped over Maggie's foot, then blended into the moss-covered stones along the stream. She gasped, then clung onto Gil.

"Don't worry. I'll take care of you."

She leaned in for a kiss.

"It's been a long time since someone took care of me."

The group moved past them to the edge of the trees, where Aaron stood among waist-high bushes.

"Come on, Maggie," he called out. "Check this out."

Maggie stood still, then walked slowly toward the group, leaving Gil behind.

"Here's a lesson for you. Know what this is?"

Aaron pointed to the bunch of green stalks with jagged leaves growing in pairs. Maggie gave it a glance and shook her head.

"It's very nourishing. Great for your plumbing."

Maggie cocked her head and smiled.

"My plumbing's just fine, but thanks for your concern."

Now Aaron grinned, his eyes full of mirth.

"It's got metaphysical properties too. Check it out."

He beckoned her forward, half daring, half cajoling her to take a close look at the plant.

Maggie looked back at Gil, who was dawdling along the creek, blissed out.

"Whatever, Aaron."

She approached and stood next to him, too close, trying to make him uncomfortable but nothing registered on Aaron's face. Just a cool smile and twinkling eyes. The plant looked to Maggie like just another weed that sprouted up along the roadways, in scrubland, around the perimeter of fields, like the one they were in now. A plant that didn't need to be noticed.

"Maggie—you don't have to," Frances cautioned.

Maggie, defiant, bent down and grabbed a stalk, then another one. Pain shot through her hands, tingling and prickling and making her fingers feel icy hot. She threw the weed at Aaron, who stepped aside and let it land near his feet.

"Damn you, Aaron. Damn you."

He leaned in, close, drawing all eyes on him and his ex.

"Just trying to teach you a lesson, dear Maggie. If you want to solve your problems you can't avoid them. You've just got to take a deep breath and grasp the nettle, no matter how much it hurts."

"Fuck you." Maggie spat on her palms but her hands still pulsed with the nettle's sting.

Frances came forward, chewing something. She pulled some mashed-up leaves out of her mouth and placed them in Maggie's hands, which instantly soothed them.

"It's okay, we've all gotten stung," she said quietly, then shot a glare at Aaron. "The real lesson is how you heal from it."

Chapter 19

The Thorn in His Paw

Sybylla walked out to the back field with the setting sun in her eyes. The day had been a strange one—busy, but without a rhythm. Maybe it wasn't the day, maybe it was her own lingering funk. She hoped that no one had picked up on it, although she'd left many clues. She'd let the water boil too hard when she'd made the sassafras tea, but she made a joke about it. She was distracted during yoga and almost fell over during the triangle pose. When she answered phones at the front desk, she put one caller on hold for five minutes—a struggling Buddhist trying to detach from his anger. When he called back on another line, she got an earful. Then on the weed walk—well, there really was nothing to say about Maggie and Gil and she certainly didn't want to dwell on it.

Sybylla gathered her thoughts in the back field, the site of what she hoped would become their labyrinth, their baby. Aaron's comments had clung to her throughout the day like mist, like incense. He was right. Her idea was too complicated and clever. Those walking the labyrinth could not get stuck. They needed to be guided. They needed to free their asses so their minds could follow, which is how Aaron told her described the best rock and roll.

In a meditational labyrinth, the walking meditators would enter, then follow the path to reach the center. There should be just enough disorientation for the meditator not to know what was ahead. Traditionally, this meant a hopeful expectation to meet the Lord, or to reach Enlightenment—big L, big E—at the center. Then, after pausing for reflection, there would be a great unraveling on a similar path, out and into the world.

That was the problem. Sybylla's labyrinth symbolized the phases of the moon, the sacred womb, and provided a way in to the center. But there was no way out, Aaron realized. And Sybylla needed to find an exit.

She began walking in a circle in the field aimlessly, dragging her feet so that she could retrace her steps in the overgrown patch if need be. She was thrilled about the opportunity to create this gift for the community, for her husband, yet she was stuck. Blocked. Uninspired. She sighed and continued walking.

She's here for a reason. Frances' words of foresight crept up on Sybylla like a caterpillar lightly crawling on her skin, over Sybylla's heavy shoulders to the nape of her neck. She didn't like it, but she knew it was true. But, truth be told, she didn't like Maggie, even though that went against everything she was brought up to believe in—tolerance, fairness, getting-out-of-people's-ways-ness. She preferred Maggie to be safely estranged from Aaron. It was bad enough when Maggie had just been a ghost from years past. Aaron had tons of those, and he and Sybylla lived with them. But Maggie's flesh and blood presence seemed to shift the center of gravity.

From a distance, of course.

Sybylla couldn't help but notice that Maggie's pull on people was real but not entirely pleasant. Maggie was present, but never warm. She chatted with a few people, but was always a bit removed. Unreadable but always noticed. And why was she here anyway?

Sybylla should have expected difficulty. Although she and Aaron hadn't talked much about his past with Maggie—too painful, perhaps, or too far in the past—she knew some of his feelings about his old lover. In quiet moments when they could shut out the world, Aaron had told her about his life back then, of the sense of promise and direction he'd felt when he and Maggie first formed the band, and how she gave voice to all of the difficult emotions he felt but couldn't express on his own. But that didn't last long. At some point they knew everything about each other and that knowledge became toxic. According to Aaron, they abused their intimacy. They became destroyers and takers, ravenous and withholding. There was no joy or comfort in that relationship. Aaron told Sybylla he'd felt more alone on stage and at home in the beach house he shared with Maggie than he'd felt while shooting up in some derelict apartment in any city that wasn't his own.

It took Aaron a long time to tell Sybylla these things, but she loved him more because of it. Although she was forty years his junior, she felt protective of him. It made her think of the first few months of their relationship, when she would walk into a room and Aaron would spontaneously burst into tears. He wasn't unhappy, he assured her. Quite the opposite. He was overwhelmed with the happiness he felt because she consented to be in his life. Words weren't enough, music and art weren't enough, and not even sex was enough to express his awe.

Thank you for taking the thorn out of my paw, he would whisper to her, trembling.

Sybylla sighed again as she felt an imaginary bug creep up her back. She just wanted Aaron to be happy and whole and healthy. And apparently the universe was telling her that Sage and Maggie's appearance was an opportunity for Aaron to heal. How that would happen, she didn't really know. But it reminded her of the healing work she did with Frances and the plant medicines, when sometimes things had to get worse before they could get better. Fevers had to spike before they were reduced. Infections had to force themselves out as part of the natural healing process. Watching this was scary sometimes, but more often than not, if you just hung in there and let the body do what it knew that it had to do, healing and balancing would occur.

Frances always called this "both-and" stuff, stuff that was *both* contradictory *and* true and could coexist. The body was both powerful and weak, both ill and healthy, both unbalanced and perfectly in tune, both in crisis and in control. Frances had a point. And maybe Sybylla could both welcome Maggie into their lives and not like her. Maybe Maggie could both be there and be absent. Maybe Aaron could love both Sybylla and Maggie, a state of being that Sybylla both hoped for and feared.

Sybylla paused and plucked a red clover blossom and pulled out a few thin petals, then held them to her lips and sucked out the sweet nectar, a pleasure from her childhood. She looked toward the community and its handful of cabins, the vegetable garden, the chickens, the cluster of hawthorn trees, and the freeform gazebo made out of recycled junk. As she turned east, she looked toward the creek and felt a rush of its energy.

She continued walking, her hands folded over her heart.

"Help me find my way," she said quietly. "Help me find my way," she said with each footfall. The rhythm of the words suited her and soothed her. She relaxed into it, becoming more conscious of the circle she was forming.

She focused on her mantra, sing-songing it, dragging her feet while her heart lightened. The mango- and melon-colored sunset, unusually tropical for western Wisconsin, warmed her heart, even though she knew that the splendor was due to high amounts of pollution in the air.

"Help me find my way," she said with strength.

Sybylla circled and spiraled under the setting sun, warmed with an internal fire despite the cooling air and grass. When it felt right, she changed her mantra.

"This is my way," she said. "This is my way."

She circled and spiraled some more, closing in on a patch of white and red clover, a sweet spot that made her think of nourishment and bounty. When she reached the patch of clover, she carefully made her way back to her starting point. Instead of tracing a series of moons, her feet created a loose heart with the clover at the center.

Her whole body was charged up. She ran through the field, past the hawthorns and garden and small cabins, past the orange tabby making its way to Gil's front door, to the snug rooms that she shared with Aaron, her Aaron.

Chapter 20

Pandora

Maggie pulled the key to the door to the massage room, her makeshift bedroom, from her purse. She needed some time to herself, a short nap in private, some peace, some space. She needed to put on some panties, too; Gil had grabbed the pair they'd tossed off in the soybean field, a rare fan's souvenir that Maggie hoped he'd keep private.

Just one more night in the massage room, she thought as she turned the key in the lock. *Unless I spend the night with Gil again.*

The door opened from within. There stood Frances, calm, unreactive, the citrine stud in her nostril a small gleam that never failed to surprise Maggie. She was swathed in an array of gauzy scarves over cutoff jean shorts and a dingy tank top, her hair flowing over her shoulders almost to her waist. Barefoot, of course. Composed.

The room was dimmed by the drawn rice paper shades, suffused with lavender essence misting from a diffuser, the faint sounds of mystical chanting emanating from all corners. Maggie noted the massage table was set up in the center and draped with soft white cotton sheets.

"I'm sorry. I didn't know you had an appointment."

"No worries." Frances' demeanor wasn't exactly inviting. "I was expecting you."

Maggie rubbed her forearms, suddenly chilled, although her hands and arms still felt prickly from the nettles' sting.

This is the woman Erika says knows my true horoscope, my secrets, my fate. No wonder why she creeps me out.

"I'd love it if you could stay, in fact. I'm teaching a reflexology class and need someone to demonstrate on. I think you'd get a lot out of it. Would you be willing?"

Maggie flushed, and took a step back.

"I've got so much to do. I need to make a business call."

"You've got a few minutes before class starts. I'll unlock the office for you."

Emitting some sort of magnetic pull, Frances ushered Maggie down the corridor.

"Thank you," Maggie said weakly, and sat down at the messy desk. A photo of Aaron and Sybylla stared back at her.

"I'll let you know when we're ready for you."

Maggie watched her close the door softly and exhaled.

Might as well get this over with, she thought as she dialed her banker.

"An opportunity came up, but I don't want to say too much about it until the details are clearer," she told Beth. "How big of a loan could I get my hands on?"

"Personal, or business?" she asked. Maggie could hear Beth tapping a keyboard as she spoke.

"Business."

"Could you give me a ballpark figure?"

Maggie took a sharp inhale of breath and closed her eyes. The image of Trip and Matilda bragging about their $500,000 offer—plus strings attached while they sat on the board of directors—made her nauseous.

"Half a million. Maybe more."

"Well," Beth said, trying to hide her surprise. "We'll definitely need to see some details first. And collateral. When can you come in and talk?"

"Next week, perhaps," Maggie said, hoping to put off the meeting as long as possible so that it wouldn't seem real. "Maybe sooner. I need to work a few things out."

"I'll be ready when you are. Anything else I can do?"

"Well, there is one more thing." Maggie said, fingers tingling. "Could you look into the ownership of a place in Wisconsin—the Karma Community. I'm not sure what it's incorporated as," she said as her gaze fell on the envelopes and papers surrounding her, but they blurred together in the absence of her reading glasses. "But it's in Tyler County, Wisconsin."

"Is this the business opportunity you're interested in?"

115

"No, not at all," Maggie said quickly. "I just—I just want to know."

"I'll have our legal department look into it."

Maggie looked up from the desk and was startled by Frances standing in the doorway. She hadn't heard the door open or noticed Frances appear, and wondered how much of the conversation she'd overheard. She put down the receiver with a quick thank you, then sank back in the chair.

"We're ready for you now," Frances said, warmth filling her voice.

"I'm not sure I'm up to this. I don't even know what reflexology is."

"Perfect. Then you won't have any expectations."

+++

Maggie didn't enjoy being surrounded by seven strangers watching her, inspecting her, scrutinizing her. But there she was whether she liked it or not, sitting on the massage table, legs dangling, bare under her skirt, the center of attention as Frances knelt in front of her, Maggie's left foot cradled in her strong hands.

Maggie wasn't listening to anything Frances was saying to the students. Her own thoughts—about the $500,000 risk she'd be taking, about her court date, about Gil, about Aaron and Sage—were enough to distract her and divert her attention from the gaze of the room. Besides, she had to admit that Frances' warm and oiled-up hands on her feet soothed her, lulled her, even took her mind off her raggedy pedicure.

What is it about this woman? Maggie thought. *I should run away from her, fast.*

She felt pressure on her heel as Frances dug her thumb in and held it there. Frances ran her thumb up and down the bottom of Maggie's foot, making her flinch twice, an unexpected trigger point activated somewhere. Frances returned to Maggie's heel and went in for the kill. Maggie felt a spasm deep in her pelvis—not orgasmic, not like a period cramp, not like a labor pain. More like an opening, a release somewhere.

I hope she's not doing any damage down there, Maggie thought, blushing. *This is the strangest foot massage ever.*

Maggie didn't want to look at Frances, afraid of the intimacy. Instead, she stared straight ahead at the rice paper shades, the light shadows dancing from the tree outside giving her a feeling of movement, disorientation.

Frances' thumb then slid up Maggie's heel pad and Maggie felt her gut warm, sputter. She hoped none of this would cause her to embarrass herself in front of the class, so she tautened her abs and tried to think random thoughts.

There were many. The feeling of being center stage, the focus of everyone's attention, a feeling she tried to run from for years, creating a vacuum for Felix to fill. The feeling of losing her grip, her control. She was trying to plan for the future but at this very moment she realized how ridiculous that was. She had no control over anything—not Sage or Gil, Sybylla or Aaron, Trip or Matilda. Definitely not DA Carl Olsen. She didn't even have control over the reflexes in her foot at this moment. She thought about stuffing down the sensations whirling through her as Frances pressed and pulled and strafed the bottom of her foot; she thought about letting go, not caring how it looked to the students circling her.

Maggie felt this energy roiling through her seeking release, from her foot to her pelvis to her stomach and on up to her fluttering heart. She threw her shoulders back and closed her eyes, oblivion within reach.

"I just had to know," her inner voice sang to her.

"I had to take a look,
Shine a light on demons,
Fear my feelings,
Let all reason go."

She knew "Pandora," but silenced it.

She felt the energy rise and push and cause her throat to swell, her jugular vein to boom. She felt the human version of a hair ball grow in size, blocking her breath, but she knew instinctively that coughing wouldn't dislodge it. She listened to Frances instruct her class on the properties of the throat chakra and its correspondence to the color blue while she ran her fingers along the pad under the stems of Maggie's toes, lightly, almost tickling her. Maggie felt some relief. But "Pandora" rose up again.

I just had to know.

Maggie closed her eyes. She was back in her squirrel brown braids, little Peggy O'Donnell too scared to sing the lead after her early humiliation, but too talented to hang back in the shadows.

I just had to know.

Maggie's mouth dried just as she wanted to open up and sing.

A rush of energy encircled her head like a funnel cloud, a tornado of hopes and dreams and aches repressed for too long. One more brush along the sole of her foot and Maggie was transported, her heart beating at full power as she imagined herself as the blue Hindu goddess, tongue wagging, holding the severed head of young Peggy O'Donnell and her squirrel brown braids as a trophy.

117

"Oh," the students whispered as one as Maggie shuddered and opened her eyes.

Chapter 21

Guilty, Not Guilty

The courtroom in which Maggie's case would be heard wasn't in the historic courthouse, which provided the austere focal point for New Elm's old downtown. The imposing three-story building, which must have towered over the riverfront town when it opened in 1889, surely told the good people of Tyler County that the law was all-seeing, all-knowing, and out to get you if you didn't obey. But the building was now open only on weekends as a museum, its old courtrooms shuttered, its abandoned offices housing artifacts from the county's past: trinkets from the fur trade, shellacked fish caught in the Kickapoo River, battered Union uniforms, old Scandinavian garb and farm implements, and a bone china set with mauve flowering tendrils along the rim, a wedding gift to New Elm's favorite son, a prosperous land speculator who'd died young and left an even younger widow who was forced to head back east to marry rich again.

Maggie and Erika walked briskly on the east side of the town square to the new courthouse, a late-sixties snoozer with no charm that housed the courtroom, the district attorney, various county offices and, in back, the sheriff's office and the small jail in which Maggie had been held after her accident. Maggie stiffened, refusing to acknowledge the whole affair. She clutched her purse tighter and adjusted the collar of her white blouse, which was slightly ruffled since the Karma Community didn't own an iron. She wore her khaki pants yet again, thinking that they were the most formal piece of clothing that she'd brought from Chicago. It wasn't like she could show up in court in a peasant top and turban borrowed from Frances or the cutoff jean shorts Sybylla seemed to live in.

"Right, so we're facing Judge Hinshaw. He's been pretty fair in my drunken driving cases so far. He loves to lecture the defendant, but he's not overly punitive with first offenders. I think he'll go easy on you if you look like you've learned your lesson."

Erika stopped in front of the security guard sitting at the top of the front steps, a washed-out strawberry blond who looked like he lived on a steady diet of second helpings of beer, cheese, and brats. "Here's what you can expect," Erika flashed a laminated ID card at the guard, which Maggie thought was ridiculous, as Erika probably visited the courthouse daily and grew up with the guy. "I got Carl to agree to expedite things since you live out of state. We'll work things out with the court commissioner before the proceedings. The judge will read out the charges, then Carl and I will announce our plea deal."

She stuffed her ID back into her wallet and paused. "I wanted a deferred prosecution agreement, which means that as long as you stay out of trouble for the next five years you're off the hook. That's pretty standard for a first offense. But you know Carl is running for re-election and wants to make a statement. He wants you to plead guilty to everything but the drug charges, since you'd have a pretty strong defense on those. You do have a valid prescription and you could plausibly say that you were delivering medication to Sage."

Erika scanned Maggie's face for any sign of disagreement. "So you'll keep your license, pay a hefty fine, cover the cost to repair Carl's billboard, and have some misdemeanors on your record that I'm sure you could easily explain away to anyone who asked. You'll be able to go back to Chicago this afternoon."

"So just drunken driving and property damage," Maggie said flatly.

"Well, drunken driving is a pretty serious offense, but yes. You should be relieved you didn't kill yourself—or anyone else."

Erika tucked Maggie's file folder under her arm and opened the Plexiglas door open for Maggie. The interior was dim, with just a few fluorescent lights sputtering overhead.

"Well I hope the judge is in a good—"

"Maggie!"

She turned toward the man's voice behind her, puzzled. She was greeted with a smattering of flashbulbs blinding and disorienting her.

"What the hell?" She put her hand up in front of her face to protect herself from the flashes.

"Gordon, get out of here," Erika spat.

"It's public property," the man said, walking ever closer with his camera. "Besides, it's not every day a celebrity gets busted for doing drugs and totaling her car in Tyler County."

Erika put her hand on Maggie's back and pushed her into the courtroom, shutting the door behind them to get a few steps ahead of Gordon.

"Don't turn around," Erika said through gritted teeth. She motioned Maggie to sit on a bench behind the barrier that separated the judge, attorneys, and court officials from those waiting for their day in court and the public. Maggie was breathing hard and sweating despite the gusting air conditioning. She looked down at her palms in her lap but couldn't make them out clearly since her vision was ruined by the shock of the flashbulbs.

She hadn't felt this violated in decades. Back in her Furies days, she and Aaron were the targets of celebrity photographers who couldn't get enough of a golden couple who made fame look effortless. Those early snapshots typically showed a disheveled Aaron with a protective arm around Maggie, smiling shyly and looking irresistible. Aaron's grin and Maggie's Mona Lisa smile seemed to be evidence of sex—either in the limo, the recording studio, or wherever they were exiting. Later, of course, the press became more intrusive as they got whiffs of scandal and were downright invasive after the Clark Kavanaugh affair. Aaron would hold a hand out to block the photographers and take a swing when necessary, and let Maggie fend for herself, a hand shielding her eyes from the flashbulbs, her intriguing smile frozen into a scowl. The public wanted too many pieces of her and she wouldn't offer anything for their pleasure.

Under the fluorescent lights of the courtroom, Maggie fingered her charm bracelet to take an inventory of her trinkets. The absence of the emerald in her Claddagh charm still surprised her. But what she really wanted to do was punch Gordon, whoever he was, the jerk who was settling into the bench directly behind them.

"I didn't mean to alarm you, Maggie," he said innocently, his breath puffing on the back of her neck. "I just got so excited. My parents have all of your albums."

Liar, she thought. *You're just a huge asshole.*

The door opened at the back of the room and Maggie heard heavy footsteps up the aisle to a long table in the courtroom proper, and turned around to face them.

"Morning, Erika," the man said with smooth cheer. "Ms. Morgan. Gordon."

"Good morning, Carl," Erika nodded. "See you tonight?"

"Wouldn't miss grandma's hundredth birthday party for the world."

121

"Neither would I. I think it's a newsworthy event, don't you? Yvonne Olsen turns one hundred surrounded by her family and friends. Wonder if the newspaper will send their gossip columnist to the senior center to investigate."

"Metro reporter," Gordon corrected her. "I got promoted."

Maggie's vision was starting to clear, enabling her to take a longer look at the district attorney as he and Erika spoke quietly to a prim, underweight woman behind a large desk. On his campaign billboard—or what remained of it after Maggie's crash—he presented himself as a friendly professional in a blue suit, starched white shirt, and red tie, a pillar of the community you could trust to achieve justice. In reality, Carl's stomach drooped over his belt, his moustache was crooked, and his grey suit looked more in need of an iron than Maggie's blouse. His faded blond hair was brushed into bangs, a juvenile touch. He looked like the kind of middle-aged man who needed an official title to gain respect, since he seemed like a Beta in every other way. Other than sharing bright blue eyes, it was hard to believe that he and Erika were family. But in small towns like New Elm just about everyone had to be related to everyone else, Maggie thought.

"Relax," Erika said as she returned to her seat. "You've got nothing to worry—"

"All rise."

Judge Hinshaw took his time making his way to the bench, then engaged in a quiet chat with the court reporter while everyone else settled back in their places.

"State of Wisconsin versus Margaret Morgan," the bailiff called out.

Gordon snapped a few more photos of Maggie's back as she and Erika walked up to the table designated for the defendant.

Surreal, Maggie thought as the charges against her were read out, a list that was longer than she wished.

"Your honor, if I may." Carl stood and folded his hands into a prayer position and held them up in front of his face, playing the groveling innocent as Gordon's flashbulbs ignited. "These are serious allegations and deserve serious consideration."

"Counsellor, you'll have your chance," the judge glowered. "Ms. Morgan—"

"Ms. Morgan is accused of endangering the lives of Tyler County citizens," the DA said, his voice rising, Gordon's flashbulbs pulsing like a strobe light. "She is a menace to public safety."

"Objection!" Erika bellowed, ferocious.

"Counsellor, no grandstanding."

"I have every reason to believe she was intending to distribute drugs to Tyler County citizens and the members of that—commune," Carl spat.

"Objection!"

"Counsellor." The judge reached for his gavel. "I'll have none of this in my courtroom."

"I'll have none of this in my county. I intend to prosecute Ms. Morgan to the full extent of the law." Carl's neck and face were ruby red with adrenaline.

"Objection!"

"Order," Judge Hinshaw roared as he hammered the gavel on his desk. Carl sat down, not needing to continue. He'd given the reporter the quotes and images he needed to make the front page of the newspaper, even if he did piss off the judge.

"Ms. Morgan, my apologies." The judge set aside the gavel and turned to Maggie. "How do you plead?"

Erika shot a look at Carl, then Maggie. The deal was off.

"I'd like to approach the bench, your honor."

Maggie grabbed her attorney's forearm and held her back. She stood and took a long look at Carl, letting Gordon get shots of her rising to her power. Carl was leaning back in his chair, a Cheshire cat grin on his face, and loosened the top button of his shirt. There was no way Maggie was going to let him win re-election by ripping up their agreement and exploiting her private pain.

You have no idea who you're dealing with, Maggie thought.

She straightened up and took a deep breath, then cleared the lump in her throat.

"Not guilty, your honor."

She turned and smiled into Gordon's camera, letting him get the shot that she wanted him to print. Dignified. Self-righteous. Powerful.

"Not guilty," she repeated for him. "Other than that, I have no comment."

Chapter 22

This Changes Everything

Erika looked both ways after a refrigerated truck whizzed by them, then turned onto the highway and headed toward the Karma Community. Maggie tipped the AC vents toward her to quell her anxiety, humidity, spite, and hot flashes, which were combining to produce a rash across her neck. She sighed and closed her eyes, not wanting to face Erika too directly.

"I didn't really have a choice. Your cousin was being such an asshole."

"That's just Carl," Erika said. "He did theater in high school and he loves to play to the crowd. It can be annoying if you take it seriously."

"And that photographer," she spat.

"Now, Gordon truly is an asshole. No sense of decency. Or perspective."

Maggie put her wrist in front of the vent to try to cool her blood, but she could feel her pulse jump anyway.

"So it looks like we're going to trial. Unless you want me to come up with another plea deal."

Maggie closed her eyes and felt her temple throb in the heat.

"Could we pull over? I need a moment."

+++

"Some reporter wants a comment on Maggie's outburst in the courtroom," Sybylla said tightly as she hung up the phone in the steamy office, only to have it ring again and again and again. "Did you know anything about this?"

"No."

Kneeling on the bare floor, Frances didn't look up from the piles of papers lined up so she could collate them and turn them into handouts for a workshop on healing herbs for Wild Women in midlife. The orange tabby lazed on the third stack of paper, paws tucked under his chin and purring with glee. Frances worked around him, unwilling to disturb his peace. She'd insert that page later, before stapling the piles together.

"No? Not even an inkling?" Sybylla's face was ashy with only her spray of freckles showing signs of life.

Frances continued stacking up the sheets one by one, her eyes focused on her work. She worked to keep her face blank, although her eyes sparkled brighter than the citrine in her nostril.

"Nothing I can discuss without Maggie's permission."

"So you did know." Sybylla's sense of betrayal could be heard above the constant ringing of the phone. "What did she tell you?"

"Nothing."

"So it was an inkling."

"I knew that she was going through something really heavy. That was obvious to anyone."

"Of course. But what about this trial? Something about driving drunk and getting into a car crash."

"That seems to fit," Frances paused in her labors, stretching out her back. "You'll notice that she didn't return to the Karma Community in her own car."

"No." Sybylla paused, letting herself think through the events of the past few days as the nape of her neck grew wetter with sweat. "Aaron brought her back."

"Well then." Frances resumed her paper stacking with relish. "Ask your husband."

+++

Aaron wanted to scream.

Even in the cocooned meditation room, the constant ring of the phone was disrupting his attempt to work up good energy and a healthy dose of lovingkindness and a dollop of bravery, everything he'd need before facing Freddie and having a frank discussion of the Karma Community's finances.

He wanted to shout "Fuck! Fuck! Fuck!"—a mantra for righteously angry people like him who had no other outlet for their frustration. He wanted to rampage throughout the bright, airy, sacred spaces of the Karma Community, the albatross sinking him lower into the depths and widths and lengths of despair, to stamp his feet and throw the oranges offered at the silent Buddha's feet around the foyer, tear the gauzy curtains and rice paper shades to bits, and knock down the shelves of prayer beads, books and DVDs, incense, and other tchotchkes for sale in the gift shop.

But the phone wouldn't stop ringing.

"Fuck!" he finally swore aloud, knowing that his fellow meditators felt the same way, and stomped out of the room.

Sybylla met him at the foot of the stairs, Frances close behind her, her eyes wild.

"Maggie's on trial."

Aaron took a step back, then brushed his hand through his hair.

"So soon? Nothing ever happens so fast in Tyler County."

"You knew."

Aaron held up his hands, trying to quiet his wife's accusation, wishing he could silence the phone. A crowd of students and seekers gathered around them, pulsing with frustration.

"Take the damn phone off the hook," an elderly woman snapped, then walked slowly toward the sun deck to resume her Tai Chi practice, her elaborately carved cane leading the way.

Frances ran up the stairs and suddenly they were silent.

"You knew," Sybylla said as she folded her arms in front of her chest, protecting herself, then placed her hands on her waist and spread her arms, hoping to seem more powerful.

"I knew she was arrested. I bailed her out of jail."

Aaron could feel the energy around him shift, a gasp that created a vacuum that could turn into a black hole or an eruption, depending on the next few moments.

"Mom was arrested?" Sage stepped forward from the crowd, emanating heat and the sweet sweat produced by working honestly in the sun. "For what?"

"She was dealing with it," Aaron cut in through gritted teeth, then turned to the Karma Community guests arrayed around him and raised his voice. "Everyone needs to chill. It's a private matter. Detach. It has nothing to do with you."

The front door opened, bringing with it a blast of summery heat and light.

"What's going on?" Gil asked, his sketch pad tucked under his arm, his students lined up behind him. "There's a bunch of people asking for Maggie."

+++

About a dozen cars were lined up along the road leading to the Karma Community, a pretty good crowd for a weekend afternoon, never mind a Wednesday.

"I wonder what's on the schedule?" Erika asked as she pulled into the gravel drive lined with small groups of Baby Boomers looking anxious, hopeful, alert. She slowed down as she approached the Karma Community's entrance, braking curtly when Maggie gasped.

"Oh god. They're fans."

Their energy, excitement, and behavior hadn't changed since the Four Furies' heyday, just their ages. One grey-topped man stretched out a poster of Maggie in front of a microphone, lit from behind and looking like she was caught mid-orgasm. Another man in Dockers and a short-sleeved button-down shirt held aloft Four Furies albums still in their original plastic wrap. Two women wore billowy lace tops and shook their charm bracelets at the car as if they were magical amulets. A couple held hands in their matching faded black concert T-shirts and cargo shorts.

"Damn Gordon."

Erika locked the car doors and pulled into a full stop steps away from the front porch, where it had all begun for Maggie on this section of her odyssey. Seeking Sage, then fleeing and falling and twisting her ankle as she tripped over her own anger. Then crashing and faltering and hopefully rising again.

Her eyes moved from her fans to the gravel, instinctively looking for the emerald that had come loose from her charm bracelet, knowing it would be impossible to find now, probably ground into dust. Disappeared forever.

The fans moved closer to the car, gaining speed with each footstep.

"Ready for this?"

Maggie put on her sunglasses to hide her smiling eyes.

"I never was. But it didn't stop me then."

She opened the car door and turned her face to the sun, allowing the crowd to take a lingering look. She let her admirers touch her, praise her, grovel for her attention and squeal over her, each one claiming to be her biggest fan, the one most moved by her music. She signed their souvenirs, posed for pictures, felt their heat and desperation and thrills. And when they moved in too close and became too comfortable in her presence, she swept through the heavy front door, the orange tabby shuffling under her feet, her fans left at a distance.

+++

127

The Karma Community's foyer was shady and at least ten degrees cooler than the porch, but its aura of hostility raised the temperature even higher when Maggie appeared in it. The usual suspects were assembled, waiting. Aaron, pissed off; Sybylla, stunned; Frances, stoic; Sage, baffled; and Gil, anxiety cutting into his natural mellowness. The tabby curled up in a sunbeam on the bare wood floor, oblivious to the tension.

"This is private property, you know," Aaron said, leading the attack. "You've got to get them out of here."

Maggie kept her sunglasses on and sighed, trying to seem bored by Aaron's power play.

"I had no idea they'd show up. But I guess they're not used to seeing celebrities around here."

"They're disturbing our peace," Aaron said as he pushed apart the curtains and peered through the front window.

"Are you going to jail?" Sage asked, his voice a pitch higher than he would have liked.

"Of course not. They don't have anything on me."

"Were you really arrested? Why didn't you say anything?"

Maggie waved away her son's concerns.

"I think they're trying to scapegoat me for whatever issue they have with Aaron."

"Give me a break," Aaron argued. "I wasn't the one driving drunk and crashing into the DA's billboard and almost killing myself. You can't blame me for any of that."

Maggie could feel the climate change again, ice crackling and settling in as the reality of her criminality hit them. She couldn't bear to look at Gil.

"I'm taking responsibility for my actions," she said, self-righteousness accenting her voice. "But I won't take the fall for yours."

Sybylla reached for Aaron and pulled him away from the window.

"He's done nothing wrong and you know it."

The front door opened and more humid heat flushed into the room.

"It's really you," the woman said, eyes trained on Maggie.

Maggie stepped forward, peacocking a bit, relieved to be dealing with another fan and not Aaron's bile.

"It really is." Maggie held out her hand to the woman to beckon her in. The sixty-something woman, plump in a sleeveless T-shirt, flared Capri pants, and heavy sandals, took a tentative step forward.

"You mean so much to me," she said, ignoring everyone but Maggie. "I can't begin to tell you—"

"This is private property," Aaron said, moving between the two women. "You'll have to go." He reached for her arm and she swatted it back, her demeanor changing.

"Don't you dare," she hissed. "You never let her speak for herself."

Aaron retreated, stunned, as Maggie moved in.

"Don't worry about him," she said, putting a protective arm around her fan's shoulders. "He's feeling a little territorial right now."

"I'll never forgive him for what he did to you," the fan sneered.

"It's all in the past," Maggie said as she led the woman back outside, where they stood in the full sunlight, the other fans keeping a curious distance.

"We love you, Maggie," one shouted.

She tossed a flirtatious look in the direction of the voice and smiled, then turned her back on the crowd so she could address her trembling fan quietly.

"I appreciate your good wishes, but like Aaron said—"

"You don't understand." Tears pooled in the woman's crows' feet. "You changed my life."

"I appreciate that."

"You *saved* my life."

"I'm sure you saved yourself. I didn't have anything to do with it."

"When you left Aaron—"

She couldn't complete her sentence. She threw her arms around Maggie's shoulders and sobbed.

"I owe you so much."

Chapter 23

Out for a Spin

"I think we should take this one out for a spin," Sage said as he peered into the window of a nondescript Saturn four-door sedan that would never—could never—replace Maggie's beloved Saab, elegant and practical at the same time.

"Thirty-three-thousand miles, just off a lease. You'll never need to do more than regular maintenance on it."

There was absolutely no shade on Arne Janssen's used-car lot, located on the outskirts of New Elm in the parking lot of an old Tasty Time ice cream stand. Maggie could see the back of Arne's short-sleeve work shirt dampen in the heat as he talked to Sage quietly, the sunburned nape of his neck looking painful. Never mind that Maggie would be plunking down the money for a new used car—Arne assumed that Sage would be the decision-maker in this transaction.

Then they were off, Sage driving, Maggie pressing the manual knobs and buttons on the dashboard, seeking to crank the AC in a futile battle against the eighty-nine-degree heat and almost solid humidity, the kind of humidity that wilts whatever it doesn't swell up to painful proportions. The car wasn't as technologically advanced as her dearly departed Saab—no power windows, few amenities, plastic everywhere—but it was the best Arne had to offer.

Maggie turned on the radio to hear the closing bars of "One More Night," Clark Kavanaugh's notorious love-sick song for her.

But Sage ignored all of that as he drove the highway out of town.

"When are you going back to Chicago?"

"Tomorrow, probably. As soon as I've got a car."

"Does your arrest screw up your deal with Trip?"

Maggie scoffed. "I doubt it. Actually, no. They'll never find out about some legal trouble in the backwoods of Wisconsin."

"Hopefully those zombie Furies fans will keep their mouths shut."

"Do you really see them trekking to Chicago? I think they'll stay put."

"They need to learn to let go. I mean, we're all falling babies." Sage paused for a beat, trying to remember how Aaron had explained the concept to him. "Like, falling through the universe at different speeds. You can't hang on to anyone. You've got to keep falling."

Maggie rolled her eyes and fixed her hair in the mirror on the back of the passenger's sun visor.

"Now you're sounding like a Karma Community zombie."

"It's not all bullshit," Sage shot back. "We've got a lot of cool stuff going on."

Maggie could feel Sage's woundedness as she shielded her eyes from the sun.

"Okay, okay. It's not totally horrible," she soothed, trying to lighten her son's mood. "The lentil burgers are growing on me."

"I'm not going to miss those things," Sage groaned. "Speaking of which."

He pulled into the drive through of a local burger chain and ordered enough food for both of them, and then some. Double cheeseburgers, fries, onion rings, chocolate malts, and gigantic neon slushies to beat the heat.

"Be careful," Maggie said as Sage stuffed a burger into his mouth before he got out of the parking lot, a trickle of mayo and ketchup trickling down the side of his wrist. "If we get the car all greasy I'll have to buy it."

They drove along the winding roads, both chomping on their burgers and slurping down their thick malts, a salty-sweet combo that lit up all of their pleasure receptors in a way a lentil burger and lemon balm tea never could. They drove past soybean farms, Erika's house and law office, a cratering one-room schoolhouse right up on the edge of the road, and a stretch of homes huddled together, probably on a few acres of land a farmer had to sell to stay afloat.

Maggie's stomach clenched as she realized where they were heading. The swoop of the highway was familiar, a body memory she probably wouldn't ever shake.

Sage pulled over at the foot of the banged-up billboard, DA Carl Olsen's crumpled face grinning down at them. Maggie wondered if Carl was allowing the demented sign to remain as it was as a reminder to all who passed how horrible Maggie's crime was, how badly victimized he was by the zombies over at the Karma Community.

"Damn, mom."

Sage stepped out of the car, the thirty-two-ounce plastic tumbler of icy fruit punch clutched in his fist. Maggie followed, her sunglasses pushed up the bridge of her nose, her face blank except for a slight twitch at the corner of her right eye.

"It looks worse than it really was."

"You're lucky your air bag worked. You could have killed yourself."

Maggie shrugged and leaned against the radiating hood of the car. Her temple throbbed, tightening the scab reaching out of her hairline.

"When were you going to tell me about your arrest?" he asked, his eyes firmly on the Carl's distorted face.

"Soon, I guess. I didn't think it was going to be a big deal."

"Really."

"Yes. I was going to pay my fine and go back to Chicago, but good old Carl up here was a jerk and decided to complicate things."

"So you were staying at the Karma Community just to kill time. You know. Not to learn anything."

"I just—" Maggie wanted to craft her response carefully. "I needed to take some time out."

Sage put his hand, chilled from his supersized slushy, on her shoulder, the scent of the chicken run and second-day T-shirt and burgers emanating from him. He didn't smell like his former Chicago self anymore.

"You can always talk to me, you know," he said, his voice betraying some tenderness. "Just, like, say something."

Maggie leaned in to him and gave him a brief hug, as long as he would allow.

Both turned as a car pulled up on the shoulder of the opposite side of the road, a camera poking out of the driver's window. Maggie felt a cold sheer blast up her spine.

"Fuck you!" she yelled, then stooped to pick up a handful of gravel to throw at him.

Gordon kept clicking away, getting the shots of Maggie Morgan at the scene of her crime in a full-on tantrum that confirmed her bad reputation.

Chapter 24

If Maggie Morgan Can Do It

Safe.

Maggie had made it through the line of fans along the entrance of the Karma Community, Sage leading the way in his car, Maggie in her new Saturn. She had kept her sunglasses pushed up high, hoping to be as opaque as possible. It hadn't occurred to her to buy a car with tinted windows—not that one would have been available in Tyler County—but now wished she had asked for it.

Oh well. I'm off to Chicago tomorrow.

She ignored everyone in the Karma Community as she went directly upstairs to the massage room to hopefully find a little peace in the late afternoon. The elongated summer days had given her the feeling of endless possibility, of being able to pack everything into a day. But now she just wanted the sun to set so she could be alone. Well, to be alone with Gil for one last night.

The shades were drawn in the massage room, where the scent of Nag Champa incense still lingered. She laid down on the massage table and took a deep breath, her hand on her abdomen, taking in the cool atmosphere of the room, the clean cotton flannel sheet under her sticky legs and arms. She closed her eyes and tried to focus.

Just a minute before I get back to work. Call Keith, set up an appointment with Trip and Matilda. Sketch out my pitch for them. Call the banker. Leave.

A faint whoosh took her out of thoughts. An envelope, slid under the door like a hotel bill.

She closed her eyes again, but couldn't stop thinking of the envelope.

Damnit.

She hopped back onto the massage table and pulled her knees under her chin.

Dear Maggie—

I'm the woman who spoke to you today. I should say I'm the woman who tried to speak to you today, because I was so overcome with emotion I couldn't talk. I have so much to say to you, so I thought I'd write you a letter.

I was a huge fan of the Four Furies. My husband and I had all of your albums, and we saw your show in Minneapolis in 1975. It was incredible. It was like you were singing only for us.

That's a happy memory. Unfortunately, many of my other memories from that time were terrible. So bad, in fact, that I've blocked them so that I don't fall apart all the time.

Like you, I was in a terrible relationship back then. When I listened to you sing, I could understand everything you were going through. You had so much love for Aaron and he took advantage of that and tried to humiliate you. But you always seemed to rise above that. Yes, he hurt you. But you were dignified. You were a queen, even if he didn't always treat you the way he should have.

That's sort of how I felt back then. My husband and I weren't glamorous like you and Aaron, but we had the same issues. We loved each other hard, but we fought hard, too. Eventually, we fought more than we loved. Then he started hitting me. I think he was just trying to scare me at first. You know, to show that I couldn't control him because he was bigger and stronger than me. And he felt really bad afterwards. But it happened again. And then it kept happening. I had to wear long sleeves and pants all the time. I learned how to cover my bruises with makeup. I called the cops on him, but nobody helped me. Nobody believed me, anyway, because we were still living in the dark ages back then, so I wouldn't talk about it. I had to come up with excuses for my kids for why I was hurting so much and crying all the time. That was the worst part. I didn't want them to think that what was going on in our house was normal, because it wasn't.

I thought that this was how my life was going to play out. I felt so stuck that I even thought about killing myself just to end my misery and give my kids the chance of growing up in a different home.

And then, you punched Aaron and left him. I stood up and cheered when I saw the pictures in Rolling Stone. *I know it's not right to hit someone, after all, I was on the receiving end of a lot of punches, but this was different. He had it coming.*

I thought, if Maggie Morgan can do it, why can't I?

No, I didn't punch my ex. But I came up with a plan to leave him. I saved up spare change and stole money from his wallet for weeks. After he left for work I packed our suitcases, put the kids in the car, and left. After we crossed state lines, I left the car in a grocery store parking lot, bought one-way Greyhound tickets, and kept going. The kids cried a lot in the beginning, but I told them it was a big adventure. They eventually stopped asking about their dad when we started having fun without him.

We settled in Wisconsin and I'm proud to say that I made a peaceful, happy home for them. I still listen to the Four Furies all the time, although I sometimes skip the sadder songs. I run a support group for women who've been abused, my chance to help other women who are trying desperately to live a better life.

Ironic that I've been Aaron's neighbor for years. I've never spoken to him and never want to. He reminds me too much of my ex. Perhaps he's changed. I guess you wouldn't be spending time over at the Karma Community if he hasn't. I've spoken to his wife here and there in town and she seems like a sweet girl who is probably in over her head, the poor thing.

That's my story. I know I'm not the only one out there who saw you as an inspiration. I wanted to thank you for showing me I could leave my abusive husband and start a new life, even if I wasn't rich and famous like you.

Sincerely, Your Fan,

Susan

PS: Your son seems like a very nice young man. Pity he looks just like Aaron.

Maggie read the letter three times. The first, stunned. The second, with tears blurring her vision. The third time she let the force of the words finally touch her.

I'm not worthy of this kind of respect.

She put her hand to her throat, feeling a tightness there that had been missing since Frances' otherworldly foot massage. This fan, Susan, spoke from the heart. She changed her life because of Maggie's example. For the better, of course, but it was astounding to have that much influence over a stranger's life.

And all because of a misunderstanding.

Maggie hadn't left Aaron because he abused her. Yes, he cheated on her. She cheated on him. He could play mind games and, as Susan put it, they loved hard and they fought hard. But he never laid a hand on her—never. Maggie was his muse, the lover who lifted him from a life as a petty drug dealer to an international star. He loved her, he revered her. But somehow the legend that Aaron was abusive took hold.

Fueling the legend was her own actions. Maggie hated doing interviews, was too insecure and shy to do them. So Aaron dominated their press, while Maggie was the ephemeral beauty who appeared to be silenced by him. Besides, when she was recording and touring she spoke as little as possible to save her voice, always a fragile instrument. Without her voice, the Four Furies were doomed.

She never told her side of the story, and let the fans fill in the blanks.

Chapter 25

The Friends and Lovers of the Karma Community

"Are we copacetic?"

Frances took a sweeping view of the orange cloth spread out on the unruly grass, then took a deep yoga breath and lit the incense.

"Copacetic," Sybylla confirmed.

Aaron began beating on his drum slowly, then, swaying side to side, picked up the pace a bit. His eyes caught Sage's and the two men beat out a percolating rhythm.

"Blessed be," Frances chanted in a minor key.

"Blessed be," Sybylla repeated.

"Join us here," Frances added, raising her palms to the nighttime sky.

"Join us here," Aaron, Sybylla, and Sage intoned.

"Mother Earth."

"Mother Earth."

"Father Sky."

"Father Sky."

"Join us here."

"Shining sun, waxing moon, you are welcome here."

Frances let the last note trail off. Then, when only the drums could be heard, she picked up her brass bowl with burning sage leaves and walked to each participant, waving the smoke over each person's energy field, cleansing them. Sybylla took the bowl from her cousin and bathed Frances head to toe in the white smoke.

Frances took the brass bowl from Sybylla and walked to the orange cloth in the center of the circle, where a stack of papers lay, surrounded by oversized white elder flowers, fragrant beyond fragrant, an age-old sign of magic and vitality. Frances held the incense above the papers, then intoned:

"Father Earth, Mother Sky, shining sun, waxing moon, you are in trine, winking at each other in your sacred dance. Flow your energy into this proposal so that it finds a harmonious reader. Energize our labyrinth so that we can share it with all. Guide us to the right resources and allies who will support our healing work. Let us live in abundance and honor your bounty and beauty. Blessed be."

Frances put the bowl on top of the papers and lifted the heavy Mason jar full of decadent rose tea. She took a big sip, then held it to Aaron's lips, then to Sybylla's and Sage's, then took another sip and put it back down on the orange cloth, next to the business proposal. She then pulled a home-rolled cigarette out of her back pocket and lit it. It wasn't pot. She'd never do that to Aaron. But when you picked and dried this weed at just the right time, it could take you to another place. It was a common enough weed that grew in every parking lot, vacant space, and sidewalk crack; it was also a sacred gift from the plant kingdom to those who knew her secrets. If only the authorities knew. But they didn't.

Frances lit the joint and inhaled deeply, then handed it off to Aaron, keeping eye contact with him the whole time he toked up, drawing on years of experience—some of it good, some of it horrendous. He closed his eyes and smiled, letting the smoke enter every cell of his being. He took another drag, laughed, and with his eyebrows wiggling, handed it off to Sybylla, who accepted it warily, puffed it daintily, then passed it over to Sage, who held it between his thumb and index finger, careful not to mush the moistened end, and then held it to his lips, the smoke filling his lungs and almost—almost—making him choke, but he held it in like a champ before handing it back to Frances and resuming to beat on his drum.

The four of them swayed and hummed, prayed and giggled. They sent white light and blue light to each other, then concentrated on the business proposal they passed around like a sacred relic. They imagined the opportunities it presented, not just for them personally, but for the Karma Community and all who would participate.

Aaron, Frances, Sybylla, and Sage had worked hard on it. They'd brainstormed and swore in frustration while putting it together in front of the computer, and paced in the meadow to clear their heads. Like the labyrinth itself, the proposal was a true collaboration.

The labyrinth is as old as humankind, it began. *As long as humans could walk, we have been purposefully setting our tracks in the earth. These tracks became ceremonial and an essential part of ritual in almost every culture. Eventually, the labyrinth took certain semi-formal patterns, but almost all have seven turns or nine turns before reaching the center—to symbolize enlightenment, or catharsis, or peace, or love.*

We, the Friends and Lovers of the Karma Community, seek to build our own labyrinth. It will draw more guests to the Karma Community. It will aid their spiritual and emotional journeys. It will be a magnet to all seekers. It will be a power spot in an area being increasingly threatened by big box retailers, McMansions, and an overloaded electrical grid. It will, in short, add to the Karma Community's mission and boost its profitability.

Frances and Sybylla thought that last bit was tacky, but Aaron fought to keep it in, arguing Freddie only cared about the bottom line. But, in the end, they agreed with him, and now the finished proposal lay on the tapestry, soaking up the group's magic.

As the drumbeats raised their spirits to the sky, Aaron did a jig, then collapsed on the grass.

"I love life!" he shouted into the universe.

Everyone laughed, high on the smoke.

Aaron laughed, too.

"No, I mean it," he said, a bit more together than before. "I love life."

They laughed again.

Aaron suddenly grew serious and ran his hands through his dark hair.

"This isn't enough," he said. "I love life and this isn't enough."

He sat up and pulled off his hiking boots. Then he took off his shirt, stood up, and took off his jeans.

"Come on!" he shouted, completely naked. "Love life!"

He laughed and ran around like a tiger being chased by a bee that was drunk on nectar. His laughter—manic and joyful and utterly uncontrollable—echoed through the gently rolling hills.

"Love life, people!" he shouted. "You're a slave to your clothes! You're a slave to your limits! Put some magic into the labyrinth! Electrify the labyrinth! Love life!"

Everyone laughed again. Frances and Sybylla started peeling off their clothes.

Aaron whooped, thrilled. He ran toward the creek, blazing on life itself. Frances and Sybylla followed. Sage, embarrassed and intrigued, removed his clothes too, and trailed behind the women, their pale skin glowing in the dimming light.

By the time Sage got to the creek, the other three were already splashing around. Shaking off his shyness, Sage jumped into the cold water with clenched abs. But the water felt delicious. As it rushed past his legs and made his entire body both numb and awake at the same time, Sage felt truly free.

"All right Sage!" Aaron yelled over to him. "Awesome!"

Sage dove into the water, grabbed a hold of a few rocks, and did a handstand and exposed himself to the universe.

Oh crap, he thought. He came up for air, hoping that nobody noticed. He tried to seem cool as he swam over to the others, who were bobbing in the water and laughing.

"Good for you, Sage," Frances said, smiling and sparkling in a way Sage had never seen before. She always seemed so composed and serene at the Karma Community. But naked and high and in love with life, as Aaron commanded, Frances seemed to find a new dimension in the water.

Aaron and Sybylla seemed just as transformed. Relaxed and silly, completely unburdened and uninhibited.

Sage realized than none of them was hung up on anything.

He whooped for joy, then raised his hands above his head.

"Come to Jesus," he said in a slow Southern drawl. "Come to the water and wash away your sins."

Aaron laughed. "That would take some of us a bit longer than others." He grabbed his wife, then lifted her above the water and slowly dunked her head and shoulders in it.

"I'm saved!" she said through her giggles when she came up for air. Aaron dunked her again and again, making her laugh even more.

Oh crap, Sage thought as he watched Sybylla's naked body in the moonlight. *She is my stepmother. She is my stepmother,* he repeated to himself as he bobbed in the creek, trying to keep everything under control. *Even if we are the same age. Even if she is hot.*

She is my stepmother, he reminded himself one more time.

Frances swam over to him. "Don't you need to be saved?" she asked, a gleam in her eye.

Sage took a long look at her and felt a chill go down into his bones at the same time his face flushed. He felt himself become sober and clear. A lot of weird stuff was happening under the surface and he wasn't quite sure he wanted it to show.

Frances looked right through him.

"I'm glad you're here," she said.

Sage smiled back at her, feeling their vibe connecting in a way it hadn't before.

Does she feel that? he asked himself. *Of course she does. She's psychic. She feels everything.*

Frances inched a bit closer to him, invading enough of his space to make him uncomfortable. Sage looked down, trying to avoid her naked body, then looked over at Aaron and his stepmother.

"What are they doing?" he asked Frances.

Aaron and Sybylla were standing in waist-high water nearer to the shore. Aaron had willow branches wrapped around his hair and Sybylla was pressing wet elm leaves on his face and shoulders.

"Welcome, Green Man!" Frances shouted over to them.

"Who?" Sage asked.

"Yeah!" Aaron shouted, trying not to let the leaves come unglued from his face. "Fuck Jesus! I'm the Green Man!"

"He's weird," Sage said, not understanding the language of the Karma Community even after weeks of being immersed in it.

"He's just a Green Man," Frances said knowingly.

Sage shook his head.

"He's high."

Sage dove back into the deeper part of the creek, trying to avoid getting tangled in the brambles and muck.

Is this what mom had to deal with?

He grabbed hold of a small rock and pulled it free.

Frances slowly swam over to him like a sleek silver fish.

"It's okay, Sage," she said with smoke in her voice. "It's part of ritual. Aaron knows that. And getting high isn't a habit for him, or for any of us. All of us needed to push past our limits. We had to challenge ourselves. That's why we smoked. And that's why Aaron had us get naked."

Sage looked directly into her big brown eyes, darker than the night, darker than his fears.

"You've got to trust me," Frances said. "And Aaron, too."

Trusting Aaron went against everything Sage had been taught in his twenty years, both by Maggie and his own experiences—up until the past month or so. Don't trust Aaron: he'll disappoint you. Don't trust Aaron: he's only interested in his own needs. Don't trust Aaron: he has no self-control, whether it's with money, or women, or drugs. Don't trust Aaron: his grand plans always go bust.

Trusting Frances. I'll think about that.

Sage dove under the water again, his eyes closed and the rock in his left hand. He came up for air while Frances was swimming toward the shore. He followed her.

Aaron and Sybylla were lost in their world of giggles and Green Men. Frances clung to a rock, the water of the creek gently flowing past her and waking up her skin. Sage looked at her from the deepest part of the creek and thought, and thought.

Frances reached into the water and caught a willow branch floating in the current. She shook the excess water from it, then began winding it around her head, tucking the ends around themselves to secure it.

"Sage," she called out like a song, softly, but Sage heard her. "Don't you think I'd make a great Green Woman?"

He did.

He swam over to her and offered his stone to the emerging goddess. She smiled. He was grateful. He plucked more leaves out of the water and placed them ever so gently on her shoulders, on her neck, on her breasts, and in her hair. Every once in a while he would brush up against her—deliberately, perhaps, or not. They smiled, making Frances more beautiful and Sage more nervous.

When they walked to Frances' cabin, Frances still had leaves in her hair and Sage was still nervous. Their clothes and drums and proposal and tea stayed out in the field, gathering dew in the night and completing their transformation.

Chapter 26

Give Me Another Night

"What's that racket?" Maggie mumbled softly into her lover's ear.

"Hmmm…" Gil said, on the edge of sleep and being awake in the big soft bed. "Drums."

"It's more than drums," she said with ice in her voice. "Something weird is going on."

Gil clung to her a little more tightly, trying to pull her into a more relaxed mood.

"It's nothing to worry about. It's probably just a ritual."

"A what?"

"A ritual," he said. "Some sort of prayer or celebration. There's always something like that going on near the full moon."

Maggie tensed while Gil tried to drift back to sleep.

"Whatever it is, I hope Sage isn't caught up in it," she said firmly. "I know Aaron's the ringleader, whatever it is."

"Probably," Gil murmured. "He gets a kick out of it. He gets a kick out of everything."

"That hasn't changed," Maggie said.

"That's what it's all about, isn't it?" Gil said. "I mean, especially if you're a rock star."

Maggie thought she could still hear the faint drumbeat on the hills and tried to detach herself from the old memories and her current worries. Despite the excitement from being cherished by her new lover, the ghosts still clung to Maggie and prevented her from finding peace.

"Can't they do that in private?"

Gil smoothed back her hair, letting the gold and silver and artfully concealed drab blond flow through his fingers and onto her bare neck.

"They're expressing themselves," he said reasonably. "If they kept it to themselves they wouldn't be communicating. Besides, some things are meant to be communal—prayer, ritual, celebration. Didn't you feel a difference when you sang onstage and when you just sang around the house?"

Maggie thought for a moment. Of course Gil was right, and any performer would agree. Some activities were meant to be shared. But there was danger in that, too, Maggie knew, if one could only perform in public. That dependency on others for a heightened burst of energy or passion or validation could be as much of a drug as any weed or powder or pill. It could go over the edge into hedonism or abandon. It had the power to create anything—events as magical as Woodstock or as frightening as Altamont.

Maggie looked at Gil, peaceful as always, the man who spent his days and nights worshipping her, partly because they shared a lusty spark, partly because he wanted to be involved with Maggie Morgan from the Four Furies. She knew this and didn't discourage it. Surprising herself, she found power in it. As she had decades ago when she seduced men who were not Aaron.

"I need to talk to you," she said quietly.

Gil rolled over on his side.

"I'm leaving in the morning. I have to go back to Chicago."

He flicked the ends of her lank hair between his fingers, lightly, as if he was plumping up a paintbrush before dipping it in his palette.

"Don't I have a say in this?"

Maggie took a deep breath and braced herself.

"No. I'm sorry, but you don't. I need to leave."

"But you'll be back for your court case."

"Yes."

"We'll see each other then, right?"

"Of course," Maggie said. But she wasn't so sure. In fact, she hadn't really considered continuing her affair with Gil. The next court date was some sort of fuzzy blot on the far horizon, a mirage she didn't quite believe would materialize. First, she needed to wrest the firm from the talons of Trip and Matilda, then reinvent it as Morgan & Fellows Designs. Her trial, if it happened, was something of a worst-case scenario that would only come about if Erika and Carl couldn't agree to a plea, or at least recommit to the plea they'd crafted before Carl threw his hissy fit for the reporter's benefit.

Seeing Gil again was even fuzzier than her court date, something she couldn't even envision in her mind's eye.

"Give me another night."

He slid his hand down her neck, her shoulder, down her arm to the hollow at her pelvis, along the curve of her hip, raising the slight hairs on her flesh. He kissed her eyelids, then created a trail down her jawline and into the deep recess of her collarbone.

"Just one more night."

He drew her closer.

"I hope you've gotten whatever you needed here," he whispered.

"It's been wonderful," Maggie said, needing to tell a slight lie to let her lover down gently. "But you've been the best part."

He kissed her longer than she wanted. "Life is simple here," he whispered in her ear. "Wake up, contribute in some way, be kind, open your heart. Leave the Earth a better place than you found it. I'm sure it's quite different than your life in Chicago."

Maggie took in his words, quietly admitting they were true.

"You must have seen the transformation in people. I mean, look at Sage."

"Sage?" Maggie asked with sincere surprise. "Sage hasn't changed."

"You don't think so?"

"No. Sage has been stuck for a while. He gets overwhelmed easily. He's very sensitive. And he has a hard time dealing with his emotions in a safe way."

"Really? I would never describe him that way," Gil said softly.

"He's a sweet young man, but I wish he'd just find something he's good at and stick with it. It doesn't matter what it is as long as he likes it."

"I was watching him in yoga yesterday. He gets it. He's a natural. The teacher makes one small correction to his posture and Sage understands completely. Like, yesterday, Sage was in the warrior pose. I've done the warrior a thousand times, and it's deceptively easy. People use it as a resting pose, but it's anything but. There's a lot of tension there, a lot of movement under the surface. And I could see that Sage got it. He was still, but he wasn't at rest. He was working, but it appeared to be effortless."

Maggie listened and imagined Sage as a yogi, a punk rock yogi who thrashed instead of meditated.

"I think the Karma Community is good for him."

The words punched Maggie.

"And it must be great for him to get to know Aaron after all of these years."

Those words hurt even more.

"Give me another night," he whispered, his adoration a balm for her unsettled nerves.

"I will," she promised.

Chapter 27

The Beginning of a Great Adventure

Aaron was a little bit wobbly and weak from the night before. He was skipping yoga and breakfast in favor of a solitary run through the woods and the hills. He'd be a little bit late for the early staff meeting, but that wouldn't be a problem. Sybylla and Frances would cover for him.

Aaron wasn't a devoted runner. He didn't own proper running shoes and never looked at a watch or kept track of miles. He never denied himself the pleasure of walking when others would push themselves. He was no athlete or marathoner—his old body had been through way too much for that—but in his own way he was a natural runner. He could usually fall right into a run, relaxed and at his own pace, even if he hadn't set foot to path in weeks. He never tensed, never felt his pace become uneven, never labored to breathe. He eased up when he needed to, sped up when he had extra steam, and let the course take him where he needed to go.

That's exactly what he needed this morning—some movement, some understanding, a good old sweat that would tamp down the fire behind his eyes, the devils that now sat on both of his shoulders, having pushed off the guiding angel that would balance everything out.

Aaron kept running although he still felt weak. The sun was soft overhead and he was in no rush. He tried hard to make each footfall connect with the earth, to feel supported and steady in his stride.

For the first time in years, his footfalls beat out the rhythm of one of his old songs. Unlike most of the Four Furies' hits, he sang "Running Reds" alone without Maggie. Subconsciously, he didn't want to tarnish her with his drug-dealing past and present, when money got tight. His mumbled growl was at turns confessional, defiant, self-pitying. The rest of the band grooved into a no-worries bluesy shuffle.

"Running reds
One light ahead of the law
Nobody knows how we get there
Just be there for the show.
Running reds
Right foot on the pedal
Hands on cash and stash and your number
I'll always be a rebel.
Running reds
Speeding away from trouble.
Running reds
Speeding straight for trouble.
Running reds
Make mine a double."

He turned into the woods, where a path had been cleared by others who came long before him. It was cool and green, overgrown and unruly. *Think of the Green Man, Aaron Fields. Find the path. If you stay on it, you'll come out of here just fine, just like the labyrinth, just like life. Stay on the path, you old man,* he reminded himself.

Aaron kept his eyes trained on the ground before him, careful to step over fallen branches and pushed-up, twisted roots. In doing so, he was missing the rabbits napping in the underbrush to his right; the cardinal touching down on a branch here and a branch there; the ladylike but spicy wood violets that carpeted the shady ground; and the light but welcome breeze that kept the entire woods in motion, even when they were at rest.

Aaron knew that the lushness surrounded him, but he tried hard to not let himself feel it and be tempted by it. It was all too much right now. He knew that the trees and plants could heal him, but they could destroy him, too. That damn part of his brain that would light up like a pinball machine at the thought of drugs was tilting full-on. He craved another high. He had to kill that part of his brain that created that craving or give in and give that fucker what he wanted. The choice was his.

As he ran, he tried to think of his wife, now a safe distance behind him and busy with her morning routine and he hoped, however unlikely, that she had no idea how close he'd come last night to rebirthing the Aaron of old, Aaron the addict. He knew that Maggie and Sage were watching and waiting for him to lose it and confirm their most negative thoughts.

He focused on the path. He knew in his bones and didn't need to see with his eyes all of the plants that he craved and feared. To his left, there was a patch of greens whose root would get him stoned and mellow. Up ahead was a cluster of tall weeds that, if turned into a tea made with its fresh leaves and stems, would produce hallucinations. And that tree, not far from where he was now, has a soft inside bark that, when nibbled, would dry up his mouth but send a rush through his blood and bones. And everywhere—everywhere—grew the weed they'd smoked last night, the taste of which was now turning his legs and his resolve to jelly.

Stay on the path, Aaron Fields.

+++

Sage had been watching Frances from the hammock on the sun deck. He was restless, calm, proud, and freaked out about what had happened the night before—what happened between him and Frances, that is.

She was gone when he woke up in her bed, an overstuffed futon with layers of batik cloth draped over it instead of proper blankets. He felt lost in them, but that was fine. It was a nice kind of lost to be lost in Frances' world.

The sex last night was great. His mind was still blown. He never could have predicted that they'd end up together. Frances was unlike anyone he'd ever been with. She wasn't into the things that a normal person would be into. She didn't watch TV and had never heard of the bands that he liked. She said weird stuff sometimes and, truth be told, Sage had always kind of avoided her because of it.

He was bursting to tell someone about last night, but who? Aaron and Sybylla—forget it. Besides, they probably already knew. Maggie—never. No way. Maggie would send Sage back home if she knew he'd messed around with some crunchy psychic hippie witch.

Then again, maybe he should tell Maggie just to freak her out.

Sage swung the hammock a bit to help him think. As he watched Frances pin T-shirts to the clothesline, he thought that she looked really normal, like Susie Homemaker normal.

Frances must have heard the hammock creak because she turned around and smiled at him. *She probably knew I was here the whole time,* Sage thought. Her smile was an invitation, but part of him wanted to run in the other direction.

"It's only me, Sage," she called out to him. "Don't be afraid."

He walked over to her, trying to find coolness and confidence on his way over. She kept smiling at him, unnerving him.

"Sleep well?" she asked innocently.

He laughed.

"I didn't get much sleep," he said, squinting at her in an attempt to avoid both her eyes and the sunlight.

Frances laughed and handed him the edge of a wet bed sheet. She opened the bundle and searched for the other end of the sheet. When she did, she backed away from Sage, pulling it taut. Then Frances put her side of the sheet over the clothesline, grabbed a few clothespins, and secured it to the line. The linen blew in the breeze. She picked up a pale yellow sheet, found a corner, then handed it to Sage and repeated the process.

"Feel like a Green Man this morning?" Frances teased, breaking their silence.

Sage blanched. "I still don't know what is, but sure. I do feel like one."

Frances ran her hands along the damp sheets, then ducked behind an unruly one. "Well," she began slowly, relishing her time in the sun. "The Green Man is legendary. He's the personification of the forest—of plant life made human. You've probably seen him everywhere but didn't know what you were looking at. His face pokes out from a bunch of leaves and flowers, almost as if he's a lion and the plant kingdom is his mane. He's a very popular figure in gardens and on buildings. There's one hanging up on the garden shed in the back, in case you haven't noticed."

Sage nodded. "Yeah, right. The Green Man, totally."

Frances played along with it. "So, Sage," she said. "Now that you know what one is, do you feel like a Green Man?"

Sage hesitated, then grinned. "Totally."

Frances grinned back, delighted with his enthusiasm.

"I think this is the beginning of a great adventure."

Chapter 28

Be in the Moment

Aaron checked his reflection in the octagonal mirror, an object that, according to Feng Shui principles, could deflect negativity and send it flying. But all that appeared in the mirror was Aaron, casual as always in a blue work shirt and faded Levi's. A leather strand hung around his neck, which held a hunk of sea-blue lapis lazuli, a personal talisman for close to thirty years.

Aaron checked his reflection not out of vanity. He was spooked. But the ghosts didn't show up in the mirror, he was relieved to see. Just Aaron—preoccupied, focused, pushy, and passive Aaron.

The morning had not gone well. Aaron hadn't slept and had kept up Sybylla with his restlessness.

"Just be in the moment," Sybylla had told him as she tied back her clean long hair in the soft morning light. "You've prepared enough. The crisis will help you be spontaneous. Don't fear it. Feel it."

Aaron needed that encouragement. Frederick arrived with his usual drama, but with a new girlfriend in tow. This one was an overly made-up Russian painter, Tanya.

Aaron and Frederick had met at a hot springs resort in Utah, where Freddie—Frederick Christiansen, to be exact—was cooling his jets after finalizing various contracts with his clients. At the time of their meeting, he was attempting to unwind in the sulfurous pool with a drop-dead view of the mountains, but he couldn't relax. He'd pay for someone to do it for him, he'd told Aaron, amusing himself with the idea of barking "Relax my shoulders!" to a team of relaxation professionals wearing taupe linen lab coats and hemp sandals. "Paradise," he'd said.

Now, at the Karma Community, Freddie was being a dick, a needle making track marks up and down Aaron's back. He and Tanya had been rude to Sybylla and Frances and he'd claimed the chamomile tea had steeped too long and was too bitter to drink. Unable to take it anymore, Sybylla stomped out onto the sun deck, furious. Frances just sat silently, angrily keeping her composure.

As Aaron inspected his eyes in the mirror, he realized that the morning planned so carefully was falling apart. Freddie, sitting at the teak table in the sunny tea room with his feet propped up on a purple meditation cushion, had the upper hand. As Aaron walked through the cool hallway to go back to Freddie and Tanya, he told himself to rise above the pettiness and not allow his ego to lead him to be spiteful, disdainful, or abusive. If he were truly honest with Freddie, the Karma Community would collapse.

+++

As she settled into a downward dog, Maggie regretted that extra cup of coffee that morning. The liquid and acid and caffeine agitated her stomach, making it impossible to focus on her yoga practice.

"Breathe," the impossibly beautiful guest instructor intoned. "Breathe into your joints, your muscles, the tight spaces you want to open up."

Maggie inhaled and wondered if she could rest on her borrowed mat for the rest of the class, or simply walk across the sun deck to her car and drive away from this place forever. But she'd promised Gil one more night together, and she just couldn't be a jerk to him. And there he was on the mat next to her, the guy who'd made love to her last night and again this morning, then fetched her beloved coffee so she could sip it quietly in his bed and not be bothered by the attention of the fans who continued to line the driveway of the Karma Community. Gil had suggested a yoga class to distract her for an hour, a way for her to switch off her brain and leave her troubles on her mat.

She lowered onto her knees for the cow pose and felt a nerve pinch in the small of her back as her face and butt tilted upwards and her abs sunk toward her mat. She eased the tension by rolling her hips back to center and taking a deep breath. She was tighter than she'd realized, tighter than usual, despite the vigorous sex she was having with Gil.

I'm going to miss him when I leave. But not enough to stick around.

The class shifted into cat pose, and Maggie felt relief, more open, less clenched as she curved her spine upward and focused on her hands pressing into her mat. She rolled back into cow pose, wishing the instructor could allow her to flow between the two positions for the rest of the hour.

Her mind darted from the sight of Gil's lean, strong shoulders to the variety of body types in the group—supple young women and gymnastic men, older men and women with scars and knee wraps and loose pants covering varicose veins, Sage in the front row alert and in the zone. She closed her eyes as a cumulous cloud drifted overhead, bringing a bit of relief from the heat. Tomorrow she'd be back in Chicago, enveloped in air conditioning and professional clothing, stinking of stress hormones as she prepared her pitch for Trip and Matilda.

I deserve to take over the helm of Morgan & Fellows Designs because that's what Felix wanted, she wanted to tell them. *That's what he promised all these years. That's how he kept me at the firm for ten years when I could have walked away. I don't care if it wasn't in writing. Weren't those promises a contract? So, yeah. Give me the firm. I'll come up with money if that's what you want. Just give it to me.*

But she knew that honesty wouldn't pay off with those two.

As the close colleague of Felix Fellows for a decade, I am able to carry on his legacy with dignity and respect. Clients can expect a continuation of your father's legendary esthetic. The firm would be in good hands, the best hands.

She thought about the implications of that line of reasoning as she back into Downward Dog.

More of the same.

Plug and play.

Follow the blueprint.

No new ideas.

None.

Might as well be singing Furies songs night after night.

She felt lava roiling her veins, crashing out her thoughts and making her mind turn to vapor. Heart speeding along, beats doubling up against the walls of her chest. A flash down her arm. Sweat. A cold hand closing around her throat.

She tried to breathe deeply, but her throat would only allow in short, sharp gusts of hot summer air. Her muscles contracted as panic seized them. The same blanketing panic she'd felt in her squirrel brown braids as she squeaked out a solo in the Christmas concert, her voice sounding nothing like it did when she was alone, pleasing herself. The same icy hot panic she felt before going onstage with the Four Furies, stunned that anyone would want to pay to hear her. The

153

same engulfing panic she'd had to tame before shows with coke, or sex, or downers, or alcohol, or fights.

The same panic she'd pushed through each time to grab what she wanted.

I can do this.

She was out of sync with the rest of the class. She could tell from the swooshing and breathing around her that they were flowing through a quick Sun Salutation, but she was stuck upside down, ass in the air, inert. She tried inhaling again, this time imagining holding Trip's severed head in one hand, tongue wagging unmercifully, gleeful, powerful. And in her other hand: what? Her Blackberry? A checkbook? Paint samples? Upholstery swatches? None of that meant anything. Ten years of playing by the rules and nothing tangible to take pride in.

I should be proud of myself simply for surviving.

Hot air sputtered from her throat past her chapped lips as she plunked her right foot between her hands into an unsteady lunge. Another deep breath and she pushed herself into Warrior One, legs shaking as she stood up, palms reaching toward the periwinkle sky, sun a torch to be feared and revered. A laugh caught in her throat as tears dribbled from the corners of her eyes.

It's time, it's time, it's time.

+++

When Aaron re-entered the tea room, Freddie was poring over the spreadsheets Frances had prepared, the corners of his mouth turned down and creases forming at the bridge of his nose. Tanya was wandering, aimlessly, spacily dancing and humming an indistinct tune. When she heard wind chimes, she cocked her ear and pantomimed playing the piano, like a New Age mime entertaining a crowd of tourists. Frances and Sybylla sat quietly, their hands composed in their laps, silent faces, warriors at rest.

"The numbers aren't good," Freddie said plainly.

"The economy isn't good," Aaron said, trying to commiserate.

"I don't mind losing money on this temporarily," Freddie said, "but I'm not running a nonprofit."

The comment turned Sybylla's face red and struck Aaron like a blow to the kidneys. Frances didn't flinch, didn't budge.

"It's tough right now," Aaron explained as calmly as he could. "We're getting more competition from the Lotus Institute, which has started taking overnight guests and expanded their sauna, which they're passing off as a sweat lodge."

"Competition should make you better," Freddie said. "Marianne Multi-Grain leading the same old chakra workshops isn't going to cut it anymore."

Aaron paused to compose himself.

"Remember that 9/11 hit us hard. People aren't spending money on what they see as non-essentials. They don't want to leave home."

Freddie pushed the papers aside.

"I'm not buying that," he snapped. "If this were Disneyland, I would agree. But this is a spiritual retreat center, and this is a perfect time to market to people who are still traumatized. In theory, they should want to come here to get some peace. So where are they?"

"So many people lost their jobs, or they're afraid of losing their jobs," Aaron countered. "Spending a few hundred dollars on a yoga workshop is a luxury that they don't feel they can afford."

"You must make them feel that they can afford it, that they can't not afford to come here," Freddie said. "That's your job. If they are still head cases because of being afraid of terrorists, then they should come here to put themselves back together again. Aren't you networking with grief counselors? I know the Scientologists are. The *Times* prints little biographies of all of the victims. Send catalogs to the families of the deceased. Look at the obituaries, too."

Aaron wanted to punch him. He cleared his throat instead and counted to ten.

"Isn't that a little crass?" he said as diplomatically as he could. "It doesn't sound like something we'd do."

"One could argue that that's the problem."

Freddie leaned back in his chair, fully aware of his power.

"Do you offer programs for people who are grieving? Payment plans for anyone who worked at the towers? Health programs for asthma or anxiety?"

Aaron and Sybylla exchanged a look.

"I've only been here for two hours and already I've come up with more profitable ideas than the lot of you," Freddie said dismissively. "When times change you have to change too—you have to anticipate the change. Be a change agent, Aaron. You were, once."

The pinpricks made track marks all over Aaron's skin, injecting a fire into his veins.

"We do have ideas," Sybylla protested, unable to take Freddie's disrespect any longer. Aaron walked over to her and put his hand on her shoulder, trying to calm her and protect her.

"We have new instructors coming in the fall," Aaron said, trying to salvage the situation. "The equinox celebration is always a hit. And Duncan and Shifrah are coming back."

"Yawn," Freddie said. "I've heard it all before."

The two men's eyes locked. The battle for dominance was almost complete.

"They have a new workshop and book," Sybylla said, coming to the rescue of her husband.

Freddie's gaze was relentless. Tanya continued wandering around the room, enjoying each moment of the confrontation.

"Yawn again."

Aaron stepped toward his benefactor, openly hostile.

"You will not insult my wife in my home."

Freddie smirked.

"Your home?" Tanya laughed. "Frederick pays the mortgage."

White-hot flames engulfed Aaron.

"Apologize to Sybylla."

"I was only being honest."

"Apologize."

"Aaron—" Sybylla said, reaching out to him.

Frances raised her hands to cool down the situation.

"Frederick," she said. "We have a proposition for you. It's something totally unique. I think it might be what you're looking for."

"Frances, now isn't the time," Aaron said sharply, still steaming.

"What do you mean?" Freddie retorted. "Her timing is impeccable. I need a laugh."

Frances closed her eyes and imagined herself full of white light and powerful beyond powerful. She began speaking, fully aware of the risk she was taking.

"We have lost our way," she said, now looking intently into Freddie's eyes and trying as best she could to connect with him on a human level. "Not just us here at the Karma Community, but all of us. Me. You. Tanya. Aaron. Sybylla. We are totally disconnected from what we should be doing, what we can be doing, no matter how noble our intentions. We're overloaded with demands and obligations. Don't you feel overloaded, Frederick? Don't you wish that you could find your heart and soul and find the heart and soul in the rest of the world?"

She kept connecting to him, pulling him into her energy field.

"Don't you wish you could clear out all of the debris you're dragging along with you and find some clarity again?"

Freddie looked at Tanya, then out the window.

"But the Ancients didn't feel that way. They weren't lost. They knew what was important, what was sacred. They were connected to each other, and to the earth and the sky. But when they did fall off the path, they got right back on it again. They did it by walking the labyrinth. You see them all over the world, in just about every culture. You enter the labyrinth, you walk the path, you find the center—the heart, the core, the soul. Your soul. My soul. The world's soul. And you to come into balance again."

She took another deep breath, her eyes remaining fixed on Freddie. Aaron and Sybylla stood together, awed. Tanya shed a tear, silently.

"Go on," Freddie said.

She stepped toward him and took hold of both of his hands, in an instant increasing both his discomfort and his attention. She tried to channel all of the righteous anger of Aaron and Sybylla through her being and into what she was trying to communicate.

"A labyrinth, Frederick. A simple coiled path, a journey into wholeness. We want to build one here, at the Karma Community," she declared.

Frederick looked deeply into Frances' eyes, investigating them for fraud, or fear, or even some New Age lunacy that he'd come to expect from a Karma Community staffer. He found none of that.

"I'll consider it," he said, clearing his throat and squeezing her hands. "But the future of the Karma Community as it is now is over."

Chapter 29

Peace

Only two people were in the dark meditation room when Aaron cracked open the door. Well, three people, if you counted the massive brass Buddha that sat in the corner, surrounded by a dish of water, three oranges, incense, candle stubs, the tarot card of the Empress, four daisies and a packet of matches. The Buddha was just as alive and welcoming as any other creature at the community's center, and Aaron waved to him as he sat down on a purple cushion.

One meditator cracked open one eye, spied Aaron, nudged his partner, and nodded Aaron's way.

"Hey man," he said softly as Aaron settled in. "Rock on."

Aaron bowed to the man, his hands clasped in prayer at his chest.

"*Namaste*," Aaron said quietly, then closed his eyes. "Peace."

He sighed heavily. His old addict's brain was the devil on his shoulder insisting he shove something in his system to shut it all off. The taste of drugs in the ceremony in the meadow now ate into every hour of his day. More, more, more. But he knew more would never be enough. More would put him into the grave with a dirty needle, the wrong mix of pills, the fatal round of Russian roulette in a motel room you could rent by the hour. It took all of his strength and enlightenment to strangle that devil and the asshole he knew he was under the skin. A decade clean and sober meant nothing when his old addict's brain was woken up and ready to make some mayhem.

I need peace, he said to himself. *Shut off this brain, shut off this mind. Peace. Peace. Peace. Peace.*

He inhaled slowly and folded his hands over his eyes, his smallest finger fitting into the dent in his nose.

Peace. Peace. Peace. Peace.

He tried to focus on the colors lining his eyelids, tried to direct his thoughts on nothing, on emptiness.

Peace. Peace. Peace. Peace.

He imagined clouds drifting around him.

Peace.

He saw Frederick's face in front of him.

Peace.

His heart beat faster.

The numbers aren't good, Aaron remembered Frederick saying in the tea room.

Aaron placed his hands over his ears.

Peace.

In his mind's eye, Aaron saw the spreadsheets, saw Frances and Sybylla wave incense over them, hoping to infuse them with positive energy.

I have half a mind to sell this place, Aaron remembered hearing Freddie say to the women.

He exhaled as slowly as he could, trying to expel all of Frederick's negativity. He inhaled just as deeply and stifled a cough. He put one hand on his lower lung, then took another breath. He ran his hands along his arms, feeling the old scar tissue raised by years of destroying himself with needles.

He tried to focus on his mantra once again.

Peace. Peace. Peace.

The clouds reappeared.

Maggie Morgan.

Her face took shape before him, both as the woman she is now and as the younger woman he'd felt in his heart was his one true love.

Maggie.

He clasped his hands on his knees.

I was happy then. Truly happy.

He shook his head and opened his eyes. The two meditators were still there, deeply immersed in their experience. Buddha smiled down on Aaron.

+++

"I'll sign anything," Maggie said, grabbing a *Stars that Shoot and Fall* tour T-shirt out of her fan's grip. "But I won't sign that trash."

That trash was a collection of tabloids that must have appeared in grocery store check-out aisles that morning and now materialized in the possession of her fans gathered at the foot of the Karma Community's drive. That trash was getting in the way of her desire to extend her yoga practice's feel-good vibes and puff up her ego before saying goodbye to the community tonight.

"Furies' Maggie in Drug and Drink Death Wish," one screamed on the cover in acid yellow type, with Gordon's photos from the courtroom in all their grainy glory. While Maggie felt proud and self-righteous and newly powerful in the moment she faced Gordon's camera, the resulting pictures revealed her to be sneering, spiteful, raging, the same Maggie Morgan who punched out her lover on stage twenty years prior. DA Carl Olsen, on the other hand, was portrayed as a small-town hero simply motivated by his selfless care and concern for the good folk of Tyler County.

Damn that Gordon. Damn that Carl.

And this whopper, superimposed on the photo of her and Sage throwing gravel at Gordon at the foot of DA Olsen's campaign billboard: "Drunk! Fat! Out of Control! Maggie's Post-Furies Life with Aaron's Love Child." The article contained no new news, really, just a rehashing of the rise and fall of the Four Furies, plus some speculation about her life as a "portly suburban soccer mom slash office assistant."

I'm not portly. Not even close.

"Wine Bottles, Pills and Aaron: Inside Maggie Morgan's Nightmare Crash and Night in Jail," another gossiped, which Maggie thought was somewhat close to the truth. Her mugshot looked even worse than she'd imagined: blood soaking into her hairline, messy makeup, bleary eyes, gritted teeth, Pinot Noir-splashed blouse. And it was the first time she saw police photos of her wrecked Saab, its accordion-scrunched hood official evidence of how close she'd come to death.

It was an accident. I was concussed. No one asked for my side of the story.

"Messy Maggie Runs Back to Ex-Furies Aaron. But He's a Farmer with a Teen Bride!" That one included her courtroom photos as well as a shot of the exterior of Norm's Norway Inn, where Aaron had whisked Maggie after rescuing her from jail. "Or will she beg Clark Kavanaugh to take her back for another night?" the pull quote asked.

Get over it, people.

The bimonthly *New Elm Extra*, on the other hand, placed above the fold a collage of photos of Grandma Yvonne Olsen's birthday celebration, complete with birthday cake, streamers, a performance by the Tyler County 4H Glee Club dressed in old-timey costumes, and a family photo of four generations of Olsens, great-grandbaby Aidan drooling away on her knee. Maggie's smash-up was covered on the bottom of page 4 as "No Guilty Plea in Drunk Driving Crash." No photos, no sizzle.

I guess the Extra *couldn't afford Gordon's asking price.*

Gordon didn't need flashbulbs in the broad noon sunlight flooding the Karma Community, but Maggie could feel him clicking away, delighted, as he snapped her with a telephoto lens for the following week's national tabloids. Just one photo of the beloved, reclusive Maggie Morgan, losing her cool once again for his benefit, would cover a down payment on a lake cabin Up North with a private pier, pontoon boat, and two-car garage. She refused to let him have it.

+++

Aaron and Frederick took their lunch in the lavender patch in the side yard, their Adirondack chairs facing the grand swoops of the Karma Community's hilly estate. The discreet cottages linked by wildflower-lined paths, the chicken coop, and kitchen herb garden. The gazebo, the trail leading down to the creek. The organic vegetable garden, the stinking compost pile. The flat grassy stretch that Aaron, Sybylla, and their friends hoped would become the labyrinth, if only Frederick would assent. And his assent was the point of this lunch.

"There aren't too many labyrinths open to the public in Wisconsin," Aaron offered. "We'd be a novelty around here, a draw."

The two men rested their plates of lightly dressed spring greens, strawberries, and baked tempeh on their knees, but neither one ate. Aaron, because he was too angry and anxious to put anything into his bile-soaked gut; Freddie, because this kind of rabbit food disgusted him.

"This part of the Middle West is known for—what's it called? Supper clubs?" Freddie asked, placing his plate on the soft grass. "*Saveur* did a piece on them recently. Like steak houses, but chintzy. Retro. Are there any nearby?"

Aaron could have ticked off a list of a dozen supper clubs within a gravel's throw of the Karma Community, but he wouldn't take the bait.

"We do our best to be self-sustaining here," Aaron grumbled. "No Saturday night prime rib specials unless we raise and slaughter our own cows, which won't be happening anytime soon. Sybylla's gone vegan. Except for the eggs."

Freddie drank a long draught of his mint iced tea from a jelly jar, then held it to his cheek and paused.

"I'll have Tanya look into that. Grass-fed beef and all that. Organic veal. Artisanal cheese, perhaps."

161

Aaron stuffed a clump of bib lettuce and arugula into his mouth to prevent himself from responding.

"Look what I've got."

Tanya, approaching from behind them, startled both men with her news. In the exuberant noon sun she held out a crunched newspaper just inches from Freddie's nose, ignoring Aaron.

"Messy Maggie Runs Back to Ex-Furies Aaron. But He's a Farmer with a Teen Bride!" he read slowly, savoring every word. He turned to Aaron, a slow smirk spreading across his face.

"Is this true?"

Aaron snatched the tabloid from Tanya's grip, scanned it briefly, then balled it up and tossed it into the wind.

"Sybylla's not a teenager."

"So it is true. Maggie has returned to you."

"It's true, it absolutely is," Tanya interjected. Her chiffon blouse fluttered and revealed the absence of tan lines on her shoulders, just smooth, pampered, sun-kissed skin. "She's right out in front, signing autographs. Even the paparazzi are here."

Freddie stared down Aaron, almost daring him to pounce.

"You fool." Freddie rose from his chair, adjusted himself grandly, and tucked in his shirt. "This should have been part of your pitch this morning."

Tanya led the two men around the side of the main building to the front porch, where they had a clear view of about two dozen well-wishers and a photographer off to the side, his phallic lens trained on Maggie.

"She's there," Tanya said. "In the middle of the crowd."

Freddie narrowed his eyes in the sun and walked down the drive. He parted the crowd so he could extend his hand to Maggie, who, though decades from her prime, he thought, still bore traces of the world-class celebrity she once was. Regal, if dethroned and diminished. A beauty, still. A beauty, always.

"I don't believe we've met."

Her glance shifted toward the voice that wasn't awed by her, a voice that commanded her attention.

"I'm Maggie," she said, stretching out her hand.

"You're Maggie Morgan," Frederick said, almost correcting her. "I didn't know you were at the Karma Community. I haven't seen you at workshops."

"I've been keeping a low profile." She held his gaze until he broke it off.

"You shouldn't." He raked his eyes over her and broke into a wide smile, an incongruous sight on his taut, tanned face, and walked away, dismissing her, toward a fuming Aaron on the porch lighting one cigarette off the end of another. His lapis pendant bobbed against his chest.

"Quite a crowd," Freddie said slyly. "The biggest one I've seen in ages."

"They're pests," Aaron spat. "Not part of our community."

"Are you getting the band back together?"

"Not on your life."

"Isn't that why she's here?"

"No."

"I see. Then just to resume your affair, as the newspaper reported."

"Not that, either."

"Perhaps you could change her mind."

"I'm married. To Sybylla. My teenage bride."

"No, not that," Freddie said, waving away their misunderstanding. "I mean the Furies."

"The Furies' time has come and gone." Aaron spoke as he exhaled his smoke, which shrouded his face and made him squint. "There's no need to put us old geezers on display again."

"But what if—"

"No."

Aaron stood up and walked toward the front steps, knowing the damned photographer at the end of the drive could get a clear shot of him but not caring.

Freddie grabbed Aaron's taut bicep and forced him to halt.

"I'll make you a deal," he said into his employee's ear. "Give me a new Four Furies song and you can build your labyrinth. And maybe I won't sell the Karma Community out from under you next month."

Chapter 30

Damn Thing

A jar of elderflower tea was tucked under Aaron's arm, concealed by his work shirt. It reminded him of when he had snuck a bottle of poteen, Irish moonshine, through customs at Logan airport decades ago. The white lightning had been given to him by a ferry pilot who lived with his wife and two handfuls of children in rustic simplicity on the Aran Islands. It was the late sixties and Aaron had been hitchhiking, chasing some sort of dream of the road and rebellion, running away from a series of busted-up bands and a lengthening rap sheet, when the Irishman had picked him up on the side of a narrow lane, shared a pint of Guinness with him, then let Aaron sleep on his kitchen floor after a healthy supper. The poteen, which the two men drank when the kids were being put to bed, had knocked Aaron on his ass. It made fatherhood easier, no doubt, and kept the sparkle in the old man's eyes. Back in the states, Aaron only took a smuggled shot when he wanted to cry or to laugh, or to stare into the darkness alone.

The poteen was long gone. The elderflower tea would have to do.

Aaron made his way to the brace of trees just past the hill. He wanted his privacy in the coming moonlight. In his free hand he held what he always kept near him, even when he tried to ignore it.

"Damn thing," he said as he heard the acoustic guitar thump from side to side in its hard case.

Aaron hadn't opened the damned thing in years. His other instruments and equipment had been pawned, sold, lost, or junked. The albums and master tapes were who knows where, and the profits and royalties were mostly siphoned to offshore accounts for the Four Furies' ex-manager's ex-wives to enjoy. The other memorabilia—the platinum records, ticket stubs, photos, and magazine covers—were strewn around the country, a side effect of Aaron's benevolence and carelessness. In the back of his mind, he'd always hoped that Maggie had held onto the good stuff for posterity.

But Aaron still had the guitar, an object that both drew and repelled him. There had been a point in time—decades ago, actually—when the old guitar was all that he needed. It made him forget things and remember others; it helped him connect with himself and with other people, a lifeline when the world and his most intimate devils were close to swallowing him.

Aaron walked toward the clearing in the woods and put down the jar and guitar. He took out a penknife and drew a large circle around him in the soft dirt. This would be his place on the Earth for as long as necessary.

He lit a cigarette he'd bummed off Sage, then scratched his head and shrouded himself in the smoke.

Damn thing.

Aaron sat in his circle a good long time, still as a rock, as indecisive as a reed. He knew what he had to do, but he wasn't quite ready to start his Vision Quest, an inner journey taken by many Native Americans who needed answers from the universe.

Aaron put his head in his hands. The whole point of the Vision Quest was to tunnel into one's fear and discomfort, he knew. What had once been so easy—strumming his guitar, piecing together lyrics and melodies—had never overwhelmed or terrified him. It did now. But that was the point of sitting in the circle, to become so uncomfortable with his fears that he would be forced to face them and push through it and be done with it.

What he really wanted to do was to get up, pull some weeds out of the ground and chew them until he saw Venus and Mars and unknown galaxies beyond them and just escape this whole situation.

But Freddie had thrown down the gauntlet—a Four Furies song to keep the Karma Community alive.

Aaron reached for his guitar. He took a swig of tea, then restrung and tuned the guitar until it was perfect again.

He set aside the guitar and lay on the ground. He turned his head to the side and saw a plant that Frances and Sybylla had shown him once. It was just out of reach.

He rolled on his side, pushed himself to the edge of the circle, grabbed the leaves, and yanked.

Chapter 31

The Last Supper

Maggie tucked her hand under Gil's bicep as he escorted her into the full dining room, the soft setting sun tucking behind the gathering of trees on the edge of the Karma Community's property. It would be her last supper at the community, the last evening she'd promised Gil, a proper goodbye before returning to Chicago, to real life, her life, not the dreamlife that permeated this rural Wisconsin retreat.

She scanned the room seeking out Furies fans, unsure if she wanted them there or not. Her old shyness was kicking in and making her heart thump and prance as she assessed the diners. Familiar faces from yoga, from breakfast. No photographers, no tabloids unfolded on the tables. Not a bit of Four Furies memorabilia in sight. Just Sybylla welcoming guests one by one and Frances waving a hand over each platter that emerged from the kitchen to bless them. And Sage, padding on a conga in the corner, damp half-moons forming along his T-shirt's collar and armpits, eyes closed, grinning.

She caught herself looking for Aaron, but found only that curious man who'd introduced himself without offering his own name when she was signing autographs, his eyes directed on her. She felt her own blouse dampen as she turned from his gaze.

She couldn't help herself.

"Gil, who's that—"

He steered her toward an empty table in the corner near a ficus tree, pulled out a chair, and released her hand gently. The table was already set with mismatched bowls and plates, heavy estate sale-bought utensils, pitchers of iced tea, plates of cornbread, and Mason jars of wildflowers, likely Sybylla's handiwork.

"I think this is the shadiest spot in the room." He guided her into her seat and then settled her in. "You'll have a little bit of privacy away from the crowd."

She smiled, grateful, feeling the heat surrounding her dissipate.

"I don't think I've met a nicer man than you, Gilman Gorham."

"Ouch—nice," he said with a light laugh. "That isn't always a good thing."

She smiled and took a long look at him, hoping to remember each facet of his features when she was in Chicago. He was handsome, he really was. But there was some essential animating goodness that sparked his handsomeness and made him irresistible. He was kind, he was thoughtful; a gentle lover but commanding, too; a partner who didn't ask more from her than she could give. She could let down her guard with him. He understood her. Even if he was blinded by Maggie Morgan of the Furies.

"It is a good thing. You're wonderful," she said, then took a deep breath and surprised herself. "In fact, if I could have another son, I would want him to be Amish, just like you."

Gil blushed and poured two glasses of cold borage tea.

"Isn't this nice, Maggie?"

"It is."

"Wouldn't you like this moment to go on and on, and on and on, forever?"

Gil looked deep into her eyes and grabbed her right hand, tinkling the charms on her bracelet with his work-roughened fingers. He slid his thumb to her slippery palm and pressed. The pressure was sensual, insistent. He turned her palm upward, placed something nubby in it, and folded her fingers over it, then his over hers. He kissed her hand and then her lips and she didn't care who saw. Tomorrow she'd be gone.

He unfolded her hand so she could look at her gift: a gold symbol resembling a musical clef sign.

"The symbol for 'ohm,' the universal sound, the sound we make during meditation, the sound that encompasses all other sounds, in every language," he explained. "It's the sound I always thought you expressed when you sang from your heart. Transcendent."

The charm sparkled in her palm like Venus in the night sky.

"I want you to always remember our night in the meditation room. The night you changed my life."

He kissed her again and she folded into him. Folded into the moment.

"I want a commitment, Maggie," he said simply. "I don't want you to leave. I love you, and I want to marry you."

+++

Frances cracked open a bottle of merlot that she'd been given for a particularly accurate tarot reading. She didn't usually accept gifts from clients who got positive readings. It was a slippery slope; giving positive results was all about ego, not accuracy. Would someone exact revenge on her if she was wrong, or if she warned of danger ahead? But, in this case, it would have been more hurtful to return the bottle, so she kept it in case of emergencies.

And now Frances uncorked the bottle in her cozy magical cottage to celebrate the birth of the Karma Community's labyrinth. She poured out a bit in three jelly jars, hoping that Aaron would show up so she could fill the fourth.

"Chin chin," she said, raising her glass.

"To life," Sage said.

"Salut," Sybylla added.

"To the labyrinth," they said in unison, then sipped the warm wine.

"We start tomorrow, right?" Sage asked while propping himself on Frances' well-worn futon.

"I hope so," Sybylla said. "Aaron wasn't too clear about it. He just said that he got Freddie to agree to it and he would worry about the details later."

She frowned slightly.

"Then he said, 'The devil is in those details, my love,' and he left."

Sybylla took another sip of wine.

"I'm sure it meant nothing," Frances said. "You know how he feels about Freddie."

Sybylla checked her cousin's demeanor for clues about Aaron. Whether it was good or not, she wanted to know if Frances was picking up on some negativity or complications ahead. But Frances was opaque.

"Frankly, I'm surprised Freddie agreed," Sybylla said. "You know the community hasn't been bringing in enough money."

"I told you not to worry," Frances said. "All it took was some good juju."

"And a lot of creative visualization," Sybylla added.

"Dude, I'm just going to admit it now," Sage said, taking another swig and grinning. "Sometimes I have no clue what you are talking about."

The two women put their heads closer and laughed, confirming their conspiracy.

"Well, you know about the good juju," Frances said. "You were there for the ritual."

"And I pad our checkbook balance just so Aaron feels better about things," Sybylla added.

"How much padding?" Sage asked.

Sybylla took a longer sip of the wine and let the tannins rest on her sun-chapped lips.

"Thousands?"

"How many thousands?"

Sybylla nibbled on a hangnail to play at stalling for time.

"Hundreds of thousands?"

"Dude!" Sage broke into a grin, a mirror image of Aaron. "That's insane!"

"I know the truth," Sybylla shrugged. "So does Aaron. We just want to create a more positive reality, the reality we want to manifest. Why look at lines and lines of red ink when you can change your perspective and feel more rich and powerful and confident in the now?"

Sage grabbed the bottle and held it up to the lamplight, checking to see how much wine was left.

"Whatever it takes, I guess. As long as we can build the labyrinth. Did Aaron say which layout to use?"

"No."

"Cool," he said. "Let's do the craziest one. Let's build a monster labyrinth with bungees and slip and slides—an extreme labyrinth, dude."

He wiggled his eyebrows to make Sybylla laugh. It worked.

"What's a slip and slide?" she asked, completely baffled.

"Dude—you really did grow up in a tree."

"A tree house," Frances said.

"Didn't you?" Sybylla asked. "Wasn't Maggie a hippie mom?"

"Not at all," Sage said while draining his glass of wine. "My mom was a hippie before she had me, but as soon as I was born, *wham*. She became a mom. Straight, straight, straight. She was totally strict with me. But I guess she had to be."

"Why is that?" Frances asked.

"It's not like I had a dad," he said, sneaking a look at Sybylla. "And who knows what kind of crap I inherited. I come from a long line of pretty serious addicts. Aaron, for sure, plus his dad was a drunk and his mother popped pills. Maggie's dad was a drunk, too. She said that's why she and Aaron really got each other, you know?"

"So Aaron's said," Sybylla said quietly. "That's why he formed the band. To get away from all that. To prove himself."

"That's why he's always searching for utopia," Frances said. "The band, the Karma Community, even rehab. He's always wanted a safe place to be himself and be with others."

"I never thought of it that way," Sybylla said, wondering how and where, exactly, Frances got her insights.

Sage held his glass high.

"To Aaron, wherever he is," he said cheerfully.

"To Aaron."

"To Aaron."

There was a knock on Frances' door.

"Aaron?" Sybylla said, brightening.

"Sorry to interrupt," Freddie said coolly as he opened the door. "But I was taking a walk on the grounds and I got disoriented and my cell phone doesn't work out here. Then I saw your light and here I am."

He sat down close to Sybylla and Frances filled the fourth glass with wine.

"Celebrating anything special?" he asked.

Frances shot him a look, searching for humor, or malice, or cluelessness.

"Well, the labyrinth, of course," Sybylla said innocently.

"Ah, the labyrinth," Freddie said while raising the glass to his lips. He drank and grimaced, then placed the glass on the floor. "The finest Ukrainian grapes, no doubt."

He put his hand on Sybylla's shoulder and gave a squeeze. "Aaron is taking my offer? Then we've got two things to celebrate—the creation of the labyrinth and the reunion of the Four Furies."

+++

Marriage.

Insane.

I can't marry Gil, Maggie thought as she walked in circles in the grove. *I can't stay at the Karma Community. And how could I take him back to Chicago with me? It would be like caging a robin or potting a perfectly fine wildflower.*

And yet, and yet.

Maggie stopped in her tracks. Her head was spinning as she stood perfectly still.

This was her third proposal.

The first came from Jerry, a desperate tactic to keep him out of Vietnam. She went through with it, but she never gave the marriage a chance. She became Aaron's lover and ran off with the Furies instead.

The second came when Sage was six and Maggie was safely tucked under Felix's wing. She was finding her groove then, attractive and happy to be sane and stable and employed creatively again even without the Four Furies. Her boyfriend, Richard, was on his way up—a yuppie—and in the Reagan era money was on the ascendant, too, even though Maggie didn't have much herself. Maggie liked Richard's bullshit and the perks of being attached to someone solidly successful. And for a while she wanted to marry him and live the charmed life that he promised.

But he didn't.

Then she didn't and he did.

They split.

She analyzed it for years.

She'd had relationships after Richard, of course. But she always saw through them, saw the end of each affair by the time the first dinner was ordered, knew exactly the downward arc of every relationship when it was just shooting off like a rocket.

And now Gil—Gilman Gorham, a farm boy who didn't care for rockets or fireworks, who had the soul of an angel and the heart of a poet.

Maggie couldn't see the arc of their relationship even now, but marriage was absolutely out of the question.

Maggie continued walking and didn't know where she was headed, although she knew for sure that the Karma Community was behind her.

Marriage—never again.

Besides, he was too nice. Nice, yes, almost an insult. He was in love with Maggie Morgan of the Four Furies, the wounded goddess with the voice of an angel.

But that wasn't her. Never was. She was always the shy girl full of self-doubt, no matter how successful she was. The one whose inhibitions made her retreat into silence or burst into inauthentic, inexplicable bravado. Aaron knew that. He saw her transform every night from ordinary Maggie to the queen of the stage. He taught her how to do it. He knew her flaws, her fears. Hell, he drew them out of her and pounced.

But Gil? He believed the myth. He didn't see the real woman in front of him.
Marriage. Insane.

+++

Gil sat on his porch waiting for Maggie to show up for dinner or bed. He was a patient man, but he felt that he was going to wait a long time for Maggie, and even longer for an answer.

He stepped out onto the path in front of his cabin and inspected the plants before pulling a few Hosta leaves from a rosette and picking some rose hips and Black-eyed Susans. He put them on his porch and brought out some candles and beach glass he'd collected during a vacation to Cape Cod. He added some maple leaves, cracked Lenten palms, and a bowl of water to the pile, then began arranging them into a temporary art piece.

The orange tabby, sensing Gil's signal, stepped onto the porch, sniffed the leaves, and settled down on the wooden bench.

He joined the cat and inspected his work in the quick dusk. Most of it would blow away by the morning, he knew, but it didn't matter, he thought. The present moment was all he would ever have.

Chapter 32

The Ghosts Are Gone

Aaron was working his way through the first album song by song. He dropped a line or two from "Broken Morning," forgot a verse of "I'm Yours," and played one too many lines of "Turning My Back on All That," one of his favorites. He played "Home Is Where You Are" like a dirge, then a sea chanty, then a bluegrass trifle.

He moved onto the second album, "The Garden of Earthly Delights," with looser fingers and a raspier voice.

The opener, a monster hit, was "No Time for This," an almost verbatim transcript of one of his fights with Maggie. Playing it was painful each time, especially this time, as he sang Maggie's lines as well as his, but the audience always loved it and it always brought out the feisty side of Maggie onstage. That only fired up Aaron even more.

The next few songs were quieter and moodier. The tension was still there, just like in their relationship, but the songs had a groove that just chugged along. He rocked through "Changing Time," rolled through "Savannah," and lost himself in "After That Night."

It was the first time he had played any of these songs straight.

He took a long sip of the herbal tea before launching into the third album, *Stars that Shoot and Fall*, the most difficult one. Expectations had been heavy on them at the time; while writing the songs Aaron felt that the entire world was watching him and Maggie, voyeurs on a very grand scale. They had to sell albums, fill seats, look like hell in photos, and party with celebrities, all of which pulled Aaron away from what he truly loved, the music.

He didn't want to feel these songs anymore.

Detach, Aaron. You've changed, and the ghosts are gone.

He started strumming the first song. He stopped and buried his head in his hands. He didn't know how long he sat like that, but when the pain of hesitation was too much, with shaking hands he began strumming again. The songs were tormented but brilliant.

One Great Mystery kicked off with "Thought the Last Time Would Be the Last Time," rose to its peak with "Balancing the Scales" and "Finding His Way" it crashed into "Running Reds" before winding down in a wordless extended jam.

On to *Phoenix*, the one finalized while Maggie was sleeping with Clark Kavanaugh. Each song stung of betrayal, even the love songs, even the sex song. He couldn't sing any of these and let his fingers pick out the melodies instead. Too close to the bone.

He launched into *Seize the Day*, recorded when the band was barely speaking to each other. The songs were good, but none of the sessions jelled. Finally, desperately, Aaron woke up Maggie in the early morning, shoved her into the car, and drove helter-skelter through the cliffside roads to the studio. She screamed the entire way. Aaron pushed her into the recording booth and played the backing tracks one by one. The adrenaline and rage and exhaustion and terror breathed new passion into her vocals and transformed a disappointing career ender into a scorching farewell.

No wonder why she slugged me.

After "Taos" and "Fading Fast" the Four Furies' catalog was complete.

He didn't know what to do.

He heard a rustle in the soft pine needles and wondered how many forest sounds he missed through the night.

"Maggie?" he said to the shadow that was materializing before him.

"Yes."

"Maggie," he said, reaching out his hand to the one woman who could save the Karma Community. "I need you."

+++

Maggie didn't move. She was stiff and damp from a night in the open air, circling around the Karma Community's grounds freely. She'd tramped over the

175

land all night, from moonrise to pink sunrise, feeling as uninhibited and safe, for once. In California, she'd lost her anonymity and felt restricted by her fame. Then, in Chicago, she was hemmed in by her suburban yard, Sage, and normality. Out here in the Karma Community she was free again. Free to dabble, to play, to unwind, to stretch out.

She took Aaron's hand.

He cupped her fingers with both hands and brought them to his mouth, brushing her fingertips along his chapped lips, bristly whiskers, and then, ever so lightly, the tip of his tongue.

His touch sent a jolt of electricity through her weary body and woke up each atom and charged up all of the spaces between them. It was as if he'd offered her the hit of acid that bonded them thirty years ago. But this wasn't a drug.

"Damn you, Aaron," she whispered.

"I am damned," he rasped, the long night having taken its toll. "Dammed with you. Damned without you."

Maggie knelt and kissed Aaron as if he was the juiciest fruit she just had to have, then straddled him, the man she'd loved and feared and hated and adored her entire adult life. She ran her hands along his shoulders, down his scarred arms, then pushed him into the soft pine needles scattered on the damp dirt, fully in control of this old man who'd once been her young lover. The air felt clean and dirty at the same time—Aaron's musk and the clean pine needles mixed to smell earthy, primeval.

"Damn you, Aaron," she said as she rocked her hips onto his and held his shoulders firmly to the forest floor. The soft light hid their crow's feet and sags, new features on each other's bodies they'd once known as well as their own. She kissed him again, then ran her tongue down his stubbly chin, sinewy neck and past the fading guitar tattoo on his pec. She tugged at the leather cord strewn around his neck and he moaned as he slipped his hands under her T-shirt to her breasts.

"I need you," he whispered. "Only you."

She felt him harden between her legs and his eyes lit up as she ground into him.

"You old dog," she teased, then rolled off of him, trying to control her breath.

He was splayed on the ground, helpless and excited.

"Maggie. It's only ever been you. Come back."

Maggie brushed back her mussed hair and smoothed out her shirt.

"Why?"

"Because we're great together. The best."

Maggie laughed.

"We're the best when we're not the worst."

"Maggie," he said, his eyes sparkling, grinning now. "Come back to me and make this all right again."

He crawled to her like a panther on all fours and she laughed again.

"Do you want me to beg?"

"Yes."

"Then I'm begging you. Come back to me."

He stretched out to her again and cupped her breast in his hand as his other hand slid along her tight jeans encasing her thighs.

"Please," he whispered into her ear, letting his breath linger on her neck. "I still love you."

"We can't. Shouldn't."

"Come back to me," he said as he ran his tongue down her neck and began peeling off her clothes.

"Damn you," she said as he sucked on her nipple.

"Damn," she said as he pushed into her, old lovers reborn anew.

+++

As the sun rose, Frances woke Sage and Sybylla, both of whom crashed in her cabin after Freddie left. They knocked on Gil's door and after pulling on yesterday's clothes, he joined them in the shed, where they collected some shovels, string, a rake, and a bucket. The foursome walked over the hill to the back field, ready to break ground for the labyrinth.

As they reached the top of the hill, they were greeted by Aaron and Maggie, blushing and ecstatic, horrified and ashamed.

Chapter 33

The Signs Had Been There All Along

Sybylla lay perfectly still on the smooth, cool floor of the meditation room. Still was the wrong word, perhaps, because her body was in motion. Her head throbbed and her pulse could be seen clearly at her throat and temple. Her brain, although tired from lack of good sleep, scrambled to make sense of her life. She shifted her body to make full contact with the floor, anxious to feel Mother Earth's support.

Frances' hands floated above her cousin, waving the negative energy out of her body so that it could be released into the ether.

"Breathe, Sybylla," she counseled. "Our universal mother hasn't abandoned you, and she never will."

Sybylla whimpered and shut her eyes to the physical world.

The past day had been horrible. After Sybylla's discovery of—the whole world's discovery of—Aaron's betrayal with Maggie, Sybylla had kicked her husband out of their bedroom and shut the door on him with tears and shouts. They'd never fought like this; Sybylla couldn't even remember when they'd even raised their voices to each other in anger. There had never been a need to—there was nothing that a rational conversation, or a prayer, or sex couldn't solve.

Until that moment on the hill. *How could I have been so blind? Why didn't I see that Maggie was only here to win him back? Why couldn't I see that Aaron was tempted?*

The questions never ended, but she knew the answers.

Sybylla had spent the past day shut up in her room, surrounded by her favorite things—her books, charms, and plants. But without Aaron, they mocked her, each one holding a happier memory than the one she was creating.

Aaron had come to her door, of course. But he always knocked and waited for her permission to enter. She never gave it. She barely had the strength to tell him no. But she did.

She had no idea where he had spent the day. She knew that the eyes of the Karma Community were focused on him, as always, so she would have heard if Aaron had been taken in by Maggie, who was most likely cast out by Gil, another person who didn't deserve this treatment. No, Aaron was probably with Sage, his partner in crime, the center of Aaron's new world. His son.

As Sybylla lay in bed, wounded worse than she ever thought was possible, she cataloged all of Aaron's misdeeds. He was messy, at times. He was curt with her, at times. He extended himself too much, too, so that he was too busy fixing other people's problems and didn't have enough time for himself, or her. It hurt her when she caught herself smiling, unconsciously, when she thought about Aaron lying on their bed and purring like a cat while she scratched his back, endlessly devoted.

I hate him.

The strange thing, though, is that she saw everything transpire before it did but was blind to it. She had felt Aaron and Maggie's attraction; it was undeniable, even to the innocent third party in their triangle. The way they said hello in passing, didn't that say something? The way Aaron's tone softened when he talked about Maggie, or when he defended her unreasonably, surely had been a tip off. The way Aaron and Maggie avoided shedding light on their growing relationship so that they could get away with it. The signs had been there all along, but she hadn't allowed herself to read them.

Had Frances?

That thought made Sybylla feel more helpless and more alone.

If Frances had seen it coming, then why wouldn't she have warned me? Maybe I could have stopped it.

She bit her fingernail, fixated on that thought.

Unless I couldn't have stopped it. Unless it was fated, and it transcended time and place. Unless Maggie is Aaron's soul mate, not me.

Chapter 34

The Full Circle

"I want to welcome everyone to this reconciliation circle," Duncan Maguire told the group. "And I thank you for coming."

Shifrah circled the circle while waving white sage smoke over the participants.

"I know this hasn't been easy for all of you, but I want you to know that all of your feelings are honored here, no matter how negative or ugly they may be, because all feelings are valid as long as they are honest," he continued.

I honestly don't want to be here, Maggie thought. *Can we honor that?*

"Please be honest and respectful of each other, because we're going to be doing some really heavy work here," Duncan continued. "I don't want any of you to start making accusations or shut down. While this process can get messy sometimes, it will benefit all of us—perhaps not today, perhaps not next year—but what we discuss in this group is speaking truth to power and ultimately it will affect you and ultimately it will last an eternity. I also want to remind you that this circle is sacred, but you already know that."

Duncan smiled and one by one looked everyone in the eye.

"Let's begin. I would like everyone to put a word into the circle."

"Integrity," Shifrah said.

"Confusion."

"Betrayal."

"Family."

"Healing."

"Circle."

Pause. All eyes turned toward Aaron and Maggie.

Maggie closed her eyes.

"Wholeness."

All eyes turned to Aaron.

"Love," he said quietly.

Maggie warmed and felt the fuzz on her arms tingle.

Sybylla, sitting directly across from her husband, reached for a faded bandana and blinked back tears.

Aaron tensed his shoulders, then let them drop.

Duncan picked up a stick that lay in front of him. Metal cord snaked up it, then wrapped around a quartz crystal and a turkey feather at the tip. He held it with both hands, showing it off to the others, then spoke.

"This is the talking stick. Whoever holds it can speak; everyone else must listen. When everyone has had his or her turn, we'll be able to dialog freely."

He handed it to Sybylla, who sat to his right. She sighed deeply.

"This has been the worst week of my life," she began, her brown eyes pooling with tears. "My husband betrayed me and he did so in front of my friends and family. I don't even have anywhere to go! This is my home, this is my world, and you two had to destroy it."

She stared full strength at Maggie, then at Aaron, then took a long drink of borage tea, which Frances had suggested she take in large quantities, along with lemon balm and oat straw infusions.

"And I don't understand why," she said with a wail in her voice. "Maggie, I welcomed you here and made you as comfortable as possible. And Aaron—I have done nothing but love you, support you, and heal you. I thought that was enough, but I guess I was wrong."

She took another drink of tea while Maggie felt guilt creep up on her.

"I've done a lot of thinking and I just can't understand why you did this, Aaron, why you had to ruin what we had. All I can think of is that you're selfish or that you never loved me. Maybe we shouldn't have gotten married."

She looked at him long and hard. His fists were clenched and he flattened them, then shoved them in his back pockets and sat on them. He avoided her eyes.

"Why wasn't my love enough?"

Sybylla finally broke down in sobs.

"Why am *I* not enough?"

181

She buried her face in the bandana, muffling her pain.

Duncan rubbed her back as she cried. She trembled and gulped for air, no longer able to defy her fears.

Take a pill and a long nap, Sybylla, Maggie thought. *You shouldn't get so worked up over this. When you live with Aaron, you have to cope with a lot of betrayal, a lot of questions.*

When Sybylla regained at least some composure, she handed the talking stick to Gil.

"Sybylla, I'm sad to see you so unhappy," he said with brotherly concern. "I've witnessed your life with Aaron almost as soon as it began, and I know how happy you were, and I'm sorry—for many reasons—that it's hitting a rough patch."

He cleared his throat.

"Maggie," he said quietly, his eyes finally meeting hers.

"I forgive you."

Her eyes lowered, while his lingered.

"I love you and I still want to marry you. I've known since I first met you— first heard you—that you were my perfect woman. I still think so, even if you don't see it right now. I have faith that you will see it."

He wouldn't take his eyes off Maggie as his face flushed under the scrutiny of the room.

He turned to Aaron.

"Aaron, you are still my friend."

Aaron exhaled.

"I'm trying to forgive you. But it's tough. Really tough. I know you and Maggie have a ton to work out, so I will give you the time and space you need to do it. I want Maggie to come back to me, but it must be her choice made of her own free will."

Maggie smiled, but still didn't dare to look at Gil. She kept her eyes locked on a knot in the pine floor that looked like an Irish harp riding a wave.

Damn right it'll be my choice.

Gil ran his hand over his scraggly chin and cleared his throat.

"Sage, I don't know what you're feeling right now, but I would like to be your friend, and I would be honored to be your stepfather."

Sage laughed, then grinned.

"It would be like being a stepfather to Sean Lennon. You have such an incredible musical lineage. I hope you appreciate it."

Maggie, Aaron, and Sage exchanged smiles, the royal family at the center of their court.

182

"I hope you keep drumming," Gil added.

Maggie beamed, then mouthed the words "thank you" to Gil. Their eyes caught, and she turned crimson.

He handed the talking stick to Shifrah.

"I don't know where to begin."

She looked at everyone in the circle, taking stock of the group's energy.

"I would like to honor all of you here. Sybylla, you are such a gentle, wise, and trusting creature. I hope that this situation doesn't change your essential nature. That is your true self. Treasure it."

Sybylla managed a smile, one without conviction.

"You asked why your love isn't enough. Sybylla, Aaron is a wounded man. He is an addict. Even if he doesn't smoke dope, or drink alcohol, he is still an addict. He may be a sex addict, in fact. Perhaps even a chaos addict. Your love will never heal him, Sybylla, it will never be enough."

Sybylla cried into her bandana, her abdomen spasming.

"It's the truth, Sybylla, a hard truth. I've known Aaron a long time. I knew him when he was abusing drugs. I saw how hard he fought to get off them. And I'm proud of his progress. But I was never so proud of him as I was on your wedding day. I'd never seen him happier. And I'd never seen him take such a great leap of faith as his marriage to you. He put everything on the line for you, Sybylla, something he'd never done before for anyone else. Is that enough for you?"

Sybylla buried her face in her hands.

"I don't know what will happen next, Sybylla, but I do know that Aaron loves you very much."

Shifrah turned to Maggie, then changed her mind and turned back to Sybylla.

"Marriage isn't easy, sweetheart. Use this crisis to discover parts of yourself that you never knew you had. It's a magical opportunity for self-exploration. It might be just what you need."

Sybylla sniffled.

Shifrah handed the talking stick to Maggie.

She took a deep breath.

How honest should I be?

She took another deep breath while making her decision.

"This isn't easy for me," she said quietly, letting the room wait for her.

"Gil, thank you. I don't know what you see in me—especially after this week."

She dropped her eyes to her lap and took another breath.

"Sybylla, I understand how you feel more than you realize."

Sybylla shot daggers at her, but Maggie knew she deserved her hatred.

"Although Aaron and I were together for ten years, it was never an easy relationship. At first I was hurt by what I thought were his constant betrayals. We were so in love in the beginning that I couldn't imagine being with anyone else and I couldn't bear the thought of Aaron with some other woman. But now, with hindsight, I understand him a little more. I was naïve to think that Aaron could be my entire world, that the Four Furies could be my entire world. I was naïve to think that if I was the perfect girlfriend that Aaron would love me and be faithful.

"But cheating and escaping was easy, you know? Easy for him, if you consider our lifestyle. And easy for me, too, since I could blame Aaron for all of our problems, just because he was the one with the most visible issues. The bad boy. The lightning rod. But now, so many years later, I'm sorry that I did put all of the blame on him."

She took a deep breath as Sybylla's tears dried.

"I had lovers, of course, but that wasn't the answer. I was asking Aaron for something that he couldn't give. He never promised it, either. It was never mine."

She closed her eyes and sat still for a moment, fully aware of her hold on the circle.

"It reminds me of a song I can't get out of my head lately."

She took a deep breath.

"*I just had to know,*" she sang, her voice as clear and unaffected as the early days of the Furies.

"I had to take a look
Shine a light on demons
Fear my feelings
Let all reason go.
Don't say no.
Pandora.
I just unleashed a blazing star
I had to take it too far
Tumble over the edge
Say farewell to my friends
Live with the scars.
My rebel heart.
Pandora.
Pandora."

The room was stunned, silenced by the singing voice of Maggie Morgan, formerly of the legendary Four Furies. The same Maggie Morgan who hadn't sung since leaving the Furies two decades ago. Refused to. Said it wasn't possible. Yet there is was. The voice that seduced millions, released. Unleashed.

"Wow," Duncan said, speaking for the group. "Just wow."

"I wrote that," she admitted. "But I've never sung it for anyone, and we certainly never recorded it. Aaron was the songwriter, not me. But it's been running through my mind for years. Years. And it says everything I've ever wanted to say."

She turned to Aaron, who sat just inches away from her.

"Aaron, I forgive you."

He swallowed hard and swept his hand across his brow.

She handed him the talking stick and they exchanged grim smiles.

Aaron cleared his throat and reached for the lapis around his neck, then sighed.

"I've been in a lot of these reconciliation circles, especially when I was in recovery, but this one is the hardest."

He shifted on the floor and resettled in place.

"Gil, my friend, I'm sorry that we both love the same woman."

He took a deep breath and closed his eyes. He turned toward his wife and clasped his hands around his knees.

"I'm sorry that I hurt you, Sybylla. If I could take away your hurt, I would move heaven and earth to do it."

He stretched out his legs in front of him, his skin showing through the rip in his jeans.

"Do I owe you an explanation? You seem to want one. I don't know that I have one. But you can be damned sure that I didn't make love to Maggie because I'm a sex addict. I hate labels. I refuse to be labeled," he spat.

He reached toward Sage's cigarettes, then lit one and held it close to his lips, before rubbing the dent in his nose with his calloused index finger.

"I am what I am, Syb, take it or leave it. I was on this earth for almost sixty years before I even met you. I was around the world a few times before you were born, and I've been with more women than you can imagine."

Sybylla turned scarlet.

"I'm not saying this to hurt you, but to get you to understand that I had a life that I fully lived. I am a man. I am an artist. I am a rebel, at heart."

"You're a husband, too," Sybylla shot back.

"Sybylla, please," Duncan cautioned, hushing her. "You'll have your turn again."

185

"It doesn't matter, Duncan. She's right. I'm a husband, too—I'm Sybylla's husband. And I don't know that I should be."

His words hung in the air.

He took a deep drag on his cigarette.

"I hate labels, I hate rules, I hate being told that I can't do something. I've been fighting against rules my whole life. There are so many different ways to be, you know? Why can't I just be myself?"

He inhaled his cigarette and let the smoke out in a steady stream that shot through the sunlight filtering in from the south. The smoke curled at the ends, then disappeared.

"Marriage is only one kind of relationship. There are so many others. Marriage is too idealized by society, and it's unnatural. As if saying vows will make a relationship right or wrong. That's horseshit."

Sybylla shook her head at him and scowled, stifling another outburst.

"That doesn't mean that I don't love you, Syb, or that I don't take our marriage vows seriously," he said, his eyes boring into her. "I do. But I don't think I'm the marrying kind."

Sybylla balled up the bandana and threw it at him.

"How can you do this to me?"

Aaron stubbed out his smoke in a chipped tea cup.

"I'm not doing anything to you. Life is complicated. It seems very simple when your whole world exists here at the Karma Community, where everything is pretty and safe, but the real world is complicated, and real people are even worse. I'm an old man, Syb. I have a son, I have an ex, I have talent, and fuck I'm ambitious. I went through hell because I lost all of that, you know that. Can you understand why I want to reunite with my family? My *family*, Syb. This is a twenty-year-old wound. It has nothing to do with you. I love you, but it has absolutely nothing to do with you."

He looked out the window and Maggie placed her hand on his shoulder.

"I'm fucked up, Syb. You should run away from me as fast as you can."

Sybylla crumpled up into a ball. Aaron kept looking out the window. When he felt strong enough, he handed the talking stick to Sage.

"I'm blown away by this. Are you and mom getting back together?"

Maggie looked at Aaron, whose eyes fell to the floor. When no answer was forthcoming, Sage lit a Marlboro.

"That's crazy. Crazy in a good way. It's just, I mean, I can't imagine it. I mean, I can imagine it. It's all I thought about as a kid. You know, I'd come up with these wild schemes to get you guys back together, just kid stuff, you know?"

Aaron laughed.

Sage grinned.

"Rock and roll, dude."

He handed the talking stick to Frances. She looked around the room, checked out each person's aura, then sat silently until she felt centered.

"I'm sorry that all of this happened, Sybylla," she said simply. "But I think we need to make room for Maggie."

Chapter 35

Home Sweet Home Part 1

Maggie was slightly headachy as she turned the key in the lock of the back door of her Oak Park home for the first time in weeks.

"Well, this is it," she said, trepidation and excitement mingling in her voice. "Home sweet home."

"Sweet," Sage said, rushing past her and into the dim dining room. Piles of mail were stacked up on the cherry wood table, thanks to Keith. Her devoted assistant had also watered the plants while she'd been gone, she noticed as she walked through the house, but other than that, nothing had changed since she'd left after Felix's funeral. Dishes were stacked on the drying rack; the multiple remotes were tumbled into a wicker basket next to the couch; the heavy antique furniture still sat in their well-worn grooves; the family photos were still poised on the shelves and end tables amid the bric-a-brac.

Aaron took it all in, room by room, touching each piece of furniture, opening cupboards to scrutinize labels, inspecting knickknacks, witnessing Maggie's love of order. He stopped at a painting of a still life on a heavy wooden table, a dead pheasant slung next to a platter laden with squash, potatoes, and bread.

"Wasn't this in your parents' house?"

"You remember that?" Maggie asked, genuinely surprised.

"How could I forget? Your old man made me feel just like that bird when I told him I was in love with his daughter. I'll always remember Old Joe saying,

'But she's married to another young man, and he has a job.' As if picking up a paycheck has anything to do with love. As if I didn't deserve you because I wasn't willing to conform to some bullshit system he lived and breathed and ate up and farted out."

Aaron raked his hands through his hair, aware of being surrounded by a load of bad memories.

"Isn't that the old man's chair?

Maggie walked toward him and took his hand.

"It is. Almost everything in this room was theirs. I didn't know what to do with it when they died, so that's that."

"That's that," Aaron said, encircling her in his arms. "That's that, plus a lot of bad fucking memories."

He clinched her even tighter.

"Whoa, weird," Sage said as he entered the room. "I'm gonna have to get used to you being together."

Aaron grinned while Maggie blushed, laughing off her embarrassment.

"I'm starving. What's for lunch?"

Sage picked up the phone, ordered some pizza, turned on the TV, and shut out his parents.

+++

Sybylla retreated to her room. She pulled the I Ching from the shelf and fished three pennies from an old coin dish. She threw them, then checked out their configuration in the book. "The Clinging. Cling to what is true and right," it counseled.

Easy for you to say. I don't know what's true and right anymore. If I did, I'd be clinging to it for dear life.

She threw the coins again. No change.

Stuck.

She went over to her astrology books and pulled out her chart, as well as Aaron's. She knew them like the back of her hand, but she wanted to be sure.

His moon is on my Jupiter. My midheaven is on his sun. I open him up, he is my destiny.

She reached for her mythology book and opened to a random page, something she liked to do to find synchronicities. She opened to the story of Hera, Zeus' wife, the protector of marriage and married women. Hera was a jealous thing, but then, Zeus was always seducing every woman in his tracks.

Oh Aaron. Will we ever be happy again?

+++

"I can't tell you the last time I had real pizza."

Aaron's face drew down, silently, as he chewed.

"I can't say that I miss that tofu shit, dude," Sage said. "There's nothing like the real thing."

Aaron took another bite and closed his eyes.

"The best pizza in the world is at Ray's in Hell's Kitchen. 1984. Not a nice neighborhood. I wasn't eating much in those days, but when I did, that was it for me."

"You miss it, hey?"

"I've had a good life," Aaron said, taking another bite. "It's been fucked up, but it's been great."

Father and son chewed in silence.

"You miss Sybylla?"

Aaron filled a glass with water and grabbed some ice cubes from the freezer.

"We've only been gone a few hours."

"Did you miss mom?"

"Yes."

Sage lifted the pizza box top and checked the rest of the pie.

"Did you miss me?"

"Yes."

"But you didn't really know me, you know."

"I know. That's what I missed. I wondered who you were."

Sage kicked the breakfast bar with his foot.

"And?"

"And I'm getting to know you."

"And?"

"And what?"

"And are we going to be a family now? Are you moving in?"

"Maggie and I haven't discussed that yet. One step at a time."

"Do I have a say in it?"

Their eyes locked.

"I mean, if you move in, that affects me, too. If you want to be my dad, that's something I've got to think about."

"Haven't I been a dad to you this summer?"

"Yes," Sage said, drawing out the word. "But that's different. This is real."

"And our time together at the Karma Community was fake?"

"No, but it wasn't all that real. It's easy to live at the Karma Community, you know?"

"It is. That's the point. Create a safe space to bring out a person's best."

"Okay, whatever. But if you want to move in here and be my dad or whatever, I think I should have a say in that."

"Well, I'm going to have to adjust to it, too. I haven't lived in a regular house in years. And I don't know if I can be domesticated."

Maggie walked in, fresh from a shower and wrapped in a thick white terry robe.

"Our first meal as a family," she said, lifting the pizza box top. "And it's pizza? Eaten standing up?"

"New York style," Aaron said, hoping to break the tension. He walked toward her and rubbed her shoulders, then pulled her to his side.

"Aaron was telling me all about how screwed up he was," Sage said. "You know, the heroin and money problems and all that stuff. So I guess that my issues aren't so bad. You know, in comparison to being a junkie and a deadbeat dad."

Maggie sighed. "I guess you're still finding yourself."

Sage clicked through the channels of the kitchen-counter TV.

"Maybe that's why you felt so comfortable at the Karma Community, Sage," Aaron said, trying to pull his family together again.

"Yeah, those people aren't doing anything either," Sage said, full of defiance and self-pity. "They're stuck, just like me."

Maggie took a bite of pizza, tired of another conversation about Sage's lack of direction.

"Doing something positive would help you get unstuck, you know," she said. "It would take you out of yourself, make you realize that there are a lot of people out there who have a lot less than you and they're doing a lot more with it."

"Enough with the lecture," he said, turning up the volume of the TV.

"Something to think about," Maggie snapped.

"The Karma Community doesn't do charity stuff like that, so why should I?" Sage spat back.

"Hey, hey, hey," Aaron said. "We do—they do—some stuff like that, Sage. We offer some scholarships and work-study programs for people who can't afford the tuition. And we've done some fundraising things for other organizations."

Maggie grimaced.

"But mostly it's just rich white people navel gazing and being totally self-absorbed," she said. "Chanting their way to happiness."

"Is that what you did there?" Aaron retorted, his anger rising to Maggie's challenge.

"Pretty much."

Her words hung in the air, smothering the noise from the TV.

"Sometimes you have to heal yourself before you can heal the world," Aaron said. "Part of the problem in the seventies is that we were so fucked up as individuals that we offered fucked-up solutions to society's problems."

Sage clicked through more channels, sneaking glances at his parents.

"Screwed up," he said. "Watch your language in this house or mom will be all over you."

Maggie glared at him.

He turned off the TV and stomped up the stairs to his room.

+++

Frederick propped his feet up on the desk in the office, half bemused, half frustrated. He'd spent the morning with Gil, the most rational person in the Karma Community at the moment, trying to make sense of its spreadsheets. No matter how hard he'd tried to convince the business office—or what passed for the business office at the Karma Community—to get organized, he'd always been thwarted.

No wonder why these people ended up here. They'd never make it in the real world. They're still working on the barter system and saving pennies under their mattresses.

He looked up at a poster of a bird in flight, with a quote from Ralph Waldo Emerson written in calligraphy below it.

"I'm sorry I can't be of much help to you," Gil said, sincerely. "But I try not to have anything to do with money. I just focus on my artwork, and Aaron and Sybylla and Frances handle the rest."

"Well, they're out of commission at the moment, so you'll have to step up and help me. This could be a real opportunity for you, actually. I need someone to help me work with Aaron. Well, that's assuming he's coming back."

He picked up the labyrinth proposal.

"How much do you know about this?"

"A little. I know that they've invested a lot of their hopes in it."

Freddie leafed through it. *God, what amateurs. This thing will cost less than lunch, and they're worried about it. But at least they're seeking my approval.*

It's barely worth my time, but they're afraid to do anything without my consent. Besides, I could own the Four Furies when Aaron and Maggie get back together.

"Bah."

Frederick tossed the spreadsheets onto the desk and picked up the manila envelope that he knew would brighten his mood. It had been a while since he'd had background checks conducted on the Karma Community's core staff, but he always liked to know more about others than they knew about him. He always got a chuckle out of it, too.

Aaron Edward Fields. Not much new to report, Frederick saw. Property, none. Car loans, none. Investments, a few—a few hundred dollars in an eco-friendly mutual fund, some CDs drawing very little interest. Income, almost nil. Taxes owed—very little at this point, thanks to a Brooklyn-based accountant who owed Aaron a favor after many years and helped clean things up with the IRS.

An arrest in Jackson, Nevada. Drug charges littered across California, then the Midwest, then the Southwest. Obscenity charges threatened after that filthy song with him and Maggie having sex in the background. Sixty days in the county jail in Faulkton, South Dakota. Resisting arrest in Washington, D.C. Driver's license revocation. Another arrest in Lexington, Kentucky. Disturbing the peace in Seaside Bay, Florida. Court-ordered rehab in the Quad Cities.

Missing from the report was what was rightfully Aaron's—royalties, commissions, profits from a healthy back catalog, money streaming in from ads and videos and concerts. All of that was lost when Aaron had been lost, when he signed away the rights to this and that to make all of his problems go away.

The Four Furies' fortune was all gone.

Sage Sequoia Morgan-Fields. This report was new to Frederick. Two credit cards, a small car loan, no real estate, portfolio, or significant income. No trust fund, allowance, or inheritance.

A dry stone.

Sybylla Blair Pinckney Fields. No credit cards, car, real estate, investments, or debt. A small savings account that hadn't been active in years. Cited for resisting arrest in Washington, D.C.

Frances Eleanor Blair. No credit cards, no property, no debt. *No change there*, Frederick thought. Resisting arrest in Madison. Trespassing in Madison. Vandalism in Baraboo. Resisting arrest in Washington, D.C. Petty stuff, political stuff.

What a waste, Freddie muttered. *Pawns. They own nothing, they have nothing to bargain with. Just the clothes on their backs and their tarot cards and drums. Their feelings. Their intentions.*

He turned to the report that intrigued him the most, the one that was surprisingly thick.

Margaret Mary O'Donnell Morgan. Steadily employed at Felix Ingles Fellows II Designs. Mortgage, yes, on her primary residence in Oak Park, Illinois. Taxes paid up. A stake in the Diana Fund; an investor in Mother Lee's Day Care Center and Spotlight Dance Studio in Chicago. A big donor to Early Literacy Chicago, Planned Parenthood, Young Artists Group, and St. Dymphna's Community Mental Health Clinic.

Missing, as well, was any sign of the Four Furies. No royalties, no payments, no income.

Maggie, dear Maggie, nice, respectable, middle-class Maggie. You should have managed the band, not Aaron. Why did you hand over control to someone who has no need for money?

He cast the report aside.

"Where's Maggie?" he asked, looking up from the report.

"I wish I knew," Gil said sadly.

"I guess you didn't talk much," Frederick leered.

Gil hesitated.

"Come on. What does it matter now? She's gone."

Gil shifted in his chair.

"So? Just pillow talk between you two?"

Gil folded his hands together, trying to keep poised.

"We talked about the Four Furies a lot."

"Oh?" Frederick said, clearly pleased. "Fondly? Were those happy times for her?"

"I guess. I think that seeing Aaron again brought back a lot of memories and she probably needed someone safe to talk to. Besides, I'm a fan."

"But you were more than that to her, weren't you?" Frederick said, moving closer toward his prey. "You were lovers, no? You had a 'connection,' as they would say here."

"I thought we did," Gil said, his voice trailing away.

"And you want her back, right?"

"If that's the right thing to do. I wouldn't want to push her into anything."

"And the Four Furies? Wouldn't you love to hear them again?"

"Of course," Gil said, unable to hide his enthusiasm. "And I'm not the only one. You saw the fans on the driveway. All hell would break loose if the Furies got back together."

Frederick put his hands on Gil's shoulders.

"Then help me find Maggie."

Chapter 36

Home Sweet Home Part 2

Aaron flicked on the old flashlight, unable to stand up straight in the attic of Maggie's Tudor cottage. The small crawl space was stuffed with boxes, but Maggie, unsurprisingly, had arranged them neatly.

He shone the beam on one stack of boxes, then walked toward them. Maggie had marked each one with her label-maker: "mom's floral china," "mom's blue china," "mom's crystal," and more. Aaron moved to the next stack: "linen," "early watercolors," "sheet music," and "misc. candlesticks and vases" the plastic strips announced.

He moved through more boxes, the detritus of Maggie's life, Sage's childhood, and her parents' history. In the back corner, he found the boxes he had a hunch Maggie had held onto: "Furies: albums," "Furies: '73 tour," "Furies: clothes," "Furies: gifts," "Furies: awards," "Furies: bootlegs and masters," "Furies: posters," "Furies: photos." He zeroed in on one that he was surprised she'd kept: "Furies: Aaron."

He shoved the others aside, lit a cigarette that sparked up some dust motes, and broke the seal of the crumbling packing tape with his thumbnail.

Aaron opened the box to find his seventeen-year-old self staring back at him, with a shiny, tall pompadour and an acoustic guitar slung over his shoulder, his best scowl defacing his good looks. He was skinny, but he had presence.

"Eat your heart out, Ricky Nelson," he said to the photo.

196

He took another drag on his cigarette and dove back into the box. Guitar picks. Love letters to Maggie. His beloved spaniel's collar. Boy Scout badges. His baby book. His favorite pipe.

Aaron stubbed his cigarette on a wood beam, then flicked it onto a tuft of faded pink insulation. A striped spider walked along the toe of his work boot, then hid among its laces. Aaron left it there. He pulled out a photo of him as a pre-teen, his arms around his parents' shoulders, a Mustang in the background. Another photo, of Aaron and his gang assembled on the steps of the town library, named for his grandfather. Yet another snapshot of an eight-year-old Aaron, learning to ice skate on the pond marking the land that his mother's family had owned since they stole it from the Mohegans.

"Mayflower bores," Aaron said bitterly, and lit another smoke. "Damn judges and bankers and teachers and puritans."

He lifted his father's death notice, then tossed it back in the box.

"My whole damn life I've been trying to get away from you. How was I supposed to be myself when the whole damn town was the damn Fields family?"

He kicked the box into the pile of Furies' debris, then opened one final box.

"Furies: me," the label read.

Giant clouds of lace. Mother of pearl hair combs. Slinky suede boots with the heels that kicked him in his final humiliation. Her own watercolors of their beach house. A tambourine with a tangle of ribbons. A valentine he'd made out of a lace handkerchief pasted onto a sheet of music, which he mailed to her while she was waiting in Reno for her divorce. Cocktail napkins from the Chateau Marmont, the Whiskey A Go Go, Max's Kansas City. A pack of matches from the Russian Tea Room. A double-exposed Polaroid of Maggie vamping on their private plane. A mash note to Pete. A home pregnancy test kit.

All of it still smelled like Maggie Morgan of the Four Furies. Roses. Musk. Sandalwood.

He held the box and shook it to hear the jangle of what he knew would be in there.

He reached in and pulled out the Elsa Peretti necklace Clark Kavanaugh had sent to her after their affair.

"Damn Clark." He threw Maggie's betrayal across the attic into a puff of insulation.

He reached in again and found the sterling silver charm bracelet that became Maggie's trademark. It was heavier than he'd remembered, heavier than her current gold charm bracelet, but its weight held all of Maggie's history with the Four Furies. The heart charm he'd given to her when they were creating the band in Colorado. A globe, a piano. Faith, hope, and charity. The Eiffel Tower. "Love" accented with a ruby. Trinkets and tokens of their life on the road so that they'd always remember it.

Aaron sat in the dust and held the charms to his chest for a very long time.

+++

The ants were in Sage's legs again.

Lying on his bed, curtains shutting out the noontime sun, the ants prickled his legs and burned his toes. He tried to whisk them off, but his shoulders were too tight. A pill or a joint would settle him down.

He stared at the ceiling for a long, long time.

What would Frances do? he dared to wonder.

He stared at the ceiling some more, then took a deep breath and shoved himself off the bed. He pulled a pillow with him, flattened it on the floor, and after a few attempts he managed to get into a decent shoulder stand, just as he learned to do in yoga class at the Karma Community.

His bedroom, now upside down, revealed itself in a completely new way. Now, the drum kit seemed to hang from the ceiling. The TV set floated in mid-air, and the heap of clothes on the floor turned into a dark cloud.

The blood drained from Sage's toes, so he wiggled them and realigned himself.

"Ohm," he said softly, articulating all of the sounds in the universe.

"Ohm," he continued after a deep, cleansing breath.

His heartbeat slowed, the space between his shoulder blades opened, and his mind stilled.

He lowered his feet behind his head, into the plow position, stretching his hamstrings. He breathed in for seven counts, exhaled for twelve. He inhaled for nine, exhaled for fourteen.

I can do this, he thought between breaths. *I am doing this.*

He kicked his legs back in the air and settled into another shoulder stand. In the next breath, he heard footsteps above him, then a dragging sound, a thud, and silence.

"Ohm," Sage chanted, temporarily shutting out the noise in the attic.

"Ohm," he continued.

He couldn't hear Aaron anymore, but Sage felt his father everywhere—in his anxiety, in his dreams. There was no escaping Aaron.

More footsteps fell above Sage.

He curled down and threw the pillow back on the messy bed.

"Damn Aaron," he muttered as he sat at his drums. Then he beat them with no reason or rhythm, just instinct.

+++

"Sage!" Maggie shouted from the foot of the stairs, knowing full well that her son couldn't hear her. "Knock it off!"

Maggie grabbed her coffee cup and went to the solarium, where the drums weren't so intrusive. She opened the notebook Sybylla had given her, now stuffed with drawings from her early classes with Gil, dried sprigs of lavender, a flyer on the history of the Tyler County courthouse, and other flotsam from her time at the Karma Community. She took a long slurp of her coffee, then began to write what would become the blueprint of her future:

The best way to ensure the legacy of Felix Fellows is to place his firm in the hands of his most devoted assistant. I worked alongside Felix for ten years and understand his creative process, his aesthetic, and his high regard for both good design and good business.

She flipped the page over and began again.

What I bring to Felix Ingles Fellows II Designs:

A deep understanding of the Felix's aesthetic

A sense of comfort and predictability with long-standing clients

An easy transition for staff

Her pen hovered over the next line.

My own celebrity

She ripped that page in half and crumpled it in her fist.

She stared at the blank page, took a deep breath, and conjured up her drawing class with Gil. *Breathe, just breathe,* she instructed herself. *Don't worry about the end result. Let it flow. Flow.*

She looked out the window at a zaftig cloud hovering over her neighbor's house. She observed it stretching on its easternmost side, then condensing to the north, then being pulled west as if by a magnet. She let her hand follow its circumference, then its path across her page. It was a scribble, a dabble, but that didn't matter. She drew the roof line of the Jaegers' house, then the ivy lacing its way upward to the eaves. A mundane picture, almost a child's first drawing. No matter. The business proposal would solve itself. The money would come for the right proposal. She just needed to be free to fail first.

Chapter 37

Time to Return to Life

The bathroom light was unusually harsh as Aaron looked into the mirror. His eyelids were slightly puffy after a long night making love to Maggie, but his blue eyes sparkled, showing signs of life. His whiskers, more silver than ebony, prickled him as he ran his hand along his cheeks and chin.

He opened the medicine cabinet to look for a razor.

He found labels. Twenty-four-hour eye cream. Wrinkle filler. Vitamin C gel. Vitamin E lotion. Exfoliating mousse. Dead Sea mud goop. Cucumber peel-off mask. Six bottles of skin-colored foundation. Pink makeup. Lilac makeup. Tubes and pencils and lipsticks.

"Maggie," Aaron shouted roughly into the adjoining bedroom. "You don't need this stuff."

"What stuff?"

"Creams! Gels! Perfume!" Aaron sounded like a carnival barker trying to teach a second-grade class a lesson. "You're beautiful without this crap."

Maggie laughed.

"How would you know?"

"You don't need to buy into this."

"I can't help it. I'm weak."

"Look at this label," he said, poking his head and a bottle of moisturizer out the bathroom door. "You're putting all of these chemicals on your face? Your skin? The largest organ of your body is eating this toxic sludge? Would you put it on your salad?"

"Maybe the kiwi mask," Maggie said, egging him on. "It smells delicious."

"Bah." Aaron closed the door, leaving Maggie to her writing.

Aaron opened another cabinet and found a basket of Band-Aids, cotton balls, and, finally, some disposable razors. They were designed for women, but they'd do in a pinch.

He pulled the whole package from the basket, exposing what he feared he'd been looking for all along.

More labels.

He turned on the faucet to drown out the sound of his snooping.

Take every four hours, Margaret Morgan.

No refills.

Do not operate heavy machinery.

Do not drive.

Use only as directed.

Aaron opened a bottle, discovering a world of magenta and pine green capsules. Another had tiny white tablets. The third had pink octagonal pills. He inhaled their chalky, sterile musk, bringing back memories of his mother, then of high school friends and an old girlfriend, a self-medicating waitress at a Greek restaurant in Boston.

He capped the bottle quickly, shut off the water, looked in the mirror and snapped off the light.

+++

Frances appeared in Sybylla's doorway with a bucket of hot water and a basket of supplies. The morning sun stung Sybylla's eyes and she rolled over, attempting to shut out another day.

"This is it, Sybylla," her cousin said sternly. "No more hiding. It's time to get up. It's time to return to life."

She entered the room, put down the bucket and basket and threw open the curtains. Sybylla didn't budge. Frances circled the room, pushing aside stacks of books, kicking papers and rumpled clothes and waving away dust motes. Sybylla rolled onto her back and threw her blanket over her head.

Frances opened her bottle of lemon essential oil and put a few drops in the hot water.

"You can live your life, Sybylla, or it can live without you. It's time to get up."

She added rosemary oil to the water, then sniffed the small brown bottle before capping it.

"Get up. If Aaron comes back, you'll be strong. If he doesn't, you'll be strong."

"I am not."

"You are. You've just never had to show your strength."

Frances dropped a sea sponge in the water, wrung it out, and threw it at Sybylla. It landed with a thud on her thigh.

"Tell me," Sybylla said.

"Tell you what?" Frances asked as she dunked a ripped Zeppelin T-shirt, now a washrag, into the water.

"Tell me if he's coming back."

Frances drenched the rag again, then squeezed it out, watching the water run through her fingers.

"You know the answer, Sybylla."

She pulled the blanket from her face and sat up.

"No, I don't," she said petulantly. "Sometimes I think he'll come back. I can feel him, as if he were sitting at the foot of this bed, pressing down on it. Like he was here."

She shook her head.

"But sometimes he's just gone."

She laid back down.

Frances opened the window above the bed to let in some badly needed fresh air. A chill ran through Sybylla.

"Why won't you tell me where he is?"

Frances looked out the window to the side garden, where the orange tabby was sniffing a silvery yarrow frond.

"You know everything you need to know right now."

Frances turned away from the window, avoiding Sybylla's eyes, and put some scattered books—books on astrology, tarot, I Ching, divining rod instructions, and crystal power wisdom—back on the shelves.

"Is he with Maggie?"

Frances closed her eyes and gathered her thoughts in silence.

"He's doing what he needs to do at this moment. You have to trust that."

Frances sat down next to her cousin and put her fingertips on Sybylla's neck to feel her pulse. She felt two.

"Does Aaron know?"

"I didn't tell him."

A tear rolled down Sybylla's cheek.

"I never thought it would be like this. I thought we'd bring a baby into the world together. In a loving home."

More tears flowed.

"If..."

Sybylla put her hands on her belly, feeling queasy and tense, like she had a flu that just wasn't going away.

"If I decide to," she choked on a word she couldn't say. "Would you help me?"

+++

Maggie was propped up in bed, lounging amid seven pillows in cream-colored silk shams, elegant and cozy at the same time. She closed her notebook when Aaron entered the room with renewed strength.

"What are you writing?"

Maggie looked up and smiled.

"Just writing." She put the notebook on her bedside table, placing a half-full coffee cup on top of it.

"Anything juicy?" Aaron wiggled his eyebrows and laughed. "Anything about me?"

He zoomed in closer and grinned.

"About last night?"

He reached over and cupped her breast under her silk wrap, then let his whiskers graze her neck before kissing her.

"Actually, I was thinking of some of our first performances," she said, smiling into his eyes. "Remember that one in San Diego, when you wanted us to test the songs on the first record in front of an audience?"

Aaron sat on the bed and leaned against Maggie's bent knees, comfortable again.

"Remember how everything went wrong? You broke two guitar strings..."

"And Pete had a bad freak-out before going on."

"That girl showed up, the one with the boa constrictor. She told him she was pregnant."

"And he couldn't deal with it."

They laughed at the memory.

"As if it was his," Aaron said derisively.

"She also said they'd gotten married while Pete was tripping."

Their laughter faded away, and Aaron felt for her hand.

"I think I did most of that set with my back to the audience," Maggie said to fill the space of their silence. "I didn't realize everyone could see through my blouse until we got under the spotlights."

Aaron smiled and looked at her squarely.

"But you liked being on stage, right? Eventually? I know it wasn't easy at first for you. Your shyness."

Maggie leaned back, her hand unconsciously making its way to her throat.

"It never got easy for me. Everything got exaggerated, blown up. Distorted. When it was good it was great, and when it was terrible…"

More silence.

"Remember the first time we toured Scandinavia?" Aaron asked.

"God," Maggie said, grimacing. "I think I'm still drunk from it."

"One nonstop party. They really dug us."

Aaron squeezed Maggie's hand.

"You miss it, though, don't you?"

Maggie looked away, into her next-door neighbor's yard, its patio and bird bath, perfectly trimmed cedar trees and late-blooming roses.

"I liked working on new songs," Maggie admitted. "The whole creative process. Taking a few lines of a melody and having the band turn it into something special."

"I loved that, too."

"I liked the first few years," Maggie continued, slowly. "They were scary, but fun, too. I mean, I had no idea what I was doing. There weren't many women who were succeeding in the music business at that time. That was a constant struggle. But when it was just us—just the Four Furies—I fit in."

"We had chemistry."

"And some people got it, and some people didn't. But remember when the label tried to put me in a new wardrobe so that I'd look more like Cher? Like some Las Vegas lounge singer?"

Aaron stifled a laugh.

"Hey—we could have gotten our own TV show!"

Maggie shook her head.

"I don't miss being controlled. Or being misunderstood," Maggie said with finality.

"You hated talking to reporters," Aaron commiserated. "I don't blame you."

He laid his lanky body alongside her and they held each other without speaking. They were familiar old lovers, but still newlywed shy with each other after twenty years apart. Aaron tucked his left arm under Maggie's neck and gazed directly into her eyes.

"That song you sang," he purred as he let his whiskered chin roughen her check. "How did it go?"

Maggie sank deeper into her silk pillow. She knew exactly which song he was indirectly begging her to sing but she wouldn't do it.

"The one about Pandora. The one you wrote."

He hummed the melody along her bare shoulder and slid his hand down her arm to her waist to her hip under the billowy duvet. She tensed, unwilling to respond.

"*I just had to know,*" he whispered, his voice barely carrying the tune. "Isn't that how it goes?"

He kissed her and moved in closer as he felt her tension release.

He hummed the rest of the melody, then gave it a twist, a natural harmony if they ever sang it together.

"Sing, Maggie. Sing with me." He moved his hand down to her thigh.

She wrapped her arms around his shoulders and felt the weight of thirty years expand and release, throb and settle.

"I'm not ready," she whispered. "But…"

"But?" Aaron asked, seeking out some hope.

She said no more as she moved on top of him, surprising both of them with her strength.

Chapter 38

The Oldest Story Ever Told

"Is this a typical Tuesday for you?" Aaron asked, squinting in the noon sunlight that both exposed every nook and cranny in his face and filled his demeanor with youthful energy.

"Sorta," Sage mumbled, hunched over his mountain bike to inspect its gears and cords and brake pads and pedals.

"Do your friends know you're back?"

"Not really."

He ran his hands over the handlebars, feeling their stickiness where his hands were usually gripped.

"Why not?"

Now Aaron hunched down, hoping to make contact with his son. "Don't you need to go back to your job? Don't you have a girlfriend?"

Sage rolled his eyes.

"I've got some good news," Aaron said, trying again. "I think your mom and I are going to get the band back together again."

"Hooray for you."

"Hey, Sage…"

"Hooray for fucking you."

The words smacked Aaron in the face.

Sage walked into the garage, seething. Aaron stayed fixed on the apron of the driveway, not knowing what had set off Sage, although Sage had been sour-tempered the whole time they'd been in Chicago. He heard Sage bang around in the garage, sliding boxes across the floor, clanking metal on metal, cursing audibly but not clearly.

Sage returned to the bike with an air pump.

"What's the matter?"

"You."

"Me? What did I ever do to you?"

Almost immediately he regretted asking.

"What did you ever do to me?" Sage said, dropping the pump with anger. "What didn't you do to me? You fucked me up."

The two men locked stares, one with disbelief, one with hatred.

"You ignored me. You lied to me when you weren't ignoring me."

He took a step closer.

"What do you think it was like to see you in the papers or hear about your fucked-up life. You were a rock star, cool as shit, the world at your feet. But you had no time for me, and I'm your son."

Aaron turned white.

"You made mom miserable and you're going to make her miserable again."

Sage spat on the ground, disgusted. Aaron took a step back.

"Hey, hey, cool down. I thought we were working through that. I thought we were forming a relationship."

"Bullshit."

Sage seethed.

"Fuck you. Fuck you and your hippie shit."

Aaron let it wash over him.

"Sage, cool down, man. You're the one who found me, remember? You're the one who reached out to me."

"Exactly. You couldn't even do that."

Both men were shaking.

"Get the fuck out of here you self-centered asshole. You've done enough damage. I won't let you hurt us again."

"Sage, please."

Aaron took a step forward, as if to hug his son. Sage roared, grabbed Aaron's shoulders, and pushed him to the ground. Aaron rolled onto his side to get up, but Sage crouched down and looked him directly in the eyes.

"I've always wanted to do this," Sage hissed as his fist landed squarely on Aaron's jaw.

+++

Frances was slicing tomatoes when she got the twinge. With each pulpy slice the twinge grew stronger, more urgent. It started in her pelvis, as if an artery was bubbling and roiling, full of hot blood. It couldn't be ignored when it became a full-blown spasm, unlike any she'd had in years—since the business office was robbed, in fact.

She sat down and held her stomach. She closed her eyes and rocked from side to side.

Mother Earth, healing earth, she chanted. *Help us here.*

She continued rocking, losing herself in a trance.

Mother Earth, healing earth, help us here.

The chant was in a minor key.

She stood up and walked around the kitchen holding her belly.

She looked out the window and into the sky, noting the shapeshifting clouds. She saw Gil on the hillside, carrying a shovel and rake to the site of the labyrinth.

A breeze entered the room.

She walked over to the sink, now humming her chant, and filled a shallow bowl with water. She stared into it for a long while, watching the ripples settle and become still. She saw the sun's reflection in it, and her own.

With her mind's eye, she saw much more.

Mother Earth, changing earth, she whispered. *Change us here.*

+++

"Isn't that?" whispered Karen to her fellow nurse, Elaine.

"It can't be." Elaine's eyes darted to the bloody man on the examining table and the worried woman at his side.

"I knew she still lived in the area," Karen said in a hushed tone. "My friend once saw her at a charity event, all cleaned up. You never would have known."

"God, I was so into that band when I was a teenager. I wanted to look just like her."

"They're all over the tabloids right now. They're back together."

Karen flipped the chart and took a second look at it.

"Yep, that's him."

"I guess bad boys never change."

"Wait till the blood work comes back. Who knows what's in his system."

They smirked, satisfied.

"Now Mr. …" Karen checked the chart again and raised her voice. "Fields? You got dinged up pretty good, but you're going to be okay."

"No broken bones?" Maggie asked.

"No, just a few bruised ribs, and bruises everywhere else."

Karen eyed Maggie up and down.

"Now, Mrs. Fields…"

"Morgan. Ms. Morgan."

"Ms. Morgan," Karen corrected herself while secretly delighted that she'd been able to make the connection. "Ms. Morgan, we're going to tape his ribs real tight, but he'll have to heal on his own."

Karen turned to Aaron, who held an icepack to his swollen face.

"Mr. Fields, I'm going to stitch you up. But don't worry, you won't feel a thing."

He moaned.

"I can give you some pain pills to take home."

Her smirk reappeared.

"I don't want any," he said through loose teeth, cracked lips, and thick tongue. "I don't want any pills. I can do this on my own."

"Okay, whatever you want," Karen said while gathering gauze and bandages.

Maggie grabbed Aaron's hand and looked away as he clung to her.

+++

The sun was almost rising when Sage tapped on Frances' window. She was up, anyway, sensing that she had to be alert at all times during these difficult days.

She waved him to the door, then let him in with relief.

"I missed you," she whispered into his ear.

"I missed you, too."

They couldn't let go of each other.

"Where have you been?"

"Home."

"Are you okay?"

"No."

She held him tighter.

"I think I killed my father," he said, his voice shaking. "Aaron," he clarified.

She patted down his hair.

"You didn't, Sage, you didn't. You roughed him up, but he's still alive."

Sage didn't ask how she knew, didn't really want to know if Maggie called, looking for him and telling everyone about the fight, or if Frances was doing her psychic thing again.

"Can you love someone and hate him at the same time?"

"Of course. Especially if it's family."

Sage coughed, stifling a sniffle.

"He told me they were going to get the Four Furies back together, and I just snapped. I hate that band. I hate their music. I just want my life to be back to the way it was."

"You can't go back, Sage. No one can ever go back. You've always got to move forward. Make peace with things you can't change and change the things that ask for your attention."

She smoothed out the tension in his back.

"I don't know anyone who talks like you," he said with his head still resting on her shoulder. "I don't get half of the things you say, either."

Frances laughed.

"I'm pretty used to that."

Sage fought back a tear.

"What do you see in me, anyway? I'm so fucked up. Just a fucking loser who needs to be medicated."

They were quiet for a while.

"I think you're a Green Man. You're not aware of it yet, but you're going to do great things."

She pulled back and looked at him with all of her attention. "Keep your innocence. Keep your idealism. Don't let them get you stuck in a world you feel powerless to change. Feel your fear. Feel your pain. Just don't get overwhelmed. You can connect with other people's fear and pain and heal them."

Sage trembled, but Frances was as solid as an oak.

"I believe in you, Sage."

That's all he needed to hear.

+++

Aaron's bruises and cuts were a mask that Maggie saw through, even when she wasn't looking at him. It wasn't the first time she'd cleaned him up after a fight.

Drama. Comedy and tragedy. The young prince killing the old king to usher in a new era—it was the oldest story ever told.

Aaron winced as he lay in bed next to her, a purple towel covering the pillow.

And Sage was gone, again.

Drama.

Was it worth it? Maggie wondered. *Couldn't Aaron just tiptoe into our lives and settle in quietly?*

She shivered when she thought of Sybylla, and Gil, and Frances, people who Aaron and Maggie still weren't able to talk about but whose presence or absence was felt in every moment. Somehow they'd contained Aaron's worst impulses and kept him in check, like lion tamers, like mother hens. Left to his own devices, Aaron knew no limits. Even marriage vows dissolved when he wanted them to disappear.

But Maggie couldn't ignore her own role in Aaron's drama. She was a willing partner, too. *It's chemistry, it's love, first love,* she told herself. *Plus jealousy and revenge and lust and hatred, too,* she had to admit.

I wanted to know that he still wanted me.

She leaned over and kissed his forehead like a mother.

I just had to know, Pandora.

Chapter 39

You're Not the Only One Who's Changed

Maggie spooned the soft scrambled eggs past Aaron's cut lips, careful not to break open the gash at the corner of his mouth.

"Free range?" he mumbled.

"What?" Maggie chopped the eggs into even smaller bits.

"Free range. It's better for the chickens."

"Oh," she said, catching on. "I don't think so. But I can check the carton."

"How far I've fallen." He managed a sort of smile but winced when it reached his blackened eye and deeply bruised jaw.

Maggie put down the dish and handed him a cup of chamomile tea, blowing on it to cool it down.

"So what started it?"

"The fight?" He took a quick sip. "Sage hates me."

"He doesn't."

"He does. He unleashed twenty years of hatred on me." Aaron closed his eyes and sank back into the comfy pillows, trying to distance himself from the blows, the kicks, the spitting, the venom. He was grateful that he couldn't remember chunks of it.

"And that came out of nowhere?"

Aaron sighed. "I told him the Furies were getting back together."

Aaron looked down at his scraped knuckles. He couldn't remember if he'd returned Sage's punches or just defended himself from them.

"Are we?" Maggie pushed the plate just a little bit further from the edge of the bedside table.

"I thought we'd agreed."

"I don't remember that."

Maggie pushed herself back on the bed, tucking her knees under her chin and wrapping her arms around her legs.

"I have my own life now. I've worked really hard for it."

"So have I," Aaron said. "You're not the only one who's changed."

"Oh? Looking at you now I don't know that you have."

Aaron leaned forward, as if Maggie had punched him in the gut.

"Sorry, sorry," she reached out to touch his shoulder, then his puffy, purple eyelid and scuffed-up cheek. "I didn't mean that. I know you're trying to make things right. It's just that trouble always seems to find you."

"Some would call it excitement." Aaron searched for her hand. "Maybe you need a little."

Maggie stiffened, drawing her legs closer still.

"Let's do it, Maggie. We could do it right this time. We're adults. We've matured."

Maggie put her forehead on her knees.

"We appreciate each other now." Aaron pushed further still.

He reached out as far as his beaten body would allow.

"We need each other. We're best when we're together, remember?"

Maggie rested her cheek on her knee and looked at Aaron.

"I don't have time for this," she said, backing away. "I've got to make my big pitch in a few hours. I don't know how I'll do it, but I will."

"Fuck 'em. Come back to the Furies."

"And there's Sage."

"Who hates me, but we'll muddle through."

"And Sybylla?"

"Ah."

"And?"

It hurt Maggie, but it had to be said. It hadn't escaped her notice that Aaron hadn't mentioned his wife since they'd fled the Karma Community. Whether it was guilt, or a short attention span, or merely Aaron's inability to deal with his own messes, she didn't know. *Is that how he dealt with me when he'd wander away and into another woman's life? Did he forget me as soon as he was gone?*

213

"That's something I need to work out when the time is right."

The two were quiet for a moment, listening to a lone car pass by the house and a dog bark in the distance. Aaron put his hand on the nape of her neck to soothe her.

"I appreciate you, Maggie. Don't ever forget that."

Maggie smiled.

"I do."

They grew quiet again. Neither one of them could say the word *love*.

+++

Sage followed Gil up the hill to the site of the labyrinth. The scene was rough, more a work in progress than a budding maze. Grass had been torn up and pushed aside. Stakes had been posted with twine running between them to delineate the pattern. It was obvious to Sage that they'd been uprooted a few times.

"Dude," Sage said. "This is a mess."

"I know. There are more rocks in the soil than we thought, and I've been doing this on my own, since Sybylla and Frances have been busy, doing—well, I don't know what they've been doing. But I don't mind. It's been kind of therapeutic."

Sage curled his still-sore hands into fists, then unclenched them and put them in his back pockets.

"You must be pissed," he said, turning toward Gil.

Gil squinted in the sun, the light picking up threads of amber in his hair.

"I don't know if pissed is the right word. I feel a loss, but I know that everything that happens is meant to happen."

"You think so?"

"I do. If I was going to lose Maggie to anyone, it may as well be Aaron. I just hope that he's good to her this time around."

"I doubt it. Look at what he's done to Sybylla. I stopped by to say hello to her this morning and she looks terrible. And she doesn't deserve it."

"She doesn't, that's true. But maybe she can get through this without developing too much scar tissue."

"He didn't hurt her—not physically, right?" Worry crept into Sage's voice.

"No, no. She just has some psychic wounds. Haven't you ever gone through a bad breakup?"

Gill grabbed a shovel and picked at the dirt near his feet.

"I am worried about her," he finally admitted. "She spends too much time alone. She's taking it so hard. And when I do see her, she just tells me to do something different with the labyrinth. First it was going to be heart-shaped. Then she said that was hypocritical and wanted it to be a traditional Cretan labyrinth. Fine. So I laid it out that way. Then she said that she wanted it to be like a coiled serpent, with a long tail at the south for the entrance and the mouth, the exit, pointing east. Okay. I drew that out for her and she just burst into tears. I don't know what to do."

Sage kicked at a clot of grass.

"Can we just let it go wild for a while?"

"I'm all for that."

Sage picked up a rake and moved some of the dirt to a long but shallow hole.

"It's too bad. This thing was going to rock."

"I know. But maybe this isn't the right time."

Sage snuck a look at Gil, the man who once said that he'd be proud to be Sage's stepfather. None of Maggie's old boyfriends had said that, not even when they were trying to win Sage over. Their attention to him followed a pattern—good-natured ribbing and forced friendliness, then a slow pulling away when they realized that Maggie's son would always come first in her life. Dating a single mom eventually became inconvenient.

"I was really happy this summer, you know? Everything was smooth. No worries."

"I know. Sometimes it feels like a dream. Maggie..." Gil caught himself. "How is she?" he asked cautiously.

Sage continued smoothing the dirt, erasing the labyrinth.

"She's okay. She's working on her business plan and Aaron's going through all of the old Furies junk in the attic."

Sage ran his hand through his hair and squinted into the sun.

"Aaron said they're going to get the band back together."

"Really?" Gil's voice betrayed his enthusiasm. "Wow. They were a great band. I don't know if you can appreciate it, but they were..." he thought for a moment, looking for the right word. "Magic."

Sage stared a Gil in disbelief.

"They're really fucked up."

"No more so than any other couple," Gil said philosophically. "They just put it out there for the whole world to see and hear."

Sage laughed.

"Dude, you are a fucking Buddha. Don't you care that Aaron stole your girlfriend?"

Gil dug a little deeper into the fresh dirt. "I do care, I do. But what can I do? You can't push a river. You can't fight the Four Furies."

"You could try to win her back. She seemed happy with you. Calm."

Gil rested his shovel on his boot.

"Did Frederick call the house?" he asked, growing serious.

"I don't think so."

Gil hesitated, then decided to level with Sage.

"You know that he and Aaron did a deal. If Maggie and Aaron would record a song and give all the rights to it to Freddie, then he'd let Aaron build this labyrinth."

"Dude."

"And then when he saw the financials for the whole Karma Community, Freddie said that Aaron would have to leave altogether if he didn't record anything, and that he'd put this place up for sale and kick all of us out and that would be the end of everything."

"Whoa."

"Aaron agreed but didn't tell us. He really put his butt on the line for everyone here."

Sage began raking again, this time with a bit more urgency.

"So mom's going to save the Karma Community?"

"If Aaron holds up his end of the bargain and convinces her to do it."

The two men raked and shoveled, did and undid, for another hour or so.

Chapter 40

Charmed

"The board members will see you now."

Maggie looked up from her desk at Felix Ingles Fellows II Designs' office, feeling unready but unable to stall any longer. *It's time, it's time,* she told herself. *I've earned this. It's what Felix wanted. Let's get it over with and move on.*

The walk to the conference room seemed longer than any entrance to a stadium stage. No applause and chants of "Maggie, Maggie, Maggie." No adrenaline-pumping pep talk with the other Furies along the way. No quickie sex with Aaron, no drugs to get her in the right state of mind, no vocal warmups or last-minute set list changes to cater to the crowd.

But the panic remained.

She walked along the softly carpeted corridor and took deep yoga breaths as she thought about the years of labor that had gotten her here. Learning the basics of good design and recognizing quality craftsmanship. Paying her dues with her colleagues to earn their trust. Receiving Felix's wisdom during late-night tea drinking sessions. Strategizing her next steps from the bottom rung of the ladder and biding her time until now.

Her breaths became shallower as the heavy doors opened before her.

She entered, armed only with her briefcase of documents, her portfolio, and samples, dressed in a Michael Kors dove-grey jersey suit, coral silk blouse, and

217

alligator-skin sling-backs that were already killing her feet. The colors were Felix's favorites; the shoes a statement that needed to be made. Her gold charm bracelet rattled as she opened her briefcase and hoped for the best.

Missing from her materials was any kind of statement assuring her ability to match the half-million dollars Trip and Matilda had already been offered. But Aaron wanted to get back together, and his little hippie community was worth far more than this legendary design firm, unbelievably.

I should have brought the Karma Community's checkbook to prove I could get my hands on however much money they want, Maggie thought. *Bankers and stockbrokers be damned.*

The directors didn't bother to stop their hushed chattering as she entered the room. A cell phone beeped and was checked. Papers were manhandled and ruffled. A cheese Danish was munched discreetly and washed down with fresh-squeezed orange juice and a San Pellegrino chaser.

"How good of you to speak to us, Maggie," Trip oozed from his father's armchair at the tip of the long conference table. "Commence as you wish when you are ready."

She took two long breaths as she scanned the six faces arranged around the table. There was no microphone stand to cling to, no support from a band. No backbeat to align her heartbeat to. No adoring audience. No grandfatherly Felix to hide behind.

"Thank you for meeting with me this afternoon." Her voice shook as she adjusted its tone and tenor for Trip, Matilda, and four board members. "This has been a difficult few weeks for all of us. But I am confident that together we can create a smooth transition to the next incarnation of Felix's life work."

She passed around the copies of her proposal with trembling hands that made her charm bracelet clatter.

"As you know, I worked closely with Felix for ten years. The best ten years of my life, to be honest."

"That's not what I've been reading in the papers," Trip interrupted. "All the tabloids say you've been living a hellish existence as some sort of overweight office drone."

Maggie flicked her eyes toward him, unable to move any other muscle.

"And that you've gone back to your druggie ex-boyfriend."

"Who overdosed just yesterday," Matilda spat. "But I shouldn't have to explain that to you. You were at the hospital with him."

Maggie forced herself to breathe while her temples throbbed and her palms became coated in sweat.

"That's not true," she said. "He was in an accident."

"Just as you were in an accident. With alcohol. And drugs."

"I was concussed," Maggie explained.

"That's not what the court documents say," Trip smirked. "We've been following the proceedings keenly. Very keenly."

"And the tabloids," Matilda said. "Don't forget the tabloids."

Maggie folded her hands in front of her and focused on the jade bead that Felix had affixed to her bracelet. For luck. For prosperity. For a charmed life.

"None of that is true," she said simply. "You know the tabloids just make up stories to sell to gullible readers."

"Let's just pretend you're innocent as charged," Trip said. "Why don't you explain to us why we should allow our father's legacy to be placed in the hands of a woman who would generate this type of attention. Notoriety. My father lived an impeccable live without scandal."

He leaned back in his chair and folded his hands over his chest.

Maggie inspected him, each pallid, worthless, smug, priggish square inch of him and hated him. Hated his entitlement. Hated his power. Hated his lack of understanding of how hard it was to succeed in the real world without inherited wealth and a family name and connections that would open the doors of prep schools and an Ivy League education and secret societies and exclusive resorts and gated communities and board rooms and charity balls and the ability to squash another person's dreams just because he could.

She flipped open her briefcase and searched through its contents to stall for time. She fanned through her notebook with its sketches and plans. An envelope emerged from the mess. She didn't need to look at any of the writing to know which one it was. The letter from Susan, her fan, the one who'd followed Maggie's lead and left her abusive husband for a better life on her own.

I used to have a life, a big life. I used to mean something to people. I used to move them, change their lives. Dazzle them, create their memories. Create my own legacy. Now I'm just a passenger on the conveyer belt of life. Décor.

"It's an open secret around the office that you made some terrible investments in the past year," Trip noted, cutting into the silence. "So I'd love to hear how you plan to make us an offer that we can't refuse."

Maggie kept her eyes on Susan's letter, then leveled them on Trip.

"I can get the money," she said evenly. "You have nothing to worry about. Shall we shake on it?"

Maggie strode toward the conference table and extended her hand.

"Shall we?"

Chapter 41

Dreams of Her Own

"Please reconsider, Sybylla. Are you sure that this is what you want to do?"

Frances put her arm around her cousin, who was venturing out for the first time in a few days. No longer captive to her fears, Sybylla was able to walk, to talk, to take long looks at the land she'd loved for so long. She hadn't worked out the details yet, but in the big picture, at least, she knew that she'd be alone. No Aaron. No Karma Community. No baby.

It came to her in the middle of the night. There was a big world out there—a huge one. Why confine herself to the Karma Community? If Aaron could leave, why would she have to stay? Didn't she have dreams of her own? Goals? Well, then, she wouldn't deny them. She could be a midwife, or a doula. A Feng Shui expert or jewelry designer. Or even a dog walker. Sybylla had met one a few summers ago in a tribal dance clinic, and found her to be so peaceful and poised and healthy—maybe that was due to her work with animals.

Working with animals—that was it. She'd learn how to train dogs and cats for therapy, then go to nursing homes and hospitals and let people cuddle them and forget their troubles and let some good old-fashioned puppy love into their lives. She didn't know how she'd get there but she knew where she wanted to go.

"I've made up my mind," Sybylla told her worried cousin. "How could I bring a baby into this situation? It wouldn't know its father. And if it did—and that's unlikely—who would it meet? Aaron's no father figure."

She shivered.

Maybe Maggie was right to leave Aaron when she found out she was pregnant with Sage.

"Please reconsider. Call him."

"He was cruel to me," Sybylla said, no tears left. "He doesn't deserve to know."

"Don't do it out of revenge," Frances pleaded.

"I'm not. But I won't have Aaron's child."

"I'll help you raise the baby, Sybylla. Your parents will help you. Have you told them?"

"No."

"Your brothers?"

"No."

"Anyone?"

"No."

They stopped walking and Frances placed her palm on Sybylla's belly.

"Sybylla, this baby wants to be born. I feel such a life force. She's a tiger, an angel. Please don't sacrifice her just because you're angry right now."

Sybylla stiffened her spine, throwing back her shoulders.

"You just want me to have it."

"I do. I want you to have *her*."

Sybylla looked away.

It's a girl?

"Don't harden your heart, Sybylla. You have so much to give."

Sybylla was silent, stoic.

"Please."

No response.

"At least talk to Sage. Find out where Aaron is, what his mental state is. Give yourself a little more time."

Frances threw her arms around Sybylla, and they continued walking up the hill, where Gil and Sage were working.

"Please. Don't. I can't."

Sybylla turned away.

"I had so many hopes for this labyrinth. It was a labor of love for Aaron and me."

She gasped, taking it all in.

221

"And it's a disaster."

The men were sifting and raking, shoveling and working. What had once been an untouched field on the far side of a crest of a rolling hill was now a mass of dirt, a jumble of misguided intentions.

Sybylla faced Frances.

"Would you help me with the abortion?"

"Sybylla…"

"I want an herbal one. A natural one."

"Herbal abortions aren't easy, Sybylla. You're going against the body's wishes, even if you are doing it without chemicals or surgery."

"I know it won't be easy. But if you don't help me, I'll go to a clinic. You can't stop me."

+++

The dining room was almost empty at lunchtime, a mere shell, and one long table was filled with almost all of the current residents of the Karma Community—Sage and Gil, Frances, Freddie, Tanya, a few silent retreaters and the orange tabby, Maggie's old pal. Sybylla, feeling unwell, was sipping miso soup and carrot juice alone in her room.

"Much has changed in just a few short weeks, no?" Frederick asked Sage while inspecting the basket of warm sprouted-wheat bread. "I haven't decided if I should send out the new course catalogs or put up a For Sale sign."

Sage glared at a smug Freddie.

"I have faith that it will all work out in the end," Frances said, almost convincingly.

"The end, Frances, the end. Each day I'm more convinced that this is the end of the Karma Community."

The silent retreaters gasped at Freddie's cruelty.

"I have faith," Frances said firmly.

"If you don't like the way things have ended, then it isn't the end," Gil said gallantly.

"Well put, Gil," Frederick said, scooping up a mound of tabbouleh. "But you may want to have a Plan B in place. Let's play pretend—pretend the Karma Community has gone condo and you no longer live here. What would you do?"

The friends looked at each other, not sure if they should take the bait.

"I would continue doing art therapy, just in a different setting," Gil said.

"As long as I'm helping others I'm happy," Frances added.

Sage beamed.

222

"Me, too," he said. "I want to make a difference. I want to help people too, whatever it is."

"By doing what? Operating a labyrinth?" Frederick sneered.

Sage flushed and felt his bruised knuckles swell.

"I could work on a farm—an organic farm. I could raise chickens. I could work in a health food store. Get my band back together. Or lead a drum circle."

Frederick burst out laughing.

"Like father, like son—a fool."

Sage stood up and pushed his chair aside.

"Just in case your drum circle doesn't work out, I suggest you call your mother."

Chapter 42

Old Dog

Aaron shuffled out the back door and into the open air. At last. He wasn't used to lying in bed all day, not these days at least. The Karma Community had given him enough room to roam, enough work to keep his hands busy and his demons in hibernation.

He wasn't used to a house and yard. Maggie's house and Maggie's yard—and Sage's, too, but it was too painful to think about his son's hatred. He looked over to the spot on the driveway where Sage had pummeled him into near unconsciousness. Was there blood on the concrete? He wasn't ready to find out, and he hoped that when he was it would be washed away by rain or bleached by the sun so no evidence would be left of his family gone bust.

He stepped into the grass, overgrown but still tame. Carefully, carefully, he lowered himself onto his knees, then sat, then lay down. He bent his knees and let the soles of his feet sink into the grass.

He closed his eyes.

Help me.

He touched his bandaged ribs, still tender, still sore. He took a deep breath, then coughed, regretting the strain.

I'm fucked. And if I'm fucked, the Karma Community will be, too, and my friends will be left without a home, without a mission, scattered to the four winds.

Shit.

He squeezed his eyes shut, creating even more pain.

Sybylla must hate me. I deserve it.

+++

Maggie wasn't sure if she was looking at Aaron's corpse or Aaron in corpse pose on her lawn, his bashed and battered face shaded by her sugar maple tree and his legs in the full sun.

"Aaron," she said softly. No response. "Aaron," she said with more intensity.

She kicked off her heels and knelt next to him, slithering her skirt up her thighs to be more comfortable. His stomach rose and fell shallowly, restricted by the nurse's professional wrapping. He was alive.

"Sing for me, Maggie." His voice was as raw as his wounds.

She lay down on the cool grass and put her hand on his heart. She let her hand rise and fall with each beat, then let their breaths sync up.

"Theoretically," she said *sotto voce*, "if we were to get the band back together, how would we do it?"

He popped open one eye and squinted. She grabbed his hand and felt each fingertip roughened by thousands of guitar strings and impossible chords. His wedding ring was gone.

"Just theoretically. No promises."

"Well," he exhaled. "We'd have to rehearse. I'm out of practice and you— I'm sure your voice is still there, but—"

"But that's not what I mean. I mean, how would we split the money."

"God, Maggie."

"It would have to be different this time around," she whispered in his ear. "We're going to be equals, true partners. No secrets. Everything has to be a joint decision and split fifty-fifty. No more handshake deals or contracts written on old set lists."

Aaron trembled slightly and closed his eyes again.

"Whatever you want."

"Okay, then. Here's what I want," she said, all business. "I want a piece of the back catalog going forward. I don't care what I agreed to twenty years ago. This is what I want now."

"Maggie," Aaron's moaned.

"And I want a piece of the Karma Community, right now, since Sage and I never got a dime from you all these years."

"Maggie," Aaron's voice weakened.

225

"I'll have my lawyer call you tomorrow. Your lawyer can take it from there."

"We don't need any damn lawyers."

"I think we do."

They let the silence speak for them. Maggie rolled toward him but he was looking away. She brushed her hand along his arm, then to the bandages under his T-shirt. His belt, curled along the edge with age. His hip. An unnatural bulge.

She dug inside his front pocket. He swatted her hand away.

"Maggie, don't. Just leave it alone."

She overpowered him and pulled the bottle of her pain pills out of his pocket.

"How could you," she seethed. "Or couldn't you help yourself?"

She sat up bolt straight and shook the bottle. Empty.

"Old dog, old tricks."

Aaron blinked at her.

"Maggie, I can explain. I was about to explain."

"I've heard it all before."

"I was only trying to—"

"Well maybe you shouldn't have tried," she spat.

"I was in a jam."

"You always are."

She flashed her eyes at Aaron, silencing him.

"Fool. I don't know why I gave you a second chance. Fool me once."

"I didn't mean to hurt you."

"And you played the martyr when you refused a prescription. Just trying to impress the nurses, I'm sure."

Her hatred burned.

"The pain was horrible, Maggie. I needed to kill it. I couldn't stand it anymore."

"I can't stand it, either. That's why I left you."

She turned away from him.

"You should have known better," Aaron said as he closed his eyes. "You know I can't be around drugs. I have no self-control, especially when I'm in pain."

"Where did you get them? You haven't left the house."

"In your bathroom, in the basket."

She threw the bottle at him, not caring if it would hurt. "How deep did you have to dig to find them? They were prescribed when I had a migraine five years ago. How desperate are you?"

"Very," he whispered.

"I pity you, Aaron. A little boy trapped in an old man's body. You think the world revolves around you, but you're just a pathetic old man."

She walked into the house and locked the door behind her.

Chapter 43

Nothing Left to Lose

Frances put the kettle on the gas flame and turned down the heat so that only a small flicker of blue escaped the stovetop. She placed on the countertop the packets of herbs and roots, the ones she kept in her room, where others couldn't accidentally try them. They were for knowledgeable women—wise women—only.

And a few foolish ones, too.

She thought Sybylla was a fool. And being foolish, she wouldn't listen to contradictory opinions. *Don't make such a big decision while you're in this head space,* Frances had counseled the night before. *Don't harden your heart. Discuss it with Aaron before you go through with it.*

"He'll only talk me into having it," Sybylla replied sullenly.

Frances shook her head, remembering how stubborn Sybylla could be when she was wounded.

There's always time for forgiveness, Sybylla. This can be an opportunity for you to grow into a woman, instead of being a child bride.

"I'm a married woman, not a child. Or I was."

Millions of women have had children at imperfect times. Do you think babies only show up when it's convenient for the parents?

"It wouldn't be fair to the baby."

Nothing would persuade Sybylla.

So, reluctantly, Frances agreed to help Sybylla abort her daughter. As a healer, Frances was taught to work with her clients and not impose her personal opinions on them, as she had with her cousin. She'd been through this process before with other women, and it was never easy. But it was necessary for those with too many children, or not enough strength, for those who were abused or those who simply did not want to become mothers. Frances asked that the women take the decision seriously, and they did. And she honored their wishes and did her best to make everything as comfortable and peaceful as possible.

As the first few steam vapors escaped the kettle, Frances did the only thing she knew how to do. She threw a blanket of white light, loving light, around her cousin. She caressed her face with it, bathed her in it, made it pulse and wave and flow to infuse Sybylla with wisdom and peace and love.

Please, Sybylla. Make the right decision.

"A cup of tea before packing up your things?" Frederick taunted Frances, snapping her out of her reverie. He stood in the doorway, hands placed on his hips, feet confidently planted apart. He took up the entire space, both physically and psychically.

Frances' cheeks burned as she watched more steam escape the kettle.

"There's still time," she said, refusing to take Frederick's bait.

"It's a shame we never truly got to know each other, Frances. I felt as if you were just about to emerge from Aaron's shadow, and now it's come to this. Pity."

Frances stilled her mind.

"Who knows, Frederick. The Karma Community may get a second chance."

+++

Maggie gunned the engine before Aaron had completely closed the passenger side door. She'd considered tossing him out on his ear, but then realized that he'd just wind up on her doorstep again, but more stoned and beat-up than he was now, or he'd turn up in Vegas or New Orleans or Miami and cause a full-blown scandal that would derail her business pitch, much more than a family drama. Besides, she still had some business in Tyler County. Besides, she needed to find Sage.

Aaron looked out the window as they sped.

"Helpless," she muttered.

It was the last word spoken until they crossed the Illinois-Wisconsin line.

"Maggie," he said, his voice raspy from the silence. "I need to tell you something."

He turned to her, but she stared straight ahead.

"Maggie."

"I'm listening."

Aaron held his rib cage and took a deep breath.

"I'm sorry I took the pills. I was in pain. I thought I could deal with it on my own. But I guess I couldn't."

Maggie didn't flinch.

"It breaks my heart that it was Sage who beat me up. Of course, I'd always wanted to take a swing at my old man. But I never did."

He felt his bandages, fingering them up and down.

"I deserve it," he whispered.

He touched the stitches at the side of his mouth, checking for blood or scabs.

"I thought Sage and I were becoming friends. The whole summer went just fine."

He closed his eyes, thinking of the drum circle, the labyrinth, Sybylla.

"I never thought that Sage would hate me."

Maggie couldn't let that one go.

"You're kidding me," she said, biting into the words. "For twenty years you ignored him. You gave him nothing. We struggled, Aaron, and you were living a life of excess."

"I was paying off debts, Maggie. Debts that you left me with."

"We had nothing."

"You and Sage were always a part of me, Maggie. All these years. But I—"

He faltered and held his head in his hands.

"I was so ashamed for so long, Maggie. I fucked up such a good thing with you. And I knew it. I was afraid of what you and Sage thought of me. I was doped up, Maggie. I wasn't thinking clearly and I hated myself. And then I was sober, and I just couldn't face it. I couldn't face you."

"I thought that part of rehab was apologizing to the people you'd wronged."

"It is, sometimes. But I didn't think that it would have mattered to you and Sage. I mean, what's an apology worth after all that I did to you?"

Maggie took her eyes off the road and stared full strength at Aaron.

"A lot, Aaron. It would have meant the world."

"Is it too late to say I'm sorry now?" he asked quietly.

Maggie thought for another moment, another mile.

"You can let Sage decide."

Aaron sighed, his ribs aching as his lungs expanded.

"I found this. I want you to take it. I hope it holds some happy memories for you."

He held out his hand, revealing her sterling silver charm bracelet, the one she'd worn every day during her relationship with Aaron, every day she was Maggie Morgan of the Four Furies. The light caught each charm, setting off sparks within the front seat.

"You shouldn't paw through my things," Maggie said simply.

"Please don't hold a grudge," he said. "We can work this out."

"We tried working it out and we couldn't."

He set the bracelet in the cup holder and looked ahead, bracing himself.

"One more thing. About the money."

Maggie clenched the steering wheel.

"There is no money."

He drummed his knuckles against the window.

"The back catalog is gone."

Maggie scoffed.

"Where?"

"Taxes. Paying off the roadies and the band. The Four Furies were in debt, Maggie. You handed off a huge mess that had to be cleaned up."

"I paid my dues," she said defensively.

"I'm not denying that."

He turned to her, struggling with the strain of sitting in the cramped Saturn.

"But the Karma Community. You're loaded."

"Definitely not. Definitely."

"I saw the checkbook. You've got more money than I'd imagined."

"The checkbook isn't quite accurate."

"Sure, right."

"It's wishful thinking, creative visualization. We were conducting a thought experiment by padding the balance."

Maggie rolled her eyes. "Now I suppose you're going to tell me that your accountant is a falling baby, just floating through the universe on good vibes."

"I'm broke, Maggie. Stop rubbing it in."

He put his hands through his hair and squinted into the sunlight, breaking up his fresh scabs.

"And I don't know where you got the idea that I own the Karma Community, because I don't."

Maggie gunned the engine down a long lane circumnavigating a picture-perfect dairy farm, not caring what the local speed limit was. Her hands on the steering wheel almost blistered with rage.

"If you don't own it, who does? Sybylla?"

Aaron leaned back into the seat and closed his eyes.

231

"Frederick Christiansen. Some douchebag investor. A creep. You met him when you were signing autographs."

Maggie thought back to the blur of the fans' adoration and the lone man who wasn't awed by her. The one who introduced himself without introducing himself.

"Who else?"

"Just him."

"And what else?"

"And he wants to sell the place because we're broke."

"And?"

"Unless I can convince you to get the Furies back together and he can get a piece of the action. Then he'll let us stay. No Furies, no Karma Community."

Maggie eyed herself in the rearview mirror and let the truth of his statement sink in. Weeks of learning to trust him again, hoping for her just deserts, thinking he could make it all right by handing over some of his riches at last. For her, for Sage. For the design firm, Felix's legacy. And it wasn't his at all.

"You manipulative, lying, corrupt, cheating, son of a bitch."

Maggie released each word like a dagger.

"Fraud."

Her spittle landed on the dashboard.

Aaron put his hand on her forearm and she shoved it away with more force than she'd intended. The car swerved but she course-corrected quickly enough to keep it between the yellow lines and the gravel shoulder.

"I want the band to reunite," he pleaded. "I sincerely do. At first I was doing it for the Karma Community, but then I got carried away thinking about how amazing it would be."

"You always get carried away."

"I wasn't trying to manipulate you."

"If you weren't trying to manipulate me it was only because you can't see beyond the immediate moment in time."

"I want it, Maggie," he pleaded. "I want a second chance. Don't you?"

Maggie slowed to thirty-five miles an hour through a town that, with its dime store, diner, consignment shop, corner taps, and churches, could have been a mirror image of New Elm.

She pulled over in front of a hardware store and kept her eyes locked straight ahead.

"Get out."

Aaron turned, wincing, in disbelief.

"I said get out."

"Maggie, you're being irrational—"

"Get out."

Maggie shifted into drive before Aaron could close the passenger door behind him. She drove straight ahead with her eyes fixed on the road and her mind clicking through her options.

I don't need Aaron or his damn money to get what I want. I never did.

Chapter 44

I Thought I Had a Choice

Sybylla jutted out her chin, pointing it forward, to the sky.

"I mean it," she said. "I want this burned."

She kicked at a pile at her feet. Aaron's jeans, even his favorites that he rarely washed and still smelled of him. Aaron's copy of the Dalai Lama's writings, *Autobiography of a Yogi*, Emerson. A porkpie hat from Bob Dylan, a T-shirt from a Stones concert.

"Maybe we should box it up in case he comes back," Gil said.

"Or mail it to Maggie," Sage said, picking through the relics.

Sybylla snorted.

"I don't care what you do with it. Just get it out of here."

The men scooped up the entrails of Aaron's life and headed to the labyrinth.

Sybylla changed the sheets on the bed and waited for Frances to bring the tea.

+++

Gil dug a hole where the entry of the upturned labyrinth had been. It wasn't hard work—the soil had been loose from the digging and moving and sifting of the past few weeks. But it wasn't easy work, either.

"Maybe we should put this stuff in garbage bags in case he wants it again," Sage said, eyeing the jeans and the hat. "He must have held onto it for a reason."

Gil kept digging.

"Bob Dylan's hat."

"So he said. Who knows what the truth is."

Sage looked through more of Aaron's belongings, dropped all of them on the ground, and held a nicked and scratched jackknife in the palm of his hand.

"I'm sure this could tell some tales."

He flicked open the blade and sliced the air in front of him, then closed it up and inspected it further. He wiped his index finger along it.

"Check this out."

Gil stopped digging.

Sage read the faded inscription: "To Aaron. Love Mother and Dad. 1955."

He raked his hand through his hair.

"I never met my grandparents."

He put the knife in his pocket and stood silent for a while.

"I'm going for a swim."

Gil watched Sage walk down to the creek with a heavy heart and burdened shoulders. Not knowing whether to dig further, Gil walked toward the Karma Community with his arms full of Aaron's clothes and his own heart heavier still.

+++

An angel, a tiger.

Frances' words rang out in Sybylla's head.

I'm going to kill an angel.

Sybylla paced the floor of her room while she waited for Frances to bring the strong tea, ticking off each second that passed into the ether.

My angel, my tiger.

As the words worked like a mantra in her mind, Sybylla realized that Frances wasn't coming.

I thought I had a choice in this.

My angel, my tiger.

Maybe I don't have a choice.

Sybylla upended the room, stripping the bed of its fresh sheets, spilling a cup of water, knocking to the floor a vase of wildflowers. In the closet she tossed aside her old winter boots and found what she was looking for: the last remaining evidence of Aaron in the form of an old work shirt. It would have to do. She grabbed it, along with scissors and

235

a black marker, then ran down the path, past the snoozing tabby and the vegetable garden and chicken coop and the patch of wildflowers, through the open field and to her favorite tree in the grove.

There she tore the shirt in squares as big her hands, and wrote.

Come back, we're a family.

Come back, we can work it out.

Come back, I don't want to be alone.

Come back, I will listen to you.

Come back, I love you.

She tied the corners of each prayer to the tree's lower limbs, then climbed.

Chapter 45

A Meeting of the Minds

The *New Elm Extra* shared office space with Svenska Realty and Norske Notary in the ground floor of a small cottage-like building on the north side of Main Street. Maggie rang the bell and entered when she didn't get a response. Tourist pamphlets, town maps, donation jars for the local 4-H club and a calendar of Rotary Club meetings cluttered the front desk. Maggie scanned the work space behind it; office junk, dust motes, no people.

"Sorry, we're closed," she heard from a back room not open to the public. "Come back tomorrow. I'm on deadline."

"Screw your deadline," Maggie said.

Gordon emerged from the back, flushed, his belt straining against his gut. "Not when I've got such hot leads about Aaron's beating and overdose in Chicago. I'm this close to getting the name of who beat him up."

Maggie sighed and placed both hands on the desk, breathing deeply to stay in control.

"That's nothing compared to what I'm about to give you."

"You?" Gordon scoffed. "You're not going to give me anything. You hate me."

"I don't hate you," she purred. "I'm just feeling misunderstood."

She practically batted her eyelashes at him while she let him make the next move.

"Okay, I'm listening," he said, a hot lead too tempting to ignore, even if he was on deadline.

"Okay, I'm going to be straight with you. I'll tell you my story. All of it. But I want to get paid."

"I don't pay my sources," Gordon sniffed. "I'm offended you'd think any respectable journalist would."

Maggie wanted to laugh, but caught herself before she blew her offer.

"But you get paid, and I'm sure you get paid a lot from your freelance work for the tabloids."

"Yes, but that's different. I'm the writer. The reporter. The creator."

"Let me get this straight. It's my story, my life, but you get paid, and the tabloid makes money, the advertisers love it and buy more ads. Seems like I'm the only one not making money off my own life."

"Can't help you Maggie. We can talk on the record, but you're not getting paid."

Maggie leveled her eyes on him with contempt.

"If you're willing to walk away from 'Exclusive: Maggie Morgan Tells All,' by Gordon Whatever Your Last Name Is, then you're a bigger fool than I realized."

She could see a bead of sweat trickle down his temple.

"Exclusive," she confirmed, then let him fantasize about the headline, the money, the notoriety. "With photos for the right offer."

Gordon whisked away his sweat and leaned against a bookshelf laden with phone books and ancient back issues of the *Extra*.

"Call your editors and jack up the price. I'll take seventy-five percent of it and make it worth your while."

"Fifty."

"Seventy. I'll call you in an hour to see what you've got."

+++

Maggie shivered as she entered Tyler County's courthouse twenty minutes before closing time. The official manifestation of government felt weighty enough to turn her dread into despair. But she didn't have time for fear. She walked into it, legs trembling, kitten heels wobbling, but walking nevertheless.

It's got to happen sooner or later.

"I'd like to talk to Mr. District Attorney." She tried to keep the snark out of her voice.

"Do you have an appointment?" She was sure the assistant, an undernourished young man in a cheap button-down shirt and creased khakis, knew that she didn't.

"I don't. I have a court date."

"So do a lot of people here."

"Tell him Maggie Morgan wants to see him."

The assistant left Maggie waiting on a bench in the hallway long enough for her to get nervous.

Here's hoping he realizes a good thing when it's offered to him.

She took a deep breath and closed her eyes.

I hope it truly is a good thing.

"He'll see you now." The assistant held open the heavy wooden door and waited for Maggie to respond. She stiffened her back, imagined Carl Olsen's severed head in her hands, and felt the eyes of the assistant prosecutors follow her into their boss' office.

The room had a boxed-in feeling that mirrored its inhabitant, Maggie intuited. Square, organized, stifled. A mid-century artifact that survived longer than intended and was betraying its age.

"Ms. Morgan, what a surprise." The DA stretched out his hand for a long shake, too familiar for one who was trying to put her in jail to further his political ambitions. "I wasn't expecting to see you until we were back in court."

Maggie smiled sweetly to mask her intentions.

"I'm back in town a bit and wondered if you and I could chat for a few minutes."

"I don't think the judge would like that much. Or my cousin Erika, your attorney."

Maggie shrugged one shoulder and looked him straight in the eye.

"You and I are old friends by now. I doubt they could object to a friendly conversation."

Carl leaned against his desk and let his eyes linger longer than they should have on her smooth neck and hint of clavicle peeking out from her blouse. Maggie's palms perspired, her bursting adrenaline betraying the placid smile on her face.

"So what brings you back to New Elm? Did you miss our Kringle and cheese curds?"

She faked a laugh.

"Actually, I thought you and I could have a meeting of the minds."

He scratched his chin and pretended to be concerned.

"You really should have your attorney present."

"My attorney represents my wishes. I'm sure I can express them myself."

"What are they?"

A long-dormant body memory surfaced and made her flush. The feeling of standing in front of a microphone, unadorned, making her voice heard. Daring to make her voice heard. Tension suspended longer than it was comfortable, but long enough to be necessary. Tension that she once knew how to control and suit her needs.

She moved closer to him, leaving her fear behind.

"Look, we can make this mess work for both of us. It doesn't have to be adversarial. In fact, you can come off as looking like a good guy if we strike the right deal."

"If I go easy on you."

Maggie shook her head.

"Not necessarily. I'm willing to accept responsibility for my mistakes. But I'm not willing to be held to account for all of the crimes and misdemeanors of the hippie generation just so you can win re-election."

"This has nothing to do with my re-election, even though you did demolish my campaign sign," Carl said, holding out his hands in mock innocence.

Maggie ignored his protestations and moved closer to her prey.

"I want to cut a deal that makes both of us look good," she said, letting her voice fall a register. "And teaches a few lessons, too."

When she emerged from his office twenty minutes later in the still-steaming early evening she hoped her luck would hold long enough to allow Carl to keep his end of the bargain.

"Maggie," she heard from across the street.

Gordon leaned out his car window, grinning.

"How did you know I was here?" she said as she approached.

"I have my sources," he teased, his eyes lit like a comet. "I've also got good news. And even better-than-good news."

"Give me the good news first." She pulled her sunglasses down on her nose to provide some anonymity.

"The good news is that we're getting some offers. The better news is that we can get even more money, thanks to Aaron. Follow me."

Chapter 46

The End

Sage stood naked on the bank of the stream, the pocketknife clenched in his right fist. He waded in, feeling the rush of water around his ankles and shins. He was sore, he was tired.

I've messed this up too much to make it right again. I can't go home but I can't stay here, either. Frederick's serious about kicking us out.

He dove into the water, careful not to dive down too deep.

And once Frances figures me out she won't like me anymore.

He opened his eyes underwater and saw a small fish swim with the stream. He grabbed at it with his left hand but was too slow to catch it.

Some Green Man I am.

He surfaced and wiped his wet hair out of his eyes. He opened the knife and let the blade glint in the sun.

It's time to become a man.

+++

Gil startled Frances as he plopped a heap of clothing on the kitchen counter.

"This is all of it," he said. "Well, most of it. I think I've dropped a few things along the way."

He managed a weak smile as Frances turned back to the sink and the window.

"It's been a long day," she said, the strain of the past few weeks finally audible in her voice.

"Something tells me it ain't over yet," Gil said, walking over to the counter. "Do you mind? I'm awfully thirsty."

He reached for the Mason jar of drenched herbs and roots meant for Sybylla.

"Whatever you want," Frances said flatly, not focused on anything in the room, anything in the material world.

He placed a towel around the hot jar and unscrewed the top. He sniffed the contents, then dipped a finger in and tasted the bitter brown liquid.

He groaned.

"What is this? It can't be nettles. Dandelions? Black walnut?"

Frances whipped around, fire in her eyes.

"That's for Sybylla." The harshness in her voice matched the taste of the concoction. "Don't touch that."

"Sorry, sorry," Gil said, backing away.

Frances grabbed the jar and moved it to a different counter.

"I didn't mean anything, Frances," Gil said, then stopped cold.

I know Sybylla has been sick, but I've never tasted anything like this, he thought. *It's too bitter to drink, and too strong to soothe a stomach.*

"What are you up to?" he asked.

She turned her back to him and looked out the window into the late-afternoon sun shining through thin clouds stretching across the horizon.

"You shouldn't have touched that."

Frances opened a drawer and pulled out more towels, all business.

"What's wrong with Sybylla?" Gil pressed on, afraid of what the answer would be, but needing to know the truth.

She slammed the drawer shut, then buried her face in the towels. Her entire body shook and hot sweat coated her skin. Gil reached out to her and smoothed her shoulders with his broad hands.

"It's the end of us," she mumbled into the soft cloths. "The end of us. Our community."

"Frances," Gil whispered. "We've been through worse. We'll go on and do lots of different things. It won't be so bad."

She sobbed anew.

"I tried to be strong. I tried to deny it. But it's true. It's the end."

Chapter 47

Freebird

"Freebird!" the ancient biker howled as he stamped his foot on the floor of the Do-Drop Inn, a musky tavern conveniently located across the street from the entrance of Trinity Lutheran Church.

Aaron grinned through his reopened split lip, then launched into Lynyrd Skynyrd's epic crowd-pleaser on a battered acoustic guitar summoned from behind the bar. His audience was blurry, but he could feel their love, their recognition, their thrill from meeting a long-lost rock legend with not a fuck to give anymore.

He missed more notes than he hit, but Aaron was on fire. A stocky, aging fake-blonde waitress brought over another shot of Jack Daniels, not needing to tell him it was on the house.

"'Cause I'm free as a…" he croaked over the white noise of a Cubs game on the TV behind the bar, the video poker game at the end of the bar, and the jukebox playing Zeppelin's "Black Dog."

"…cannot change," he sang so intensely that he lost his balance and fell to the floor amid cheers and hoots from the crowd.

+++

"I'll handle this," Maggie said before her eyes adjusted to the dark tavern.

She strode through the room with no trace of embarrassment or discomfort but fully aware of all eyes on her. Gordon's flash illuminated her way. She pushed aside a heavy barrel chair, felt the floor's stickiness under her heels, and headed directly for Aaron. Sitting up on the edge of what passed for a stage, feet dangling, a weather-beaten blonde stood between his legs, her hands on his knees. He took a long sip of brown booze, held his empty tumbler aloft, and smiled through his cuts and bruises.

"All hail Maggie Morgan," he said with false cheer. "The voice of the Four Furies. The mother of my child. The cause of my demise."

The blonde turned around, snarling, before Aaron shoved her aside.

"What brings you here?" he slurred, then held his hand up to shield his eyes from the camera's flash.

"Nothing special," she said coolly.

"You always were a bitch," he snapped. He tossed his glass aside, shattering it against a cinder-block window, the flash lighting it up like fireworks. Maggie winced and shrunk back from the shards.

"And you always were a mess."

"And you're perfect."

"I'm not."

"But you are," he said, then let out a long sigh, then a whimper, then a sob. "You are perfect," he whispered, then crumpled into her arms. Maggie let him relax into her, his hot whiskey breath wheezing into her shoulder. The Do-Drop Inn's regulars raised their glasses and stamped their feet, cheering on their reunion. Gordon's camera caught it from every angle.

Chapter 48

The Answer Was Right Here All Along

Maggie's shoulders relaxed slightly as she realized the entrance of the Karma Community wasn't ringed with Four Furies fans wanting another piece of their idols, or Carl Olsen supporters wanting to tear them into pieces. Instead, the community looked abandoned, populated only by the plump tabby on the porch, arms folded under his chin, eyes opening and closing languidly. Gordon followed but kept a discreet distance as Maggie's Saturn pulled up to the front door. She opened the passenger door for Aaron and put a protective arm around him as he steadied himself on the gravel drive, certain that Gordon was snapping away to capture her generosity for posterity and a bigger payday.

"So this is how it ends." Aaron choked off a sob as he clung to Maggie. "The end of the Karma Community. The end of my marriage. The end of the Four Furies. I wanted to have it all and now I've got nothing."

Maggie looked into his banged-up face, bruises emerging darker and darker under his eye, cuts scabbing over, fresh blood on his split lip.

"I flew too close to the sun."

The stench of cheap whiskey permeated his breath, his skin, his clothing. Aaron was decades away from the daredevilish firebrand who'd seduced her with a tab of acid, sex, and a song, but the hint of darkness and pain she'd identified in him back then remained. It would always be part of him.

"Enough with the self-pity," she said, sounding harsher than she'd intended. "You'll live to fight another day. All of us will."

Aaron staggered and Maggie loosened her grip on his arm. He took a step on his own but his legs were too wobbly to support his weight. He collapsed into the gravel and raised a dust cloud around him. Maggie stood over him, itching to kick him in the ribs and abandon him in the dirt. But Gordon's camera compelled her to kneel down before her ex-lover, concerned, compassionate, the heroine of this story. She reached out to him and smoothed his unruly hair into a tidier mess.

"Just leave me here," Aaron croaked. "Leave me and go on with your life. I'll find a way to survive. I did it before, and I'll do it again."

"Get up, you old fool," she said through her fake smile. "You can sleep it off inside."

She helped him sit up and let him cling to her for what she hoped was the last time. The tabby ambled down the front steps and paused a few feet away, then let out a clear meow.

"Shoo," Maggie said, waving her hand to dismiss the cat. She rattled her gold charm bracelet hoping the noise would bother him. But the tabby meowed again and again and again, never budging.

She looked over Aaron's shoulder and narrowed her focus on the tabby. A green spark popped up from the dust near his foot, the unmistakable green spark of the emerald that had popped from her charm bracelet when she'd fallen on the front steps trying to leave the Karma Community the first time, trying to leave the Karma Community for good, for ever.

The front door swung open.

"We've been waiting for you," said the man Maggie now knew was Frederick Christiansen, the Karma Community's owner. "Won't you join us inside?"

Maggie gave him a good long stare while her mind went click-click-click faster than Gordon's camera.

The answer was right here all along.

"Yes," she said, feeling the Furies rising. "I'd love to."

+++

Aaron was stunned by the condition of the room he'd shared with Sybylla. It was torn up as if a hurricane had met a tornado and decided to touch down on the bed. Clothes were everywhere, water had been spilled. One of Sybylla's

246

necklaces had snapped and the pale blue beads were underfoot. But worse than that was what was missing: Sybylla and any bit of Aaron.

He shut the door behind him and, dazed, he walked to the main room. No one was there, either. The emptiness of the main hall, the dining room, the waterfall, tea room, and balcony challenged his memories.

This was my place. And now it's hollow, barren, lifeless.

He walked down the hallway to the kitchen and heard voices.

"She's at nine weeks now. She still has a little time. But just a little."

Aaron stood in the doorway and saw Frances, her face wet and red, in deep discussion with Gil, and the pile of his clothes on the long table. Neither one saw him.

"I'm shocked," Gil said. "Just shocked. I can't imagine Sybylla aborting her baby."

Aaron saw Frances place her hands on her stomach.

"I know. And she wants to do it today, before Frederick kicks us out."

Aaron rocked back, dumbfounded, and banged his fist into the wall. The thump startled Frances and Gil.

"Hush," Frances said to Gil. They waited another moment but heard nothing else.

"We'd better find Sybylla."

Frances picked up the jar of herbs and the towels, her eyes catching Gil's for just a second. Aaron stood in the doorway, trembling from his toes to his scalp. His entire being—his beaten face, shaking hands, pained eyes, wounded spirit, harsh reality piercing his alcoholic haze—shocked his old friends.

"Please," he whispered. "Forgive me. For everything."

+++

Sybylla tried to climb higher up the tree to get a better view of the land, but couldn't force herself to do it. Her cloth prayers fluttered in the branches below her.

I don't want to harm the baby, my tiger, my angel.

So she waited, hiding, yet wanting to be found.

My parents will help me, won't they? And Frances, and Sage? I could make it all work. Women do this all the time, don't they?

She ran her right hand along the smooth bark, finding little knobs here and there, like Braille for birds.

Maybe Frances will never come. Maybe I'll have to build a nest and live in here forever, even if Freddie sells the Karma Community. It'll just be me and the baby—Baby Eve. In the Garden of Eden. Munching on crab apples and thumbing our noses at the world.

She laughed a small laugh, her first in many weeks.

Who knew hormonal mood swings could be so fun?

A bird whistled and Sybylla whistled back. A crow cawed and she cawed, too, just as she did when she was a child and had spent endless hours in her treehouse with her brothers. More birds twittered and chirped, piped up and wouldn't quiet down. Sybylla called out to them, releasing her troubles.

The whistling quieted for a moment, but Sybylla continued, hoping some bird would join her in a symphony.

It did. But something was different about it. Sybylla whistled again, and again. She heard the same song back as a perfect echo of her melody line. She pushed aside one of the branches and a few of the shirt scraps of hand-written prayers to try to catch sight of this strange bird.

She looked out into the distance. Up on the hill, Aaron dropped to his knees and roared.

+++

Aaron struggled, but he insisted, so Sybylla gave it another try. He crouched low, then she climbed onto his back, he slowly straightened up, and they both laughed as he carried her, piggyback style, through the grounds of the Karma Community. But not toward any of the buildings—too likely that they'd run into Frederick, too many memories and vibes to deal with right now.

She took him back.

So on Aaron's back Sybylla rode, triumphant, like a chariot in victory flanked by Frances and Gil, laughing and crying, crying and laughing. They rambled and stumbled, not knowing where they were headed, but they knew that they were going to the stream.

+++

The foursome tumbled over the hill and saw Sage, naked, sunning himself on a rock in the middle of the stream. Glints of sunlight and steel flashed up into the sky.

He turned toward them and kept his eyes on them, his friends, his father, his foe.

He sat up, the open jackknife still in his right hand.

He stood up, squarely facing the group.

248

Aaron put down Sybylla and slowly walked toward the edge of the stream, the grass getting taller and more tangled as he edged closer.

Sage took a deep breath as he eyed his father up and down, the fresh wounds apparent even from a distance.

"Sage," Aaron began.

Sage raised his arms above his head, the blade pointed upward.

"I know things have been rocky between us."

Sage laughed a sharp laugh.

"I don't even know who you are."

"That might be the problem."

The two men stared at each other.

"I'm just a guy, Sage. Not some huge God." Aaron kicked the patch of wild mint in front of him. "Just a falling baby," he added quietly.

Sage covered his eyes with his forearm, blocking out his father.

"You just want me to love you, like you want everyone to love you."

"I do, I'll admit it," Aaron said. "It's one of my faults."

Sage kept his eyes covered.

"This is your knife," Sage said, more like a warning.

Aaron squinted.

"My old pocket knife. From my mom and dad. Did I ever tell you about them?"

Sage snorted.

"I'm sorry, Sage. I'm just so sorry."

Aaron looked Sage up and down, a kid playing hide and seek in plain sight.

He did the only thing he knew how to do.

He took off his shirt, wincing when he raised his arms. He unbuckled his belt, then bent down and pulled off his work boots. He slipped off his jeans and, naked, revealed the bruises and scrapes from their fight. He waded into the water, cool on his feet and ankles, shins, knees, and thighs. He walked closer to his son.

It might as well be now.

"I'm sorry, Sage. Could you ever forgive me?"

Chapter 49

She Knew What She Had To Do

"I owe you an apology."

The strain of the Karma Community's tumult had begun to show on Gil's typically unlined face and laid-back demeanor. He was stiffer, more self-contained. Crows' feet accented his eyes. A weariness seemed to creep into his exhales. It was as if he was afraid to hope, to plan, to think deeply about what had brought him to this point and how he was going to move forward.

Maggie. It had always been Maggie.

He opened his cabin door and allowed her to pass inside. His belongings were packed up except for the essentials. Paint brushes, charcoals. A dusty boom box, the I-Ching. The blurred image of a dandelion drawn by Maggie in their first class together, when they were drawn together by fate. There could be no other explanation for what they shared.

"I'm sorry," she said simply as she sat on his futon, where they'd made love for hours as he helped her reclaim her power night after night. "I don't know how I can possibly make this up to you."

He knelt before her and smoothed his palms onto her thighs, still a supplicant even though he was the one who'd been wronged.

"I'm sorry I got back together with Aaron," she began. "It's just something I had to do to realize that it wasn't what I wanted."

He held her hands between his.

"And I'm sorry about the Karma Community. I just spoke with Frederick. I hadn't realized the situation was so dire."

He opened her hands and kissed her palms.

"Be with me," he pleaded as he searched her eyes for agreement.

"Everything is about to change," she told him. "Everything. And I'm not sure how I'm going to pull it off."

"I can help you. As long as we hang on to each other. To this."

He gathered her in his arms and caressed her from tip to toe, covering her in kisses and his complete adoration. She didn't resist.

As she untangled herself from his long limbs in the early morning light, she knew what she had to do to make it right for Gil, for Sage, for Aaron and Sybylla. And most of all, for herself.

Chapter 50

All Rise

Sage held his mom's cold hand as she waited for the judge to take his place, then slung his arm around her shoulder. Her attorney took Maggie's other hand, but firmly. The women's relationship tensed on the phone the previous evening, when Maggie had informed Erika that a deal had been struck without her counsel.

"I hope you know what you're doing," Erika had said.

"So do I," Maggie sighed.

Maggie snuck a look at her nemesis turned partner, the DA who still could scuttle the whole agreement if he wanted to pull another stunt in court. Nothing had been committed to writing the previous day, just a handshake and the hope that both would make good on their promise.

I hope he's a reasonable man, Maggie thought. *And I hope he's leading in the polls.*

"All rise," the bailiff intoned. Maggie's joints felt stiff and her legs trembled like a sailor without his sea legs as she stood, but Sage's support kept her still. She felt the camera clicking behind her and tried to regain her poise. *Breathe, breathe,* she told herself.

"Looks like the schedule is moved around to accommodate an out-of-state defendant," the judge said, poring over the stack of papers while his reading glasses were still perched on his head.

"State of Wisconsin versus Margaret Morgan," the bailiff called out. Carl waved Maggie and Erika toward the twin desks with a gentlemanly flourish for Gordon's camera.

"Ms. Morgan, you're facing a slew of charges related to an operating while impaired charge and smashing into the district attorney's campaign sign," the judge said with what Maggie thought was a sparkle in his eye as spoke to her informally, like a fun uncle. "Are you ready to pay your debt to society?"

"Yes, your honor," she said through a clump in her throat.

"With respect to the charges," Carl cut in. "The state is offering Ms. Morgan a deferred prosecution agreement with a guilty plea. In turn, Ms. Morgan agrees to pay court costs and the cost to repair the sign, as well as record a public service announcement warning of the dangers of intoxicated driving with none other than the Tyler County District Attorney."

"That would be you," the judge needled.

"Yes. If Ms. Morgan doesn't fulfill her obligations, the deferred prosecution agreement will be rescinded and she'll face three months in confinement and twelve months on supervision, lose her driver's license for one year, and will be convicted of a felony."

"What say you, Ms. Morgan?"

"I'm grateful for the state's mercy," she said, eyes downcast but her throat and mind clear. "I agree to these terms."

"Then so agreed," the judge said, letting his gavel clap down on his desk. "Next case!"

Maggie's BlackBerry rumbled with an incoming message.

Yes, I can meet you at your attorney's office. It would be my pleasure.

+++

"As your attorney, I have to tell you that I think you're a bit nuts," Erika said as her ancient printer produced the memorandum of agreement that would change Maggie's life. "But as your fan—as your friend—I think it's amazing."

Maggie laughed and blew a stray lock of damp hair off of her forehead, revealing the healing scar from her Karma Community-incurred injuries.

"I can hardly believe it myself. In a strange way, I never truly believed I'd take over Felix's firm and make it my own. And now—"

"And now you're certain you're doing the right thing."

"I am. Absolutely. For me. For everyone."

She scanned the agreement without her reading glasses before handing it over to her silent partner in the room.

253

Chapter 51

It Might as Well Be Now

The sun was setting over the high trees as Maggie closed the Karma Community's front door behind her. She locked it behind her and stood still for a moment, taking it all in. The court hearing was done and dusted. The haggling in Erika's office was settled for now. Her marathon interview with Gordon was looming over tomorrow. Thinking about rehashing the Four Furies' history from her perspective had produced a fresh headache that had been threatening for days. Aaron wouldn't like what she had to say when the interview went global but there was no way around it. She needed to tell her side of the story to set the record straight. It was her life, not his. Her life, her creation. Besides, the money it would generate would change her life, change everything.

Maggie walked through the hallways that were emptied in advance of the community's sale. Her skin cooled under the high ceilings, walls devoid of art. No giant Buddha greeting guests. No wild goddess celebrating her fresh kills. No burbles from the waterfall. Just good, clean whitewashed walls that would offer the new owner a fresh start.

She walked toward the voices on the sun deck and took a deep breath.

It might as well be now.

She stiffened her spine and tried to appear calm, in command, which wasn't easy when ex-lovers and her son and their new partners were circled on the deck, utopian dreamers who didn't want their bubble to be pierced by reality.

Frederick was absent, but then again, she thought, why would he stick around among all of the residents he's displacing?

She stepped on to the deck and waited for them to focus their attention on her.

"Congratulations on your victory in court," Frances said magnanimously. "Sage has been telling us all about it."

"It was awesome," he said proudly. "She totally owned the DA."

Maggie smiled and laughed at Sage's insistence on turning her plea into an advantage.

"I don't know about that, but I'm glad it's over."

"We're glad you're here," Gil said, not allowing hope to creep into his voice. "Going back to Chicago tonight?"

Maggie cleared her throat as Sybylla pulled Aaron closer. He was wearing his favorite trucker's hat pulled low over his brow, but his beaten face couldn't be hidden. Since both he and Sage were sitting peacefully in the circle, she surmised they'd found a way to reconcile, again.

"Well that's what I'm here to talk to you about," Maggie said after her long pause. "I'm not going back to Chicago. I'm staying here tonight."

She saw the group puzzle out her statement. She wasn't asking if she could stay. She was telling them a fact.

"Aren't you supposed to work on your deal with Trip?" Sage asked.

She smiled as she thought about her big pitch of just a few days ago and how nervous she'd been to put herself on the line for her mentor's legacy.

"I've decided I'm not going to buy Felix's firm."

She let that fact soak in while she readied her next blow.

"But I have decided to buy something else."

She felt their eyes on her, bewildered.

"I just bought the Karma Community. Freddie and I signed the papers this afternoon."

She watched the news settle on each individual. Sage pumped his fist and gave a quick whoop. Gil had stars in his bright blue eyes. Frances leaned back in her Adirondack chair, eyes closed, broad smile, a prayer on her lips. Sybylla curled into Aaron's shoulder, sobbing, while he stared directly at his ex-lover, a shadow in the hollow of his nose. She grinned.

"Yes, Aaron. I'll be your boss."

"You'll never own me," he rasped, defiant.

"I know. No one ever will. But at least you'll have a roof over your head and green grass under your feet and friends who will get you through the night."

"And my son."

"And our son."

"And you."

Maggie laughed, relishing the release.

"I'm my own woman, Aaron. Maggie Morgan. And I just found my way."

Chapter 52

Coda

"Ready?" Aaron asked. His back was turned to Maggie and Sage as he peered out the window facing the sun deck and hills behind the Karma Community. He scanned the crowd, trying to break them up into blocks of twenty, then multiplying those blocks to estimate its size. He lost count at two hundred, three hundred. The throng surrounded the main building on three sides and stretched past the gardens to the lip of the nascent labyrinth.

"I've never been ready, you know that," Maggie sighed. Her hands shook and her knees trembled. She tried to wash the lump out of her throat with warm lemon water, but that only made her want to pee. She smoothed her hair back and wished she'd had time to highlight it. But her frizzy silver-streaked hair, delicately embroidered tunic blouse, jean capris and jaggedy nerves would have to do. She couldn't postpone it any longer. Besides, she asked for it.

Aaron opened the French doors leading out to the sun deck to allow Sage and Maggie to greet the crowd first. Sybylla and Frances made last-minute arrangements of wildflower bundles lining the deck. Maggie caught Gil's eye and smiled, then gave Sage a quick hug to a smattering of applause. Gil's hand-painted banner fluttered above her head, proudly stating "Benefit for A New Day Women's Shelter—Breaking the Cycle of Family Violence." Suzanne, Maggie's biggest fan, stood in front of the microphone, blinking away happy tears.

"Years ago, Maggie Morgan inspired me to change my life and my children's destiny," she said, the crowd quieting to hear her. "Today, she's giving me one more gift. Ladies and gentlemen, after a long hiatus, I bring you the Three Furies."

The two women embraced as Aaron strummed steady chords as Sage caught the beat on the conga. Maggie missed her first cue, then her second, then stepped toward the microphone to join them on the third run-through of "Home Is Where You Are," the Four Furies' treacly first hit.

Maggie waved away Aaron and Sage until they faded into a full, bewildered stop.

She shook her head. "I'm sorry," she said into the microphone unapologetically. Then she closed her eyes and waited a few beats until the music came back to her.

"She told me she needed to be free," she sang *a capella*, changing the gender of the narrator of "Finding His Way" to female.

"To find some answers she's seeking.
Wisdom that comes from a dream,
From chasing a vision you believe in."

She opened her eyes as Aaron stepped forward, strumming, but ceding center stage to her.

"She told me to wait for a while,
While she makes a new life and home.
She told me she's not my rival.
She's got to face the truth alone.
She's got to break tradition
To create the life she wants to live in."

Sage caught Aaron's beat as the familiar chords built into the legendary chorus, the last chorus Maggie and Aaron performed together before she conquered him on stage in 1982.

"She's finding her way," she sang, giving her voice freely to the crowd, to her future, to her family.

"She's finding her way," she sang, letting the audience absorb its truth and cheer her on.

"She's finding her way," she sang, making a promise to herself she insisted on keeping.

Resources

The alternative therapies mentioned in this book are not meant to diagnose or relieve any physical condition. Please do your homework and consult a professional before taking any remedy, whether it's a pill, tincture, syrup, or tea.

If you are in a relationship in which you feel unsafe or have experienced emotional, sexual, or physical abuse, you are never alone. Call the National Domestic Violence Hotline at 1-800-799-7233 or go to thehotline.org to chat online. Both are available 24/7. I believe survivors.

Acknowledgments

It is with a very heavy heart that as I go to press with the paperback version of this book that I do so without the companionship of shyness expert Bernardo Carducci, my longtime friend, writing partner, and mentor who recently passed away. Bernie found the hidden wisdom (and, typically, humor) in every social encounter and he showed rare sensitivity toward and care for those who didn't always feel like they belonged. I'm grateful for the profound impact he had on me personally and professionally and I'm saddened to know that I'll never be able to call him up again to check in, go over our most recent draft, or say, "Hey, let's do another book." I'm not alone in mourning his loss. My heart goes out to his family and friends during this difficult time.

That said, I could not have written (and rewritten) this novel without the support and input from a wonderful group of people who wanted me to succeed, even if they didn't understand why I couldn't let go of this story and enjoy some downtime like a normal person. Some helped me with writing, others with ideas to write about.

Alums of the Bay View Writers Group gave me critical feedback, insights, and encouragement every other Wednesday night for many years. The University of Wisconsin-Extension spring writing conferences always provided a jolt of inspiration when I needed it most. I learned how to analyze personalities and behavior from the members of the New York chapter of the National Council for Geocosmic Research. I expanded my awareness of healing and wellness at the Open Center in New York, especially in classes taught by herbalists Robin Rose Bennett and Peeka Trenkle.

More intimately, I would like to thank my family, especially my brother Andy, who was always ready to help me name a character or test a new plot twist to see if it would work. My mom is my biggest cheerleader. Madison author Steven B. Salmon totally got my drive and frustrations as I finalized the manuscript. (Buy his books!) Kristine Hansen has been my steady accountability partner for ages. And in Joseph Ohm I've found someone who just might enjoy watching rock docs more than I do. I'm grateful for his patience and understanding when I needed time alone "to work on my novel."

It's done. Finally. Thank you.

About the Author

Lisa Kaiser is a recovering journalist in Wisconsin. She has collaborated on three books with Bernardo J. Carducci, Ph.D.—*Shyness: A Bold New Approach; The Shyness Breakthrough;* and *Shyness: The Ultimate Teen Guide.* Sign up for her newsletter and get updates on the next book in the Four Furies series, *Deep Cuts,* at lisakaiserthewriter.com.

Readers' Questions for the Author

Question: Why do you say that Maggie is shy? She seems very extroverted at times and was able to perform in public for many years. To me, she didn't act the way I think shy people normally act.

Lisa: That's a great question. I was inspired to write about a rock star who is shy because I wanted to show that shy people can do anything they set out to do—even if their chosen career path doesn't seem to be an obvious one for a shy person. I wanted to show that shy people can be rock stars, if that's what they want to be.

Shy people are full of surprises. They share common traits but they can reveal those traits in unique ways. Shy people become nervous and highly self-conscious when they're in unfamiliar social situations. They sweat, get knock-kneed, stammer, clam up, and look uncomfortable (because they are uncomfortable). In the book, Maggie shows these traits when she has dinner at the Karma Community for the first time, and she often breaks out in sweat and rashes when she's under pressure. When you think about it, her stage fright is an intense form of the shyness she feels in her daily life.

Another thing to note is that shy people want to be with other people. But they feel ambivalent about their ability to connect with another person successfully. So Maggie's waffling on a singing career and her conflicting feelings about fame are yet another expression of her shyness.

Lastly, most if not all shy people can pinpoint the event that "created" their shyness. Sometimes it's being called on in class and not having the right answer, or feeling isolated after starting a new school and being the new kid, or being rejected by a potential romantic partner. For Maggie, it's being humiliated by her classmate during her big Christmas concert solo. Of course, that sets into motion her desire for revenge. Her fury.

Q: Maggie considers herself to be a feminist. But her two careers have been in partnership with stronger, older men. So, is she a feminist?

Lisa: I'm glad you asked that question. Yes, Maggie's a feminist because she says she is one. And like most if not all feminists she isn't a totally independent, self-made woman. She has worked in partnership with others; in her case, she's worked with powerful men. Her shyness and self-doubt made it difficult for her to assert herself and go solo, even though she has the smarts and talent to do so.

This part of Maggie's story drew heavily from other female rock stars of her generation. When you think about it, a lot of them were in bands or collaborated with their partners—Stevie Nicks, Christine McVie, Carly Simon, Linda Thompson, Grace Slick, Pat Benatar. I think that's due to the fact that rock bands were a relatively new phenomenon back in the seventies and eighties, and they were a wild, male-dominated, hedonistic phenomenon. Perhaps the female singers of that time worked with their partners for protection, or to create a more civilized atmosphere. I'd love to talk to them about it.

Q: Am I supposed to like Aaron? He was terrible to Maggie when they were in the band but he seems to have gotten it together after they broke up.

Lisa: Ah, Aaron. I've gotten a range of reactions to Aaron from members of my writers' group. Some hated him with a passion while others thought he had redeemed himself. I knew that their conflicting opinions meant that Aaron had become a three-dimensional character in their minds—a good thing. I have a lot of affection for Aaron—I have a lot of affection for all of the characters in this story—so I can't be objective about whether he's good or bad. He's a complicated guy in a complicated relationship with Maggie, Sage, Sybylla, and everyone else at the Karma Community.

Q: Sage's journey throughout the book intrigued me. He started out in search of his father and found him. Did he get what he wanted?

Lisa: I think he did get what he wanted. At least I hope he did. He got to know Aaron as a person instead of idolizing or demonizing him from a distance. He doesn't have to rely on Maggie's negative opinion or him, or the legend that surrounded Aaron as a guitar god. Sage's new knowledge of his father may not be totally positive, but at least it's based on Sage's own judgment and experience, not fantasy or hearsay.

Q: Why did you set the story in southwestern Wisconsin?

Lisa: Quite simply, I love this part of Wisconsin. It's absolutely gorgeous—even more beautiful than the stereotypical picture postcard—and it still feels pretty far removed from the cares of the city. I'm also intrigued by the mix of cultures in this area. It's home to generations of Scandinavians and Native Americans, plus hippies, outdoors enthusiasts, cheese makers, beer makers, wine makers, hunters, Amish, and rock-ribbed conservatives. The Karma Community seemed like it would be an anomaly in the area but fit in perfectly as well.

Plus, I wanted the characters to interact with each other and not rely on texting or phone calls. That means they'd wouldn't be able to get cell phone reception. I know my phone certainly cuts out once I'm in the Kickapoo Valley, a tech failure that I wholeheartedly welcome.

Q: Can you tell us anything about what happens in the sequel?

Lisa: All I can say is that the residents of the Karma Community are on a collision course with reality. If you're really curious, go to my website, lisakaiserthewriter.com, and you'll get a preview of the next book in the Four Furies series, *Deep Cuts*.

Made in the USA
Monee, IL
09 June 2023

35269066R00163